Praise for *Just Get Home* by Bridget Foley

"Thrilling, yes, but so much more than a thriller. Set to the tune of a life-altering (and vividly rendered) earthquake, Foley brings together two very different people who discover an ultimate commonality: knowing what matters. Written with aplomb, precision, and courage, *Just Get Home* is a breathtaking achievement."

—Josh Malerman, *New York Times* bestselling author of *Bird Box* and *Malorie*

"I turned the pages of *Just Get Home* like I was reading a flat-out thriller, at that magical couldn't-put-it-down, must-find-out-what-happens pace, but that's only the beginning of this wonder of a novel because it's also smart and insightful on timely, important, difficult ideas. Its characters and their relationships are heartbreaking and complicated in the best way, at once entirely relatable, instantly recognizable, and unlike anything you've read before.

This is addictive reading that changes you as you turn the pages and stays with you long after you've finished. It is a genre-bender in my favorite way: it has the best of everything."

—Laurie Frankel, *New York Times* bestselling author of *This Is How It Always Is* and *Goodbye for Now*

"*Just Get Home* hits the thriller trifecta: a natural disaster, danger around every corner and compelling well-drawn characters who unite to survive the most harrowing journey of their lives.

Foley effortlessly weaves together the voices of Beegie and Dessa to chronicle a night filled with devastation, terror, heartbreak and ultimately hope as they try to make it home after a deadly earthquake. Inventive, emotional and addictive, *Just Get Home* is not to be missed."

—Heather Gudenkauf, *New York Times* bestselling author of *The Weight of Silence* and *This is How I Lied*

ANYTHINK LIBRARIES / RANGEVIEW LIBRARY DISTRICT

D0181203

JUST GET HOME

BRIDGET FOLEY

mira

If you purchased this book without a cover you should be aware
that this book is stolen property. It was reported as "unsold and
destroyed" to the publisher, and neither the author nor the
publisher has received any payment for this "stripped book."

Recycling programs
for this product may
not exist in your area.

ISBN-13: 978-0-7783-3159-9

Just Get Home

Copyright © 2021 by Bridget Foley

All rights reserved. No part of this book may be used or reproduced in any manner
whatsoever without written permission except in the case of brief quotations embodied
in critical articles and reviews.

This is a work of fiction. Names, characters, places and incidents are either the product
of the author's imagination or are used fictitiously. Any resemblance to actual persons,
living or dead, businesses, companies, events or locales is entirely coincidental.

This edition published by arrangement with Harlequin Books S.A.

For questions and comments about the quality of this book, please contact us at
CustomerService@Harlequin.com.

Mira
22 Adelaide St. West, 40th Floor
Toronto, Ontario M5H 4E3, Canada
BookClubbish.com

Printed in Italy by Grafica Veneta

To my Song and my Safe Place

JUST

GET

HOME

Assist the client in gathering possessions.

She had seen it written on a sheet Kate had in her folder. An unticked box next to it.

Beegie knew what the paper meant by *possessions. Stuff.*

And since she was "the client," Beegie knew that the un-checked box was specifically about *her stuff. Possession* meant something that belonged to you.

But it was the other meaning of *possession* that soothed her as she and Kate drove away from the Greelys'.

The *darker* meaning.

That was the one she worked over and over in her head.

Beegie imagined her caseworker holding up a gray little girl, face obscured by black hair, asking, "This one yours?"

Beegie would nod. *Yes, that's my monster.*

Together they would shove one snarling, demon-filled per-son after another into the garbage bags they had been given to pack her things. Soon the bags would fill, growing translucent with strain. When they were done, she and Kate would have to push down on the snapping, bloody faces of all of Beegie's *possessions* so they could close the back of Kate's Prius.

But the box on the sheet in Kate's folder remained unticked.

Her advocate didn't get to help collect Beegie's possessions, real or unreal, because Beegie's stuff was already on the street when she got home: just two garbage bags filled with nothing supernatural, or even that special, and Kate standing next to them with her folder and its helpful advice for what to do when a foster gets kicked out of her home.

It really was nothing special.

Just everything Beegie owned in the world.

Well, almost everything.

Whatever.

After Kate dropped her off and Barb had shown her "Her New Home" and given her the rundown on "The Way It Works Here," Beegie unpacked her *possessions* into a bureau that the girl who'd lived there before her had made empty, but not clean.

The bottoms of the drawers were covered in spilled glitter. Pink and gold. Beegie had pressed the tips of her fingers into the wood to pull it up, making disco balls of her hands.

But she failed to get it all.

Months later, she would find stray squares of this other girl's glitter on her clothes. They would catch the light, drawing her back to the moment when she'd finally given up on getting the bureau any cleaner and started to unpack the garbage bags.

There had been important things missing. Their absence was intentional and malicious. Eric had claimed victory.

That, Beegie had expected.

But what she had not expected was to find two *other* neatly folded garbage bags. These were the ones she had used to move her stuff from Janelle's *to* the Greelys'. She had kept them, even though back then Mrs. Greely was all smiles and Eric seemed nice, and even Rooster would let her pet him.

Beegie had kept the bags because she'd been around long enough to know that sometimes it doesn't work out.

In fact, most times it doesn't work out.

And you need a bag to put your stuff in and you don't want to have to ask the person who doesn't want you to live with them anymore to give you one.

But when Mrs. Greely had gathered Beegie's *possessions*, she had seen those bags and thought that they were important to Beegie. It made sense to her former foster mother that a "garbage girl" would treasure a garbage bag.

This idea made Beegie imagine the sum total of all of the things that ever belonged to her or ever would belong to her piled in an enormous heap like a landfill. All of it covered with flies, seagulls swooping overhead.

Everything she ever owned was trash or one day would be.

And somehow, even though it should have enraged her, seeing things this way comforted Beegie. It made her mind less about the things that hadn't been in the bag...and other things that had been taken from her.

Beegie picked at ownership like a scab, working her way around the edges, flaking it off a bit at a time. Ridding herself of the brown crust of caring.

Because if you care about something it has power over you.

Caring can give someone else the ability to control you and the only real way to own yourself was to let go.

So she did.

Or she tried.

Some things Beegie couldn't quite shed. The *want of them* stuck to her like the glitter. The pain of their loss catching the light on her sleeves, flashing from the hem of her jeans. The *want* would wait on her body until it attracted her attention and then eluded the grasping edges of her fingers.

6 PM
VAN NUYS

6 P.M.
VAN NUYS

1

Tonight's babysitter was new.

Hailey. Holly. Kristie. *Something like that.*

Dessa felt bad for not writing it down when Jen canceled. She had booked a gig, but she *did* have a friend in her acting class who could cover for her. *If that was okay?*

Of course it was.

It had to be.

It was for this reason that Dessa decided it would be best to get Olivia ready for bed *before* the sitter came. Just to cut down on the instructions. There was no reason to open all the drawers and cabinets to their life for someone who would never work for them again.

Dessa had always thought of her life in boxes.

Her family. Her job. Her past. The present.

Keeping each aspect sorted into a different mental space made it easier to deal with them individually. The word for it was *compartmentalization*, and Dessa considered it a skill. A gift that enabled her to deal with one thing at a time.

There had been a stretch, right after Olivia's birth, when the needs of an infant and the complexities of her relationship with Joe had threatened to knock over her mind's careful contents.

Dessa hadn't felt like she was getting to know her new "mother" self as much as her *real* self was being crushed beneath things she couldn't control. Whenever anyone would ask if she was "okay" she knew they had seen the leakage of one area of her life into the next.

Her compartments were crumbling.

Joe called it "baby brain." Told her it was normal.

He kissed her temple and Dessa imagined addled gray matter beneath his lips. That night, he swaddled Ollie and bounced her into calm after ordering Dessa to bed.

He was gone in the morning.

But the baby had slept five hours, her longest bit yet. The note Joe left called them his "sleeping beauties."

She had kept it, slipping it into her jewelry box, among other precious things.

Soon after this Dessa was able to go back to the comfort of her compartments. The disparate parts of her life, neatly divvied up again. No one part unnecessarily mingling with another.

And now Ollie was a toddler, almost three and bright as a summer day.

Those long months when it had felt like Dessa's life was crumbling seemed distant and impossible. *A lifetime ago,* thought Dessa.

A short lifetime, but almost her daughter's entire.

★ ★ ★

To save time they showered together. Ollie played with the water as it fell in sheets from Dessa's body, directing a channel from her mother's hip across her small arm.

"Look! A river!"

Dessa turned to see Ollie's river break into small tributaries across her chest.

"That's lovely, sweetie."

Later, in their underwear, Dessa stood her daughter on the edge of the mattress in their bedroom and wiggled a nightgown over her damp head. Ollie bounced, threatening to tumble off and hit her crib at the foot of the bed.

"Careful, baby."

"Yes, Momma."

Dessa reached into the closet and pulled two cocktail dresses from the rack. Both sheathed in dry cleaner bags, ghostlike.

She sighed. These were artifacts. Remnants from a former life. The one she had before Ollie. Before Joe. Before everything. *Why had she even kept them?*

But, of course, tonight was the *why*. She had kept them so she could pretend to be who she used to be.

Olivia pulled at the plastic above one of the dresses. "This one. The sparkly."

Dessa peeled it free of its shroud. "Good choice!"

Back in the bathroom, Ollie aped her mother's expressions as Dessa put on her makeup; Opening her little mouth in an O while her mother painted her lips, rapidly blinking her eyes when her mother brushed on mascara.

After she was done, Dessa found herself pulling Joe's gifts out of her jewelry box.

Three diamonds. Two for her ears. One for her finger.

Ollie played with the ring box. *Open, close. Open.*

"Careful, baby."

Dessa took a step back. The earrings were too much. Especially with the dress. Ostentatious. Just large enough that one questioned whether or not they were real.

She considered taking them off.

A simple hoop would be a better choice.

But then she thought about the looks that would pass between her friends tonight. Secret messages pulsing between them.

Dessa gestured for Ollie to hand her the box.

"Okay... It's time for Momma to put on her ring."

They were reading a bedtime story when a message from an unidentified caller chimed:

ON MY WAY. TEN BEHIND. SORRY.

There was a happy face tacked on the end.

Ollie tapped the book. Impatient.

"Sorry. Where were we?"

"The tree."

Though she did not say *tree*. She said, *twee*, which was wonderful.

Dessa pulled her closer. On the page a mother tree reached leafy limbs toward her child in flight.

To keep from infecting Olivia with her own rising anxiety about the time, Dessa resorted to giving her piggyback rides. Her daughter squealed, hands clasped in front of Dessa's throat. Little knees braced against rough sequins.

"Hold on with your legs, baby!"

A knock came. *Finally.*

Dessa answered it. The babysitter was blonde. Thin. Petite. Pretty.

Which didn't surprise her. Pretty girls in Los Angeles are the least surprising thing of all.

"I couldn't find parking," the girl said. "Sorry!"

Dessa smiled. If she got out of here in five minutes, she had a shot at not being late. "Holly?"

"Hailey."

"Yes. Sorry. Hailey. I forgot."

Dessa let Ollie slide to the floor. Her daughter clung to her legs as she let this new person into their home. "Olivia, this is Hailey. She's going to take care of you while Momma's away."

Ollie stuck her thumb in her mouth and gave them both a hard look. Her eyes flickering between her mother and the babysitter.

"She's all ready for bed, so all I need you to do is give her dinner. I'm guessing hot dogs are okay?"

"Um. I'm a vegetarian...so...uh..."

It took Dessa a moment to realize what Hailey was implying. Not that she didn't want to eat the hot dogs, but that she didn't want to handle the meat in order that *Ollie* could eat them. Dessa was running out of time. She pivoted.

"Got it." She opened the fridge. "Any objection to grilled cheese?"

Ollie refused to relinquish hold of her mother at their apartment door, and so Hailey was forced to accompany them the full three flights down to Dessa's car. The sound of Dessa's heels reverberated around the dim concrete stairwell.

"I'll be downtown, and obviously I'll have my cell—but just in case, I left the restaurant's number on the counter." Dessa looked back to make sure Hailey was listening. The girl was eyeing the shabby, chipping paint on the walls.

Someone else noticing the details that Dessa assured herself did not matter.

She knew that *Olivia* didn't mind where they lived. She didn't see the chips on the walls or the stains on the carpet. She didn't know it was unusual to smell ammonia when your next-door neighbor bleached her hair, or to fall asleep to the lullabies of bad actors rehearsing the same scene over and over again.

What was the expression?

Fish don't know that water is wet.

Ollie was her fish. Only Dessa knew how wet the water they lived in was.

They reached the fire door at the bottom of the stairwell. Dessa pushed her hip against it, flooding them in late afternoon sunlight.

Hailey winced.

The sound of a Korean soap opera bled from one of the apartments cantilevered above. Dessa led them to her assigned space, eyes on her daughter's shadowy form. "Ollie's father will be by around ten, but just to check in. He's probably going to have to head back out again."

"Wow. What does your husband do?"

Dessa looked away. Why bother correcting her?

"He's a lawyer."

"That sucks to have to work so late."

Dessa's eyes hurt from the adjustment of watching her daughter in the dark to the sun reflecting off Hailey's face. She shrugged.

"You can learn to live with just about anything."

A gentle pressure applied itself to Dessa's leg. Ollie staring up. Big eyes.

"I want to go, Momma."

"Momma has to go by herself. But tomorrow you and I can go on an adventure."

"To the zoo?"

Dessa pictured herself the next day, hungover from lack of sleep, pushing Ollie up the zoo's interminable hills. Melting in the city's interminable sun. "Really? Again?"

Olivia nodded, her breath a little pant.

"Okay. We will go. Again." She wrapped her arms around her daughter. "I love you more than the whole wide world."

2

Dessa turned right for what felt like the seventeenth time, circling the block, yet again. LOT FULL signs abounded. She was sure she had looked on this block before, but after a while the old movie theaters and jewelry stores began to blur into each other.

Between the key kiosks and falafel stands, Dessa could make out the odd mix that was downtown L.A.: Hispanic families, wheeling babies with impossibly thick hair in collapsible strollers; Chinese immigrants shouting in Spanish, stacks of plexi boxes holding miniature turtles at their feet; Orthodox Jews closing up their jewelry shops for the night, sweating primly in their wool suits.

Dessa loved this about Los Angeles. When she had first moved, she had tried to lend it all a sense of adventure while on the phone with her mother. *All these improbable people, wending their way through each other. Making their lives next to each other.*

It was the future. So exciting. So American.

"Sounds messy," said her mother.

A car pulled out of a space in front of her and Dessa's heart leaped. She was not in purgatory after all.

She took a deep breath, shifting herself, as well as her car, from Drive into something else. Readying herself to see her... her...

Was *friends* the right word to describe Heidi and Laurel?

Maybe there was some middle word, an in-between word, for someone who is no longer a friend but also not a former friend. Something that bridges the distance of past cohesion and current apathy.

The Germans probably had a word for it.

And Gretch? Was *friend* the right word for their relationship either?

No. The word was insufficient for her too.

Gretchen was so much more.

Dessa's name rang out over the dining room. Heidi's unmistakable holler.

She shrank. The restaurants' quieter inhabitants eyed her as she made her way past their tables toward Gretchen, Heidi and Laurel.

Gretchen stood. Giving her a hug. "The bride is already two in," she whispered.

That much was obvious.

Heidi's face was flushed. "Tell them I don't have to wear the veil."

"The veil?" Dessa was confused.

Heidi held up a flimsy piece of netting attached to a bedazzled plastic tiara.

"I told you to put it on, or I will pull out the giant inflatable penis I have in my bag," Gretchen said flatly.

The bride made a face and wedged the crown on her head.

"You're getting off easy," Laurel said. "You can't imagine the things we would have done to you in Vegas."

Dessa sat back.

She was the reason they were here and not in Vegas. She flushed at the memory of having to call Gretchen after she had gone increasingly quiet on the emails listing nightclubs, performances, spa treatments and airline tickets.

"Gretch, even if I could get someone to watch Ollie, I can't afford it," she'd finally admitted.

"I'll spot you."

"Heidi doesn't need me there anyway."

"You guys are good. She wants you there."

Dessa didn't buy it.

When was the last time she had a good time with Heidi and Laurel?

It had to have been before Olivia. Before she was pregnant. Before Joe. Before everything that constituted her life now had begun.

Heidi and Laurel had a way of talking about Ollie like she was some kind of accessory Dessa had chosen to wear. Or a lifestyle choice she had whimsically decided to pursue.

But, of course, having a child is nothing like getting your nose pierced or trying out veganism.

Gretchen, though, was different. She never treated Ollie like less than a person.

Mortified by the veil, Heidi hid her face behind her hands. Something flashed on her finger. Gretchen grabbed it. "Are you wearing your wedding band already?"

Heidi demurred. "We just got them today."

"Isn't that bad luck?" Dessa asked.

24

They stared at her. The things you don't say to a bride. She course corrected, "I'm an idiot. Don't listen to me."

"It's gorgeous." Laurel pulled Heidi's hand out of Gretchen's and toward her own face.

"Yes," Dessa added. "It really is."

"Thank you," Heidi said. "I couldn't help myself… It just looks so good and I know this is totally superficial, but…it makes the diamond look so much bigger."

"The bigger, the better." Gretchen aped Groucho Marx wiggling an imaginary cigar by her mouth. At least Dessa assumed it was a cigar.

The ring was now in front of Heidi's face, casting sparkles across her nose as she admired it. "I mean, I know it's not as big as Des's…but…you know…"

Heidi looked up after a moment, as if she had only just heard what she herself had just said. Everyone at the table suddenly aware of the three carats that occupied the real estate of Dessa's left hand.

Why the hell had she put this stupid thing on? What kind of person pleads poverty while wearing a college tuition's worth of diamonds?

"Yeah…well…" Gretchen sighed. They all knew. No one wanted to talk about it.

"I'm so sorry, Dessa." Heidi leaned toward her, laying her right hand over Dessa's left.

Envy, followed by pity.

"Nothing to be sorry for." Dessa smiled. "I think I could use a drink."

3

The music at the club was terrible.

On the dance floor, Dessa felt assaulted by it. This was music that simulated migraines. The auditory equivalent of pressing your thumbs against your eyeballs...

"This must be what the young people are listening to," Dessa shouted at Gretchen over the din. Her friend flashed a pained smile. Maybe she hadn't heard.

Or maybe it was a lame joke.

We're still years from thirty. We are "young people."

Dessa sighed.

It's only me who feels old.

She turned to make this observation to Gretchen, but her friend was gone. Dessa caught sight of the back of her head, as Gretchen wended her way through the throng of dancers.

Maybe she was chasing after Heidi and Laurel. Making sure they didn't get themselves into trouble.

Or maybe she was fleeing her best friend, a woman who was now incapable of just having fun for a few hours.

They had met in Venice Beach, five weeks after Dessa had moved to California.

Her college roommate's older sister had invited Dessa to a party, with a tone that, at least over email, conveyed less an invitation than a favor.

What Dessa's former roommate's sister's email had not mentioned was that the party would be on the roof of a building only a block from the beach.

Dessa had dressed for cocktails.

She was shivering before she even made her way up to the roof deck. From the edge of the building you could make out the white crests of the waves as they rolled in. Cheap string lights swayed in the wind. Dessa had searched for her friend's sister in the clumps of party guests, hoping there would be some family resemblance as a clue. Everyone else seemed to have gotten the memo that it would be both cold and casual.

"Jesus, did you know you're fucking blue?"

That was the first thing Gretchen said to her.

"I didn't know it was an outside party." Dessa tried to hide the shivering.

"Barbecues usually are. You know, outside."

Gretchen *was* dressed for the weather. Several layers. Oversize sweater, Jeans. Dessa already felt lame. She didn't want to make it worse by explaining that she hadn't known it was a barbecue.

Gretch pulled a bottle of whiskey from the collection on the table. A woodland fowl on the label, something smaller than a turkey. A quail or a grouse. Off brand of the off brand. She flexed her grip on the container, the plastic popping. "That's how you know you've got the really good stuff. The sound." She poured herself a shallow glassful of the cheap stuff, sipping it. "Fucking law students."

"What do you do?" Dessa asked.

"I'm a fucking law student."

Dessa had snorted at that. Not laughed but snorted. The sound deep and porcine. Nothing cute about it.

If it had been in front of a man, Dessa would have been embarrassed. But in front of this woman, who seemed so at ease with herself, Dessa just let it go.

Gretchen thought it was hilarious.

"I like you," she said. Like it was a normal thing to say.

Sometimes there is a recognition between two people that hastens their transition from strangers to friends. Like falling in love, but without the hormones.

For Dessa and Gretchen it was friends at first sight.

Gretch was "not a lesbian" but she didn't mind if people thought she was. She called herself a "power bitch," but to Dessa she seemed less bitchy than filterless. She did none of the usual feminine bullshit of opening a critique with a compliment.

"The compliment is that I've deemed you worthy of my fucking time," she would say if anyone complained.

She smoked real cigarettes unapologetically, which is difficult to do in a place like L.A., where people confirm that their food is pesticide free before making appointments to put poison into their faces. Gretchen drank brown liquor, owned a pit bull name Kitty and loved bad television.

Dessa thought she was amazing.

They discovered that they lived only three blocks from each other. They went to the same coffee place. Ate breakfast in the same diner. They had probably been in the same room dozens of times before, but they had had to travel all the way to Venice to actually meet.

It was Gretchen who took her to drinks when Dessa finally got a job that would net her enough to live in her own place. Who dragged her to Italy, Vietnam and the World's Largest Ball of Twine. When Dessa complained about a boy—because they were all still boys in the beginning—it was Gretchen who tapped her painfully on the side of the head.

"Stop it," she'd say. "Be more interesting."

And from someone else that would have been mean, but from Gretchen it was just the thing Dessa needed to hear. Either sort your shit out or shut up about it. Being around Gretchen made Dessa want to be smarter and stronger. Weak women complained about the way they were treated. Strong ones changed the way they were treated or shut the fuck up about it.

Gretchen was strong.

She was the friend who flew to Pennsylvania when Dessa's mother died. Who had helped iron out the worst of the estate tangles before taking a red-eye back to Los Angeles.

After the interment she had found Dessa sobbing on the floor of her mother's closet. Gretchen had gotten on the ground then and wrapped her arms around her.

"Being an orphan is a motherfucker," she had finally said.

And Dessa had laughed, her face red and wet.

That was how she was. How they were.

Dessa found Gretchen by the bar and then followed her eyes to where Heidi sat upon it, a shot glass topped with whipped cream pinned between her legs. A group of men gathered around her.

"It's called a Muff Diver," Gretchen yelled at her.

One of the men dipped his head between Heidi's legs, his friends cheering. He popped back up again, the shot glass in his mouth, fists held high. His friend handed him a fresh cocktail. This, he offered to Heidi like a knight presenting a favor to his lady.

"Lighten up, Dessa." Gretchen was right next to her. Mouth to ear. Her friend's face was serious.

Dessa's expression watching Heidi must have revealed something. Some judgment on her part. The humorless, unsexy, unfun part of herself that had been born with Olivia.

"Sorry."

"Don't be. Just fix it." Gretchen tapped her back. "Can someone buy this woman a drink?" she shouted to the crowd. Heidi's acolytes snapped to.

Quickly, Dessa had a vodka *something* settled into her hands. An unwise second cocktail. The one she would regret tomorrow morning when Ollie refused to curl up in bed past 7:00 a.m. The one she would feel when her daughter started pushing her eyelids open. "Up, Momma. Up!"

And then they were back on the dance floor. Gretchen, Laurel, Heidi. And Dessa. Hips dropping and rolling. Fingertips brushing her own thighs. Finding the hem of her own dress. Not so old after all. She sipped her drink, *slowly...*

But still it was disappearing a little faster than it should.

She would need to drive home, after all. She didn't even want to think about what an Uber to The Valley would cost on a Friday night.

Just then Dessa felt a vibration against her hip. Could be her phone. Or a phantom ring. There was too much sensory input here to be able to sort out the details.

She stepped away from Heidi's grinding body and reached into her purse. Her phone *was* ringing. The screen filled with a vaguely familiar set of numbers.

"Hailey?" she shouted after picking up. "Hold on! I'm moving to where I can hear you."

Dessa mouthed "Olivia" to Gretchen as she made her way back toward the entrance. More people had come in the interim. Dessa brushed against an army of sweaty bare shoulders on her way to fresh air.

"I don't know if it was the grilled cheese...or if the milk was bad..."

Hailey's voice was finally audible as Dessa crested the door.

"I mean, it was mainly grilled cheese. The throw-up."

Dessa filled in the details for herself. Ollie had woken up. Vomited. In the background, Dessa could hear her daughter whimpering a little.

"Hold on... Does she have a fever?"

There was silence for a moment. Presumably while Hailey felt Olivia's forehead. "Um. Well. She's warm...but I don't know if she's like fever warm."

Jesus. This girl was an idiot.

"Okay...just keep her comfortable. Give her little sips of water...but nothing else."

Dessa looked up the street, calculating. She was a least a fifteen-minute walk from her car. She could call a car to get her there, but who was to say that wouldn't take just as long. It was a thirty-minute drive down the 101. Less if there was no traffic and she pushed it.

"Did..." She hesitated. "Has Olivia's dad been by yet?"

"Not yet."

It was almost ten. He could still be on his way.

"I'll get there as soon as I can."

Dessa hung up and scrolled Recents for Joe's number. A picture of him with Olivia as an infant appeared on the screen. Her favorite photo of the two of them. Olivia all rolls and creases. Her father, eyes crinkly and happy.

It rang for a moment. Then dropped to voice mail.

"Shit."

"Everything okay?"

Dessa turned to see Gretchen. Leaning against the building. Lit cigarette in her hand. She had been watching.

Dessa shrugged. "Olivia's sick."

"And he's *working*."

They both knew who she was talking about. The way she had said *working*, Dessa knew she meant something else.

"Yeah. Maybe. I don't know."

Gretchen took a drag, and Dessa stepped into her cloud. This was how it had always been with them.

Four years before, when Dessa first told her best friend that she was moving to Van Nuys, there had been a moment, a gap, between Gretchen's true reaction and the one she gave.

In that brief silence sat evidence of how much Dessa's friend loved her.

Because she did not say *any* of the million-million things she truly wanted to say.

Instead, she had paused. Breathed.

And then her voice pitched up an octave. "That's great!"

The high voice is the lie voice. It was something they said to each other often. Calling each other out. They both knew Gretchen did not think it was great.

But sometimes love is in the lies.

"It's cheaper, so..." Dessa shrugged. She ran out of words before she reached the end of her sentence. Her friend nodded, eager not to have to talk about it. Another kindness.

Gretchen offered to help her move. But Dessa turned her down. She didn't want to see her friend's face as they drove past the dingbats of her new neighborhood, taking in the iron bars on the first *and* second floors. She knew Gretchen would be measuring the distance from one check cashing place to the next.

Helping her move would make it too hard for her friend not to say those million-million things.

The things Dessa had already told her she did not want to hear.

When she did come over for the first time, Gretchen was careful with Dessa in a way she had never been before. She treated their years-old friendship like a pair of new shoes she was breaking in.

Dessa gave a tour of her half-furnished home, relieved that her friend said nothing about chipped tiles or curling linoleum. Instead Gretch had remarked on what great light came in the living room and pulled a flat-pack containing the crib away from the wall. Inside the mesh of the base resounded.

"When were you planning on getting this together? Clock's a'tickin, Momma."

This was Gretchen's version of a peace offering—an acknowledgment of all the ways Dessa's life *had* and *would* be changed.

They spent the morning assembling the crib, cursing the instructions and repeatedly losing the Allen wrench.

"You know I love you," Gretchen said after they wedged the crib into a corner of the apartment's single bedroom.

"I do."

"You know I love you."

"Yeah."

Gretchen paused. Deciding. Up the street, a car lay on its horn.

She unlatched her purse and pulled a slip of paper from its recesses. Yellow legal. The curl of it bounced from Gretchen's hand.

The million-million things.

"I know you didn't want this…but…I looked up his salary. Plus bonuses from the past five years."

"Gretchen."

"What I'm saying is, I'd rep you for free. I'll probably have to go find a new firm to work at first…but it would all go to you and Ollie."

Dessa stared at the piece of paper. Gretchen's neat scrawl, columns of numbers pushing their way toward the bottom. Another string of digits, this one with a heavy comma, like Gretchen had darkened it for emphasis, was ringed at the bottom.

Dessa's chest felt hard. Why was she pushing this now? Battering at Dessa's well-constructed walls. Breaking their unspoken agreement.

"No."

"Do you not see how fucked-up this is, Dessa? You're broke. He's not. He's Olivia's fucking father."

Dessa did not want to crack this open, not now. "I can't do it without him."

"You *are* doing it without him."

"No. I am doing it without his money. It is *not* the same thing." Dessa felt her control slipping. Wobbling. The drink that had relaxed her now made her feel soggy and weak. Too close to the edges of her barriers.

"My decision, Gretchen. My shit to sort out. Not yours."

Gretch studied her face for a beat. Took a drag. "Right." She exhaled.

The tension between them went slack. Gretchen retreating behind Dessa's barriers. It would be okay. "Jesus. Go home, Momma." Gretchen dropped the stub and pulled Dessa into a hug. Kissed the top of her head. "Sick baby beats drunk girlfriends. I'll tell the girls you had to go."

Dessa yelled, "Thank you," as she crossed the street. "I love you!"

"You should love me! I'm awesome!" Gretchen called back before turning and heading back into the bar.

4

Dessa's feet hurt. If she were in her car, she likely wouldn't even consider the street she was on a hill…but in heels the incline seemed nearly impossible. Her calves burned, the balls of her feet protesting the capricious demands of women's fashion.

She considered taking her shoes off, but the thought of her bare soles touching Los Angeles pavement drew to her mind her mother's face, lips sour with disapproval. A blister was beginning to wear itself between the back of her heel and her shoe.

But she would not be taking it off.

Dessa could hear the cars on the 110 cutting their way through the skyscrapers. A persistent hum indicating that traffic was at the very least moving. Small groups of pedestrians, Hollywood types, in L.A. proper for a change of pace, made their way past her. This was what Friday night was like downtown, not so many people out that the sidewalks were crowded, but not so few that they were creepy.

Her phone rang. Joe.

"You know, you could have saved me a lot of flak if you had answered your phone five minutes ago," she told him.

"I was in the car! Aren't you always telling me not to answer the phone when I'm in the car?" On the defense…but playful.

"Where are you now?"

"In the car."

Dessa giggled, despite herself. She pinned her phone between her shoulder and her ear and kept walking.

"I'm almost there."

Dessa flooded with relief. "Oh thank God. Olivia threw up and this babysitter is a complete bimbo."

"Then I shall send this bimbo home and stay with the bug." Joe was clearly amused by her concern. But Dessa was thrilled that Ollie wouldn't have to stay with a stranger for much longer.

"Thanks. I'm leaving now, but it could take me a bit to get there."

Up ahead, a group of six men were walking toward her. Nice jeans and button-downs. Tipsy, grinning backslappers… The closer they got the less they looked like *men* to Dessa and the more they looked like *guys*. And she could pinpoint the exact moment that they noticed her walking toward them. The subtle changes in their postures as some unvocalized signal was sent through the pack.

Dessa pushed the phone into her ear. Trying to make the fact that she was on it more conspicuous.

It didn't work.

One of the pack—the Alpha, Dessa supposed—shouted at her as they approached, "Hey! You're headed the wrong way." Dessa glanced at them, her eyes meeting his for a brief moment. An accidental connection that would have caused him to look away quickly if he had been sober. But he was not.

"Sounds like I have a little competition," Joe gauged.

"I wouldn't worry about it." Dessa sighed. She didn't feel threatened by these overgrown boys...just kind of tired.

They passed her, but Alpha wasn't giving up. He turned and walked backward, shouting at her. "You look like you like schnapps!" He exaggerated the word, somehow achieving a guttural *a*. His friends burst into laughter. Clearly this performance was for them. "C'mon, I'll buy you schnapps!" Shhhh-N-Ahhhpps.

Dessa smiled. In spite of herself.

"There is something to be said for persistence though," she said into the phone, her tone playful. Joe was silent. Her flirty serve left unreturned. "Honey?"

A series of beeps interrupted Joe's silence. Call failed.

Dessa looked at the screen. A dim caul lay over the picture of Olivia and Joe. Try again? She took another step—

And stumbled. Ankle awkward, a dip to the side.

Dessa swore, righting herself. It couldn't have looked good. Wobbling like some sorority reject, too drunk for heels.

But then she looked up.

The street was *rolling*. Gentle waves cresting and falling, pushing their way through the pavement. Dessa wasn't exactly sure of what she was witnessing.

"Schnapps! Hey, Schnapps! We're having an earthquake!"

Dessa looked back toward the group of guys, who were paused in the middle of the sidewalk. They seemed thrilled with this new turn of events. High-fiving each other. Like the tectonic movements of the earth happened at just that moment so they would have something to reminisce about.

At the terminus of the street Dessa could make out the

bouncers at the bar where she had left the girls. They were waving the entire line of hopeful patrons inside.

The ground was still rolling. Dessa finally aware that she was rising and falling with it.

"Pussies!" the Alpha screamed. Dessa's eyes searched the area, looking for his new target and saw that across the street other more cautious pedestrians were rushing into buildings, their faces concerned but not panicked.

"This is a three-five. Maybe a four, tops."

His friends joined in the fun. Shouting, "Earthquake!" in mock horror. Waving their hands like frightened little girls. Dessa wondered what qualified their leader to rate the severity of the tremor.

But it was true, nothing about this lolling sine wave of a quake seemed particularly dangerous. Like the final hallway in the fun house she had gone to as a girl. The floor lifted and canted as you made your way toward the exit, hands wrapped around the banisters on the walls. Cars and taxis still drove by them on the street, probably unaware the earth was even moving.

Dessa wondered if she should head into one of the buildings. A bunch of drunk dudes in the street weren't necessarily the best role models.

But then the rolling slowed…coming to a stop.

"See, Schnapps! Just a cute little baby earthquake."

One of his friends threw an arm around his shoulders, "Hey! Since we're all about to die, would you mind having sex with him? He's got a really small penis. You'll barely feel it." The two of them curled over. Their laughter devolving into a heady hiss.

Dessa sighed, and turned back around. Tired of boys, of earthquakes and friends' expectations. She just wanted to get home to her baby and her man and go to sleep. To nurse a mild hangover in the morning and go to the zoo. To call Gretchen and pretend she had no memory of their last conversation.

She turned back up the hill, her feet biting their way toward the overpass.

There was an audible *smack*…like the tail end of a rug snapping. A loud reverberating crack.

Dessa fell forward, less down than *out*. Like the earth was rising up toward her. The skin of her palms tore into the pavement as she fell, just barely keeping her chin from impacting.

Then the world began to scream.

The roar blew toward Dessa, rising around her as she lay on the ground. Something monstrous pushing its way up from under the city.

Everything began to thrum. Harmonically attuned to the coming disaster. Windows trembling. Concrete grinding. Metal straining against stone…louder…louder…

Dessa braced herself against the building next to her, gaining her feet. From the street came a blare of horns as drivers suddenly became aware of the new movements of the earth, dislocating itself from under their tires.

There was a slick motion under Dessa's hand and she yanked it toward herself. The building next to her was *moving,* shuddering like a traumatized animal.

And then it *jumped*. The whole building leaped up, pulling at the restraints of its foundation.

The pavement beneath her began to heave and shudder. Dessa fell again, her body rocked forward, a violent shake. She screamed, looking for something to hold on to…but there was nothing but the ground that had thrown her. Forced by gravity to cling to the very thing that was betraying her.

"We have to get out of here!"

Dessa looked up. It was Alpha. His face serious now.

He held out a hand to her. Only a few feet away. She reached for him.

Twin sets of light sliced across their bodies. Dessa looked toward the street.

A car, too fast, was skidding toward them. Its wheels screamed against the road but the force of its trajectory was too strong. Dessa flinched as it swerved, its front wheel catching the curb, spinning it around.

There was a brief moment as the car flipped, a silence carried on the breeze it directed at Dessa's face.

And then it connected with Alpha's body, his hand still held out toward her. The hood of the car pinned him against the wall of the building. Alpha's friends turned to run, but before they had even taken a step, the car's tail whipped around, slamming them into the wall.

Dessa blinked, and for a moment she could still see a ghost image of Alpha's face in the lights burned into her retinas. The whole thing had taken seconds... They had been here... now they were gone.

It was not possible, but somehow it got even louder. The world ripping itself apart. Above Dessa there began a cacophony of high ringing splits. Something brushed her face as it fell from the sky. Dessa looked down as a gentle patter of crystals hit her shoulder.

A rain of glass.

Shards of falling windows battered at the arms Dessa used to cover her head. She forced herself to move. *Go*, her body demanded. *Go. GO!* There was no longer logic; there was only instinct and will.

She ran *into* the street, away from the buildings and their hail of glass.

And then it was quiet.

Dessa panted, her loud breath the only sound in her ears.

Limbs and chest beating in time with her heart, pulsing together. A pause. Dessa lifted her eyes, for the first time taking in the sight of the city beyond this street.

The silhouettes of skyscrapers swayed on the horizon. Like seaweed in the depths of the ocean. Pulled by a current beyond comprehension.

"God," Dessa heard herself say.

There had not until that moment been words. And now there was only this one. God.

Oh God. Dear God. Please God.

A prayer. An exclamation. A laying of blame. Dessa did not know. But it was the only word in Dessa's mind. The only word for this moment.

A loud crack echoed its way between the buildings. Originating from behind her. She turned.

At the bottom of the hill, the middle floors of the bar *bulged* outward horrifically. Dessa stared, trying to make sense of it. The structure looked impossible...because it was.

Muffled screaming emerged from the building. Hundreds of voices, rising in pitch. Men, women, everyone calling out in universal terror.

"Gretchen." Dessa imagined her best friend inside the club. Pressed against all that screaming humanity. Her voice wouldn't be one of them. She would be pushing her way out. She would be calm, heading for the exit. Her hands locked firm onto Heidi and Laurel. Dragging them all to safety. Dessa was sure of it. Certain it would only be a second until she would see her friends open the door, step onto the street—

The first floor gave way, disappearing under the second and the third. The building consumed itself.

Dessa screamed.

The ground came back to life. Angry. Pieces of the buildings above her began to fall. Architectural details tumbled from their moorings, cornice, molding, carved dente trans-formed on their way to the ground until they were all the same thing. Rubble. Pieces of the sky rained down on the street.

Dessa turned and ran toward the overpass, away from the buildings and their deadly debris. She reached the partition that separated the elevated city streets from the freeway below, and hauled her leg over the concrete barrier. Her heel dug into the grass of the embankment for a moment, but then she was sliding downward toward the stopped cars on the highway. Their taillights a river of red leading in the only possible di-rection. Away.

She twisted, her feet back under her. A woman watched her from inside a sedan, the shadow of the overpass making her face a dark blur.

Dessa beat at the car's window. Pleading. "Let me in! Let me in!"

The driver looked away. Shaking her head. Her hands grip-ping the wheel. She was crying.

Dessa pulled at the handle. Locked, it slipped in her hand. She pummeled the window again. Harder. "Please! Help me! Please!"

Above them a section of the overpass released a shriek as it wrenched itself free from its pylons. Inside her car the woman looked up. Horror bloomed on her face.

Dessa dropped to the ground by the car. Her hands cra-dling her neck. There was a rush of air, the mineral smell of cement and then the darkness of impact.

11 PM
DOWNTOWN

5

Beegie wakes to a world that has gone blank. Whiteness is everything. She knows this is wrong, but can't quite figure out *how* she knows it is wrong.

Right now she doesn't know how she knows anything.

She breathes and feels her breath reflecting back at her. It makes her face warm and damp. It smells like rubber and dust.

She realizes.

The whiteness is a wall. It is close to her face. And smooth. Like the color is part of it, not painted.

There is a tug on her shoe.

She realizes. Again.

She is lying down.

She is lying down and she is facing a white wall in a dim, hollow space.

There is another tug on her shoe. "Hey, Queen... Queen

Elizabeth…" says the man who is tugging on them. "You okay in there?" he says, and she nods. Her name isn't Queen Elizabeth, but her throat is too dry to tell him. She swallows and it hurts because there is no moisture in her mouth.

"C'mere," he says, and he pulls her by her feet out of the pocket she was in.

She realizes.

They are in a bus but it is…wrong.

Behind the man the roof is open, like it got punched through. There are bricks, hundreds of them, sitting on the seats and floor. Like the bricks are commuters. Like the bricks are going to Pacoima.

The man says, "Yeah, you're okay," and then he guides her to the steps. His hands are on both of her shoulders, and he is kind of pushing her out onto the street. There are people there and they look at her. They look gray, grim, ashen.

"We'll take care of her," says the man. And the people turn away. They seem happy they do not have to worry about her, like they have other problems.

"You are one lucky bitch," says Not-Charlie.

Beegie doesn't understand why she knows that that is his name. Or his *not* name.

"When you didn't get off the bus, I was sure you were toast." He laughs. "Ha. Ha. Ha."

The other man, from the bus, the Busman, puts his arm around her. He is so much bigger than her that his hand hangs awkwardly over her body. Hovering in the space between her head and her chest.

He starts to lead her away. Not-Charlie with them. A word bubbles up from somewhere in her body, "Bag," she says, "Need…bag."

"Ha. Ha. Ha," says Not-Charlie, and the Busman runs

back into the bus. He returns with her purse. He puts it on her shoulder, threading her arm through the loop. And Beegie feels better knowing it is there.

6

Dessa had experienced her "first" earthquake on Gretchen's couch.

Kitty's large head had been occupying the real estate of her lap when he suddenly perked his ears. He sat up, the muscles under the fawn-colored fur of his body taut. Dessa had enough time to wonder what was wrong before she felt it herself. A few of the framed photos on Gretchen's fireplace fell over, their edges clattering against the adobe of the mantel. And then it was over.

"You feel that?" Gretchen appeared at the door to her kitchen. A bowl of popcorn in her hands.

Dessa had giggled. Nervous energy escaping. They had warned her about earthquakes when she moved here. Not Californians. Not people who actually lived and worked and occupied the area above the San Andreas Fault line. But everyone else. It was the second thing they mentioned as soon as Dessa said she had gotten a job here. Right after they mentioned the weather.

Gretchen kicked Kitty off the couch and pulled her legs up. Dessa stared at her, trying to take a cue from her casualness. "What do we do?" Dessa finally asked, and Gretchen had laughed. Open mouth and full-bodied. A maw full of popcorn.

"Nothing. We wait. Either that was it...or..."

"Or what?"

"I don't know, Dess. There could be more. There probably won't be. We sit. We watch television. We drink cheap ass wine because we can't afford better."

Dessa knew all about aftershocks. But she had been stunned to learn about foreshocks, little quakes that could come before bigger ones. Appetizers and main courses.

"What do we do if..."

"If the *Big One* hits?" Gretchen made her voice spooky. Like she was telling a ghost story. She took a sip of her wine. "Honestly, it feels like they keep changing it. It used to be stand in a doorway. And then they were like *never* stand in a doorway. And also you weren't supposed to go outside, but then they were like, whatever, maybe outside's cool."

"Wasn't there something about a table?"

"Oh yeah. Uh...you're supposed to duck down next to a thing. Like a countertop or a table. But next to it not under it. That way if the ceiling falls, it'll fall on the thing you're next to and not you."

Dessa seemed to recall this was called "zero-point" though the phrase made no sense to her. An awkward crouch, hands on your neck, balance on the tips of your toes. If it were a yoga pose it would be called "The Coward."

Eventually she had loosened up; it was clear they weren't in any danger. Kitty jumped back on the couch, pinning their legs down under the blanket and his considerable heft. Another earthquake didn't arrive. It had been the main course, not the appetizer.

But later that night, on the porch, Gretchen grew quiet, drawing on her cigarette. Dessa swatted at bugs and looked out at Gretchen's small patch of yard. The light by the door only reached the edges of the grass, making dim mysteries out of the sad landscaping beyond.

"You know we're fucked right? If the big one really hits?" Gretchen looked at her. Serious. "All that stuff about making sure you have enough bottled water and a bugout bag? It's horse pucky. Propaganda to make it seem like the people in charge can do *anything* about it. Just wait patiently, Good Citizen. Help will arrive." She saluted, the cherry tip of her cigarette making an arc through the air. "When it happens, the fucking authorities themselves are going to be in the shit. It will be chaos for days. Weeks. There will be looting. Riots. The earthquake isn't the real disaster, Dessa. The disaster is what happens after."

"You mean like tsunamis?" Dessa was haunted by the footage she had seen from Japan. A camera positioned at the crest of a hill, picking up no sound but recording the gray line of water as it slowly pushed itself into town. People exited houses and rushed toward the hill, climbing, but Dessa knew that so many more of them were still inside. The same houses that had begun to lift and float, like ships, but not built for travel.

"No. Not tsunamis." Gretchen shook her head. "People. Panicked scared people are what make it dangerous after any disaster. And that shit is something that making sure you have enough canned food isn't going to do anything about."

Dessa laughed, trying to relieve the tension, "Jesus, Gretchen. Dark."

"Yeah, well...that's me. Mistress of the Dark."

"Tell you what, if the big one hits, I'll come over here and take care of you."

"Dessa, when the big one hits, you take care of yourself first. That's what I'll be doing."

Dessa awoke with a gasp, her breath drawing in a lungful of dust-laden air. She coughed in response, the spasm pressing her back into the large *something* that loomed above her. The blade of her forearm swept against the distinct cool of metal. The car, though Dessa could not see it. She was in a pocket. A small space between the crushed remnants of the car and the section of overpass she had seen tear itself from the bridge above.

Shaking, she reached out in front of her. Her fingers scraped the edges of something small and jagged. Stone. Concrete.

Rubble, thought Dessa. But how much? There could be dozens of feet of debris between her and the open air. The fact that she was even alive, panicked breathing in the dark, was incredible. Her limbs felt fine, sore but working.

But if she started digging, she could upset whatever delicate balance had saved her. She could lose her little pocket of safety and bring it all tumbling down.

Dessa thought about the stories of people found alive in collapsed buildings. Third world survivors pulled from the wreckage four, five, seven days after a disaster. The weak calls that brought their rescuers. The pictures of emaciated dehydrated but *living* people that accompanied the articles. The lucky ones.

Those articles never showed the multitudes pulled out before them. The not-so-lucky.

Olivia.

The image of her daughter's face flew into her mind. Her

gap-toothed smile beaming at her mother. Pretty baby. Sick before the quake. And after?

How was Ollie now?

A sound burst from Dessa's mouth. Involuntary. A plea.

This was impossible. She could not *be* here. She could not be stuck in this place while her daughter was…was…

Dessa's hand found a jagged piece. The size of a fist. She pulled it toward her, pushing it between her legs. She moved quickly. Moving the rocks into the small spaces around her feet, behind her, wedged up next to the car. She crept into the space she cleared. Pushing her way forward.

She began to sweat, the chalk from the rubble making a strange paste on her hands. The space behind her grew larger but the space before her didn't seem to have grown any smaller. Dessa imagined herself like Sisyphus or some other Greek figure, punished by the gods for a minor offense. Cursed to spend the rest of her life digging her way through some god-wrought tube of rocks. Making space for herself endlessly, circling back to the beginning until she was moving stones she had already laid her hands upon.

The car groaned, protesting under some new weight. A shift. Dessa ducked, pulling away… But to where? There was nowhere to go. She braced herself. Coward's pose. She waited.

Nothing came down.

Dessa drew shaky, desperate breaths. Each one a prayer. *Please. Please.*

The car next to her was silent. No more moans. Dessa tried to wrestle her fear. Put it in a box. Save it for later.

The only way out is through.

She began again.

She did not know how long it took until her fingertips tasted air. She had been reaching down, grasping, and then suddenly there was nothing. Dessa yelped, hope leaping. She turned her wrist feeling the bumpy edges of what had to be a section of the overpass. She moved her hand upward and it brushed something. Long and bumpy. Metal.

Rebar. The long thin poles laid down before pouring concrete. Their purpose to strengthen the structure as a whole.

Dessa swept her hand down. Scooping. A faint light struck her eyes, revealing a narrow gap between the metal bar and the pavement of the street.

It was a bit more than a foot wide, but the space between the ground and the rebar was shallow. Six or seven inches.

Dessa lay down and wiggled her way toward the hole. Far away she thought she could hear someone…wailing.

"Help!" she called. Her voice sounded strange. Hollow and weak.

The wailing continued in the distance. Uninterrupted. No one was coming.

Dessa looked up at the rebar, a carpet of gravel under her head. This was not a place she wanted to get stuck. The earth could shake again and drop the slab on her. She could squeeze her top half out, but then be stuck halfway. A magician's trick.

She took a deep breath. One arm out, then the other. Shoulders down. Head turned to the side. She pushed herself through, a strange familiarity to the action. A bar passing over her face. A year of Bar and Bat Mitzvahs over a decade ago.

Limbo loo, limbo lye.

Her breasts caught on the bar. She emptied her lungs, for the first time in her life willing them smaller. A push could send the whole thing tumbling. She closed her eyes and pressed herself backward.

A rain of dust slid down on her…but the slab held. Dessa stared up into the heavens, visible because the quake had turned out the city's lights.

"Stars, Momma," Olivia would say. Staahs.

"Of course," Momma would say. *And she would turn on the stars.*

Dessa thought it was possible Ollie had never seen real stars. Just the fake ones her mother projected onto their walls at bedtime.

Dessa angled her hips out. One side lifted then the other. Feet bare now, shoes lost beneath the wreckage, dead mother's opinions on such things be damned.

But as soon as she was out, she was reaching back in. Her arm sweeping around in the dark. Plumbing the rocks to find it. There was a moment of fear when she thought she'd left it too far in…that she'd have to go back in.

But then her hand curled around the leather strap. Fish on a line.

Her purse.

Dessa turned it over, dumping its contents on the street. Billfold, sunglasses, lipstick, car keys, tampons. Phone.

She seized it. Her fingers fumbling. "Please work, please work."

The screen flared to life. Dessa was not the only thing that had survived the quake. She pressed the string of number that would connect her to Hailey's phone.

Three low tones. Call Failed.

Joe's phone. Then Hailey's again. Again. Again. Again.

All met with that same dead line tone. No connection.

Dessa threw up.

She had not sensed it coming. Her body had given her no warning at all. One second she had been looking at her phone screen, thinking about all the implications of those tones. Could be that the network was just down. Could be it was overloaded.

Could be there were no more phones for her to connect to.

She managed to turn her head in time so that the spilled contents of her purse were not covered by the spilled contents of her stomach. The remnants of her dinner with Gretchen and Heidi and Laurel a Rorschach on the street. Food she had eaten four hours and a lifetime ago.

Gretchen, Heidi, Laurel. The *sound* that had come from the bar before it had collapsed. Dessa retched again. This time choking up bile. Her body spasming.

And then she wasn't throwing up so much as she was sobbing on her hands and knees. Wails of grief and fear and panic, coming up from her stomach and deeper places. Just as involuntary as the vomiting. As uncontrollable and inevitable as the need to push when she had had Ollie.

Olivia.

Gretchen.

The sound of a woman's voice reached her ears. A whining wail. Pathetic and feral. Uncontrolled.

It took her a moment to realize it was her own voice. Reflected back to her. Echoing off of the remaining section of the underpass, hovering above.

Dessa held her breath. Choking off the cry. The voice from the underpass ceased as well. There would be time for this later. She wiped her mouth and put the contents back into her purse.

"Just get home," she said to herself. "Just get home."

It could be her mantra. Something she could say with every step. A walking prayer. Just. Get. Home. Each word a footfall.

6 PM
(EARLIER)
LOS FELIZ

7

One of the babies got burned after dinner.

Byron Jay. With the glasses. A little red bubble blister on his forehead. Barb didn't notice him walking up behind her, sippy held up for juice. He'd walked straight into her cigarette, the ash breaking a trail down his eyebrow to his cheek. He'd started to cry, and Barb had known immediately how much she'd fucked up. Beegie could see it on her face.

Beegie took care of the other children while Barb clucked over Byron. Sitting him up on the countertop. Big worried smile. *"Oh you had an accident,"* she said, putting a bandage over the blister.

The cigarettes had started over the summer. First the smell of them from under her door after she'd "gone to bed," but now Barb was doing it openly. With her coffee in the morning. At the kitchen table at lunch. Ashing into the stacked up bowls of soggy Cheerios by the sink.

The drinking, unlike the smoking, had stayed confined to Barb's bedroom. On weekends, Beegie would watch Barb head to her room one, two, three times before lunch. By the afternoon she was slurry and loose with the littles, watching them in the front yard, slumped on the porch steps.

No good saying anything about it though. To Barb, to Kate, to anyone. If the agency knew, they'd yank everyone, and then *who knew* where Beegie would end up. So she kept her head down, chin tucked, folding laundry.

But when Byron got hurt, it was her face that betrayed her, not her mouth.

"You got a problem, Baby Girl?"

Beegie shook her head and slammed her eyes down.

"He's fine." Barb gestured, wobbly palm open, as Byron ran off to play in front of the television with the other kids. "See?"

"I didn't say anything."

"Right."

Barb leaned over and plucked the still-lit cigarette up from the edge of the sink. Stared at Beegie while she put it back in her mouth. Defiant.

"I got a phone call today... About you."

Beegie's tried to make herself small. Thought of the way Rooster used to roll on his back and pee himself to show Eric he was submissive. That's what Barb wanted her to do. Piss herself to prove she knew who was in charge.

"They said they'd been calling the people you used to live with, and finally that boy told the school that they needed to call me."

Beegie felt the back of her neck go hot. "Which boy?"

"I don't know, Beegie? The older one? It's not about that. It's about all the days you've been missing."

The school had been calling the Greelys about the days she'd skipped. Eric on the phone with them. Knowing her business.

Barb was still talking but Beegie wasn't there. She was sitting at the Greelys' dinner table, imagining them laughing at her. Mrs. Greely saying that some people can't be saved and Mr. Greely agreeing with a grunt. Eric nodding and shoving his face full of bread rolls.

"What I want to know is, what are you doing all day?"

"Nothing."

"'Cause you better not be... I can't have that around the babies."

"I never... I don't."

"'Cause you missing school like this...it makes what that family said before, it makes it seem like it was true."

A spark of something lit inside Beegie. An ember of rage and shame.

Barb kept talking. "Ten days, Beegie. You've missed ten days of school. Do you know how much trouble I could get into for that?"

"Not as much as for burning a baby with a cigarette," Beegie mumbled.

"What's that?"

"I said not as much as for burning a baby with a cigarette."

Beegie's voice was louder this time. Not shouting but audible. Each word pronounced and clear. It was a surprise for both of them.

"That was an accident."

"Just like you being drunk right now is an accident." The words flew out. She'd been holding them, wasps in her throat, bouncing and stinging against her insides until they had finally found a path out. "Just like you being wasted *every night* is an accident."

She caught Barb's hand before it connected with her head.

The older woman screamed at her, a choked cry, other arm flailing down onto her body. She called Beegie a whore. And a liar. She told her she'd have Beegie sent to a group home, like the one up in Riverside. That she knew what happened to girls who got sent up there.

The babies watched. Turned from the television and stared at them. Large-eyed and openmouthed, they witnessed Barb pummeling Beegie. Beegie trying to keep those swats from landing. At some point Beegie felt a faint tickle on the back of her neck, and she realized that Barb still held the cigarette. That the ashes from it were raining down on her, sliding into her clothes.

Beegie turned and ran. Grabbed her bag from its hook and pushed her way outside.

Beegie had that hot feeling in the back of her throat. Like she was gonna cry. Why had she done that? Said that? *Stupid, stupid.*

Her breath shuddered.

Uh-uh. None of that. She dug a hard knuckle into her eye. If there were any tears there before, there weren't after. She could be angry at herself without looking weak.

By the time the bus arrived, the hot feeling was gone and she was thinking about more practical considerations. Like where the fuck she was going to go. She couldn't go back.

Not tonight at least. Barb would only get worse after she put the kids to bed. She'd be sitting in front of the television, getting angrier and angrier and drunker and drunker. If she went back before Barb had slept some of the booze out, they'd just pick up where they'd left off.

In the morning it would be easier.

If Beegie got there when the kids were waking up, she could be cleaning the kitchen before Barb had even had her coffee.

Barb might be a drunk but that didn't mean she didn't know a good thing when she had it. Beegie made Barb's life easier.

She flared at the idea of trying to make that *woman* happy... to go back and pretend she *hadn't* hit her. To listen to her yell at her for skipping school. Yes, ma'am. Of course, ma'am.

Fuck that.

But she didn't really have any choice.

It was deal with Barb or get assigned somewhere else. And just 'cause it was somewhere else didn't mean it was better. It just meant it was somewhere else.

Like three placements ago. Janelle's. Beegie told Kate that Janelle had a boyfriend who came into her room at night. And that when Beegie asked him what the hell he was doing there, he had said he was just checking on her, but she knew what he'd been about.

And so Kate got her assigned to a new house. The Greelys this time, whose oldest son, Eric, *also* came into her room at night.

So Beegie knew better now. Frying pans and fires.

Sometimes you think you're in the fire, but you're not.

Or maybe you *are* in the fire, but it's always possible to get moved to a part of the fire that's even hotter than the part you used to be in. And now, this new place is gonna make you all crispy and charred.

Barb's house was the frying pan. Beegie could live in the frying pan. Had to live there.

But not tonight. For now she just needed to kill time.

Beegie decided she would just be on the bus for a while. Use her pass. Ride it to the end of the line then back again. Maybe she could do this all night. Back and forth, back and forth until dawn. At least she would be sitting down while she decided how she was gonna make it better with Barb.

A bus squealed up to the stop. Air brakes pitching their

two-tone whistle. Beegie clocked the route number as she climbed aboard. *This is the bus I used to take home*, she thought.

And then, *No. It wasn't home. None of them are.*

What she *should* have thought was that it was the bus that used to take her to the Greelys'. The Greelys' wasn't home. Neither was Barb's. Janelle's. Even the place she used to live with her mother, that wasn't *home*. They were places she kept her stuff. Where she slept.

Beegie made her way to the back as the bus pulled away from the stop. Lots of people on here this time of day. The sun just starting to go down. Everybody on their way back from work. All crammed together, smelling like the end of the week. Sweat and corn chips. So many people made the air on the bus clammy.

Beegie grabbed a pole just past the stairs in the back. Someone would clear out soon.

She looked out at her fellow passengers. Almost every one of them staring at something. Their phone. A book. The window. Every one of them in their own worlds. Thinking about their own lives.

The weird ones, Beegie thought, were the people who just folded their hands in their laps and stared straight forward. Like they were able to just...*take off*, go somewhere else without a book or phone screen.

Absent themselves...that was the word.

Absent...like she had been from school.

Ten days. She didn't know it had been that many.

What have you been doing, Beegie?

Nothing. Mostly.

One day she'd been walking to school from the bus...and she had just kept walking. No reason. She didn't feel like going. So she didn't.

Instead she went to the park with her book. It had been a

good one. Weird though. About a white family whose house was a little bit bigger on the inside than it was on the outside. And then one day they come home and there's a new door where there wasn't one there before and it opens into a hallway that shouldn't be there. And then everyone was freaking out 'cause this is all happening in their *home*.

It made Beegie laugh. If a mysterious room opened itself up in Barb's house, she'd probably call the agency and tell them they should approve her for more kids.

Ten days though. Beegie had only skipped when she thought she really needed it. To go to a park or the library and forget herself in something scary for a minute.

Guess I needed it a lot.

Beegie thought maybe the reason she liked scary things— movies, books, stories, whatever—was that at the end of most of them the monster was defeated. That was how the stories would go; everything was good, then a monster came, then the monster was defeated and then everything was good again.

That wasn't how things were in real life though. In real life people live *with* their monsters. In real life the monster didn't *come*...in real life the monster was already there.

The image of Eric answering the school's phone calls about her absences danced into her mind.

Fuck him. Beegie could just see the way his lips would've curled over his tiny little baby teeth at hearing she was in trouble.

The bus squealed to another stop. Beegie rocked on her feet, tightening her grip on the bar. The back doors swung open and Beegie pushed her way into a newly freed seat by the first riser.

There was a burst of loud talking from the front of the cab. Someone behind the queue of newly boarded people. "No one here's gonna tell if you take one. It's a tip!"

The crowd cleared a bit, and Beegie could make out a man leaning over the bus driver. The driver was shaking his head furiously and yanking his hand, gesturing for the man to move back. The guy shrugged and picked a heavy box up from the floor before moving on.

He was halfway back when Beegie realized that his heavy box was a case of beer. The bus rocked as it started moving again, and the man stumbled a little.

All of the emptied seats had been filled again, and so the man stopped, right above the stairs, in the space where Beegie had been standing only a minute ago. He set the case of beer down on the ground with a thud.

Beegie watched him out of the corner of her eye. He wore a button-down. Tan pants. He looked like a guy with a job. Like a guy with *people*.

But he was acting *wrong*. Like the bus was a party, not a place where everyone worked hard to pretend they were alone. Instead, this guy was smiling, trying to catch people's eyes.

He reached down through a hole ripped in the top of the box. "Anybody want a drink? I'm buying." He wielded the can above his head. "Anybody?"

Everyone ignored him. Kept staring out their windows or at their books or screens. If anything, the bus got even more quiet in response to his invitation. No one wanting to draw his attention.

He cracked the beer. The sound of the tab popping rang through the cabin.

"It's Friday, motherfuckers!" he announced before taking a big pull. Beegie watched his Adam's apple bob up and down as he swallowed.

He pulled his lips away from the can with a satisfied gasp. His eyes catching Beegie's as they opened.

"You want?" he asked, smiling.

Beegie shook her head and looked away.

But she could feel his eyes still there. Sipping his beer and watching her. She looked back, and he winked at her, before finally looking away.

Beegie looked back out the window. They were now in her old neighborhood. The place she'd accidentally called *home*.

She wished she'd thought to grab her book before she left Barb's. When she'd been running out the door. Then she could have lost herself in it now.

The bus squealed to a stop. Beegie's old one. Not much had changed in the past year.

A sudden resolve solidified inside her.

Without thinking, Beegie was launching herself out of her seat. Ducking past the Busman with the beer. He leaned back for her and she stooped under his arm. "Have a nice night," he said as her feet hit the stair. She glanced back at him, for a moment, before swinging onto the crumbly piece of sidewalk she used to come back to every afternoon.

As the bus pulled away, Beegie felt her palms go sweaty. Her limbs felt loose, elastic with a kind of wild energy. Something had happened on the bus, thinking those thoughts, seeing these old sights.

She was still angry. But not with herself anymore.

12 AM
DOWNTOWN

8

Overlay. That was the word for it.

As Dessa walked through the remains of the Jewelry District, she realized she had an *overlay* of what it should be. Her memories of the place, of what it was and what it should be, lay over what was in front of her, over her, under her bare feet.

Like the insert in the *H* edition of her grandmother's encyclopedias, Dessa's favorite one: HUMAN. Each layer of anatomy printed on a separate sheet of clear cellophane. Skin, muscle, bones. Dessa would flip them back and forth, dressing and undressing the skeleton with flesh, until her mother tsked at her and took the book away.

The building that was on fire was also not on fire. The florist stand that had toppled and cracked onto the street was also upright, a display of cheap carnations and tightly budded roses in buckets along its front. The street was filled with both the cracked remnants of buildings and moving unblemished cars. The light flickered, orange from the blaze, but it was also the pink tinged gray Dessa had walked in to get to the restaurant.

Dessa blinked hard. Trying to discipline herself to mind the physical *now*. That was what was important. This was some trick her brain must be playing on her, calling these memories up. Forcing her to look at them. Was it too early for the symptoms of post-traumatic stress? She wasn't post anything… the trauma was *ongoing*.

It had only been an hour. Almost ten when she spoke to Joe. Just past eleven when his phone and Hailey's had failed to connect with hers.

There was a hail of sparks from within the burning building. Something collapsing within. The fire leaped up in response. Licking at the edges of the other structures. The air thick with char.

The light grew brighter in response, sending the street's inhabitants' shadows jumping. It was these people for whom Dessa had no overlay, and so they were the ones she focused on.

Survivors, she supposed, all of them. But they were not all the same.

Some were victims. Their faces blank or pained.

And some were…not victims.

These others bounced around the streets with a frenetic energy that distinguished them from their counterparts. Crowbars and baseball bats hanging from their hands.

Not victims. *Opportunists.*

There were not many of them, but their whoops and calls, their *excitement* was so wrong, it terrified Dessa. Did they have no idea of the scale of what had just happened? Or did they simply not care?

A group of them rushed past her, close enough that Dessa

could feel their wind on her bare arms. They were boys really. Maybe four or five years younger than the men who had taken shots from between Heidi's legs earlier tonight, or the guys who had talked to her before the earthquake. Alpha and his friends.

Of course none of those men had survived. And these boys had.

Maybe they had a right to their gleeful looting.

One of the opportunists turned toward her. Dessa gasped at the sudden change in his direction. The swing of attention to her. She braced herself against the wall. A reflex.

The boy laughed at her bare fear. "Hey, Mama!" he said. Wagging his tongue. Fingers held up in mock devil horns on his head.

And then he was away from her. Bouncing to catch up with his friends, already bashing their way into a jewelry store.

But Dessa was still awash in the fresh panic and fear he had called up. She took a breath and watched as the group of boys heaved themselves through the smashed windows and into the dark interior of the store.

What must it be like to have that power? To *not* be afraid, but to have others be afraid of you? Not just right now on this dark street, but on all the dark streets.

Dessa reached her car about ten minutes later. The entire front section of the car, the engine, had been crushed. The front wheels splayed out beneath the heavy gravity of the *something* that had fallen on it. There was no way to identify what it was that had killed her car, and with it, any hope of her driving out of here inside of it.

Dessa stared at the vehicle, only now realizing her idiocy in even coming this way. *What roads were you planning on driving out on, Dessa?* she asked herself. *The one that fell on you?*

A flurry of voices behind her. Breaking glass. More opportunists. She needed to hide. The car door protested as she wedged it open...but it gave. Dessa swung herself inside the backseat, her heart knocking on her chest. She hit the remote. Once, twice. Two watery beeps emerged from the ruined front of the car. Locking her in.

"I can't do this." Her voice sounded so young. A teenager's whine.

Her father's face flew into her mind.

When she was fourteen, he had taken her on a canoe trip. Her mother had begged off, saying that two weeks without indoor plumbing didn't seem like her idea of a vacation. Dad had kept inviting her though, all the way until he had closed the trunk of their car. Mom had watched them from the driveway, pulling away in the dawn light.

"You knew she wouldn't come," Dessa had said.

"Yeah. But she liked that I asked." He had fixed Dessa with a conspiratorial look. "Plus if I hadn't asked, she would've insisted that she come along... And then we'd all have been miserable."

Dessa tried to imagine her well-coiffed, impeccably dressed mother on the vacation her father had described. The hikes he had called portages. The promised days of endless paddling. The mosquitoes. "Yeah, you're right."

But once she was on the trip, she worried maybe she should have stayed home with her mother. A preference she had almost never shown and was now showing less and less as an adolescent.

No doubt, it was beautiful up north. But Dad also asked more of her here. A lot more. Each day, she was expected to gather wood, throw the bear pack line and haul up the food. Rise early, put on boots still chilly wet and strike the tent. She had to carry a pack that was nearly half her weight while he carried the canoe on his shoulders down the trail.

When she finally complained about the weight of the pack, he offered to switch. The boat looked lighter on his shoulders, an easier load to carry, so she quickly agreed. At first it wasn't bad, not after the canoe was settled on her, yoke balanced on her bony shoulders, fingers forward hooked into the gunwale. It wasn't exactly easy, but she did prefer it to the formless Duluth pack she had been hunching down the trail.

"Okay, now take it down," Dessa's father said.

Dessa knew the mechanics. To push up with one hand, while gripping with the other. Swing the whole of the boat over one's head while turning your knees into it…making a flat table of them to receive the bulk of the vessel. She pushed with one arm… It was impossible.

"I can't." Dessa's voice reverberated inside the boat.

"What if I injure myself while we're on the trail? You have to be able to get yourself out of there."

She tried again. The weight of the stern shifted back, and she stumbled, pushing her fingers forward to catch and rebalance it.

"I can't do this!"

Her father didn't answer. The boat over her blocked her entire view of the world above her waist level. "Dad?"

She couldn't see his legs anywhere. "Dad?"

Her father had disappeared. Proving a point. Either she was going to do it without him or she was going to just stand there waiting until he decided she was telling the truth and she really *couldn't* do it.

Fuck you, Dad, she thought. *I can wait just as long as you can.*

She imagined him watching her from a distance. Could tell he was there, the way the insects were quiet. Still she waited, the yoke digging into the crest of her shoulders. But then the mosquitoes found her. They landed on her arms, and she could not slap them away without losing her balance and dropping the tip of the boat. She watched them on her skin, three of them. Their bodies extending with her blood.

"God damn it!" she yelled and pushed. The trick was that it was almost a throw. You only needed to get it up halfway before gravity kicked in and did the rest of the job for you, swinging it around and down. She banged her knee because she hadn't gotten it out fast enough…but she got it down.

Her father smiled at her from where he had been watching, about three yards off, close enough to intervene if she had gotten into trouble.

She wanted to tell him to go to hell. She even considered how much trouble she would get in for doing so.

But he had looked so fucking proud.

Thoughts of her father brought her down, quelled the panic. Her father before. When he was still *himself.*

"Before you say you can't do something, think of what would happen if you didn't have any choice," he had said to her.

Outside, another pack of nonvictims came jogging past the car. Dessa dropped to the leg well and tried to make herself as small as possible.

"THAT TICKLES!" said a loud voice, filling up the car.

Dessa's heart nearly stopped. She pulled a patchwork dog with an incongruous grin out from underneath her. Dessa hated this toy. The vaguely psychotic giggle. The tacky "Press Me" hands and feet. The unnerving way it went off by itself, when no one was near it. *"HAHA!"*

"HUG ME!"

A gift from Gretchen, likely picked for its offensive qualities. It smelled of raisins. Animal crackers. Baby shampoo.

It smelled like Ollie.

Dessa wiped the tears off her face with the back of her wrist. She swept her hand under the seat, pulling out a heavy metallic flashlight. The kind cops use.

She clicked it on and directed it at her foot, afraid of what she might see. The light bent on its way through a shard that had embedded itself deep in Dessa's heel, a pain she had been ignoring. Dessa took a breath. *I can't do this*, she thought once more.

And then she did.

The piece came free, releasing a stream of blood. Dessa pressed at the wound, cursing herself for not anticipating the gush. She fumbled around for the package of baby wipes she kept in the back of the car to clean up Ollie's messes. Drops of blood fell onto the floor, stains. Reflexively Dessa was upset before she realized, *It's not like I was going to drive it anymore.* She pressed the wipes down into her foot, staunching the flow.

If she was going to get anywhere, she was going to need a new pair of shoes.

7 PM

BALDWIN HILLS

7 P.M.

SELDOM IDLE

9

When no one answered the door to the Greelys' house, Beegie hopped the fence.

The Greelys had a key they left in a lockbox attached to their back porch. This was because Drew forgot his key at school a lot and Mr. Greely got tired of having to leave work to come home and let him in. Once Beegie moved in, they didn't have to worry about it anymore. She was always there when Drew got home, and she knew better than to ever forget her key.

But she knew the code.

Or at least she used to. Depended on how thorough Mrs. Greely had been in eradicating Beegie from their life.

The moon was just starting to rise, but there was enough light bleeding from the neighbors' house that Beegie didn't have any trouble making her way to the lockbox. Her fingers had pressed the first three buttons before she saw the flashes of light through the sliding glass door.

Someone *was* home. Downstairs. Watching TV.

Beegie stepped away from the box and into the shadows under the deck. She moved in for a closer look, just to see if it was Mr. Greely, who might give her what she wanted, or Mrs. Greely, who definitely wouldn't.

A sharp bark pierced the quiet, and suddenly Rooster was running up at the glass toward her. The dog's small muscular body threw itself at the glass violently, claws scrabbling to get at her. Beegie backed away.

The door slid open.

"Beegie?"

It was Drew, though he'd grown up a lot since she'd left. He was still skinny, but coming into his height. He held Rooster by the collar. The dog kept barking, his paws clawing at the air.

"What are you doing here?" he whispered, his voice lower than she remembered it.

"I left something," Beegie said. She hadn't thought about Drew. He had seemed like such a kid when she left, but he wasn't really that much younger than her. Less than a year.

"Mom and Dad are on a retreat."

Beegie knew about these. They'd taken her on a few while she'd been with them. They said it was like a vacation, but when they were there all they did was eat and listen to people talk about God. Just like going to regular church, except it never ended.

"They left you here by yourself?"

"I have a project for school. Eric's in charge."

Beegie nodded. Rooster was still growling beneath Drew's hand.

"Can I come in?" she asked.

Drew stepped aside and let Beegie pass through. He released the dog, and the creature threw himself at Beegie, his venom suddenly gone. Instead, Rooster whined and pawed at her ankles, recognizing her and begging to be loved.

Beegie ignored him. Rooster was Eric's dog.

Drew was quiet. On the TV SpongeBob yammered something to Patrick. A can of Coke sat fizzing on the coffee table, an open bag of chips on the couch.

Beegie had forgotten that…the nice things about this place. The freedom.

"What was it?"

"Huh?"

"What was it you left?"

"Uh…" Beegie stalled… Her eyes locked on the screen. She saw her first scary movie in this room. With Eric and Drew and one of their friends. Drew by the DVD player to turn it off in case Mrs. Greely came down to check on them. She was against scary movies. *Can't sit down with the angels if you feast with the devil,* she said.

What was that movie called again? Beegie wondered.

The Grudge. Beegie smiled.

"Is Eric *here*?" she asked.

"He's out with friends." Drew was still standing by the door. What had they told him about why she'd had to leave so quickly? Certainly not the truth. Couldn't have big brother looking bad… Even his lies didn't make him seem like the kind of person Mr. and Mrs. Greely would want as their son.

"It's probably in your mom's craft room," she said, even though she had no idea. "Can we…"

She gestured toward the stairs. Drew held back. Deciding.

"Look, I just want my stuff. I'm not going to do anything."

Finally, he nodded. Leading her up the stairs. Turning on

the lights as he went. Mr. Greely was brutal about making sure no one wasted electricity. The habit ingrained in Drew.

The kitchen was dark. Clean. It smelled the same as it had the day she left. Like freeze-dried coffee and the dark waxy scent of a banana before it had been peeled. Mrs. Greely always had a bunch hanging from a ceramic monkey she said was made for that purpose and very rare.

Beegie fucking hated that monkey.

After she'd moved to Barb's house, Beegie imagined smashing it. Over and over again. On the floor. With a hammer. Against a wall.

It was still there. A year later. Two sad bananas dangling from its paw.

She gave it a wide berth as Drew led her past it. She didn't trust herself not to smash it for real like she had so many other times in her imagination.

Drew flicked on the switch in his mother's sewing room, sending light flooding over her hoards of fabric and supplies. Shelf after shelf of folded material. More than anyone could use in a lifetime. Scissors and markers all neatly tucked into bins. A hundred different colors of thread, each one assigned its own peg on the wall.

Beegie's hands ached to tear it all down. To pull the shelves from the wall and empty the cabinets onto the floor. Spill the scissors and notions and all that other crap everywhere.

"Are you sure it's in here?" Drew was looking at her. He was a good kid. Dumb but good... No, not dumb. *Naive.*

Beegie had no idea what she was doing here. She had been on the bus and she had been angry and then like a gift she had been right here, in the Greelys' neighborhood. The Greelys were a target, *a real one* so she didn't have to be angry at herself.

What would she have done if Drew hadn't been here and

she'd gotten in with the key? Trashed the place? Searched for her stuff? It had probably been thrown out.

No. Her things were Eric's trophies. You don't throw out trophies.

Drew cleared his throat. Waiting.

"Why did they tell you I had to leave?" she asked Drew without looking at him. Her voice small and weird as she said it.

"They said the people…that the state or the agency or whatever it is who takes care of you decided you should stay somewhere else."

"And did you believe them?"

"Well…yeah. But it seemed weird. And then I heard…"

"What did you hear?"

"Well…someone said that boys at the school you went to were paying you to have sex with them. Like in bathrooms and outside and stuff. And that sometimes you even picked up guys…on the street."

Beegie's heart was thumping hard, smacking at her chest. She still couldn't look at Drew, didn't want to see what was on his face. "Did you think it was true?"

Drew took a breath. "I don't know, Beegie…"

"So you did. Believe it."

"Not really. 'Cause I figured if you were doing that you'd probably have a lot more money than you did, 'cause when you were here you were always broke."

"Right."

"And then Eric told me that you told him you'd give him a blow job if he paid you a hundred dollars."

Beegie exhaled. *Of course he did.*

She could hear Drew swallowing hard. The hollow sound of his saliva moving down his throat. "That's when I knew it wasn't true."

"Why?"

"'Cause Eric's a liar."

Right then, they heard the front door open. Drew's brother was home.

The first time was in the middle of the night. A couple days after her fourteenth birthday. Beegie remembered that because there was still cake left.

She had woken up with Eric's penis pushing against her lips, though she didn't know what it was at first. She lay in the dark for a moment confused. Not understanding what she was seeing, what she was feeling.

She made a little sound when she realized. What it was. Who it was. Cried out a little but that only let him push farther. He knew she was awake then, 'cause he pushed his hand down on her face, pinning her to her pillow. He pushed hard, then harder, not saying anything but increasing the pressure, until Beegie felt sure her jaw would break. And then she opened her mouth a little wider and he pushed it in as far as it could go.

Beegie gagged against him.

And then, like that was what he wanted all along he just *left*. Stopped as soon as she choked. He didn't say anything at all. Just left her room and closed the door. Like nothing had happened.

Beegie waited. But then she heard him snoring, and she sneaked downstairs for something to get rid of the taste. Birthday cake erased him from her mouth.

If not for that taste she would have thought that first time was a dream. But the taste was evidence. Mildew and Cheerios. It had happened.

Over breakfast the next morning Beegie sat across from him. He didn't seem different. Didn't say anything. Didn't even look at her. Instead he ate every strip of bacon and no one stopped him or called him greedy. Mrs. Greely just called him her "growing boy."

Beegie didn't have an appetite.

Eric had two girls with him. The three of them stumbled in the door. The girls leaned on each other and laughed, their arms filled with grocery bags.

"Ah, shit, it's little Miss Truant!" he said when he saw her. Grinning at her like seeing her in his home was a big surprise, a pleasant one. He covered his mouth and laughed before launching into a kind of little dance. Slapping his knee. The funniest thing he'd ever seen.

Eric looked past Beegie at Drew. "Ah, little bro. You should know I've already been there."

The girls laughed at this while Drew blushed. It was clear now that they were all drunk. Or if they weren't drunk, they'd been drinking. And from the way the bags the girls carried clinked in their arms they were planning on keeping the party going.

"You wanna get fucked-up with us?" Eric asked, leading the girls into the kitchen. "Mom and Dad aren't coming home till Monday morning. We've got all weekend."

"We've got all the limes," one of the girls said, and they both giggled. Whatever the fuck that meant.

Drew and Beegie followed them. Awkward and tense. They watched as one of the girls set some music to play on the little speaker Mr. Greely used to listen to his podcasts before work. Eric took a knife from the block and began slicing limes right on the counter.

Mother Greely's gonna freak, Beegie thought until she realized she didn't need to care anymore. It was an old habit. And a bad one.

"I'm here for my stuff," Beegie said.

Eric looked up at her from the slices of lime between his fingers. Behind him the other girl began opening cabinets, looking for glasses. She pulled out some of Mother Greely's favorites. Cut glass ruby red tumblers. Reserved for holidays and special occasions.

Beegie'd never had even one sip from those glasses.

"What stuff?" Eric said. All innocent.

She stared at him. Eyes hard. Everything he did was an act. All of it lies. She wasn't going to play into it.

Eric broke eye contact. "I threw it away," he said, forced casual. He pulled a bottle of tequila from the bag. Ran a slice of lime around the rim of a glass.

"No you didn't."

Beegie didn't say anything about that first time. To Kate. To Mrs. Greely. To anyone. It wasn't something they would have wanted to hear, and even worse it would mean she had to move again.

And she liked it at the Greelys'.

Yeah, they were strict. But they also always had a ton of food in the fridge, and a tablet they'd let her use when her homework was done. Mrs. Greely was even talking about sending her to the school they sent the boys to next year. Beegie liked hearing her talk about plans. *Next year, when you're fifteen we'll go to the Grand Canyon… Maybe this spring we'll go see the poppies bloom.*

She knew better than to trust any of it…at least trust it *all the way*…but that didn't mean she couldn't enjoy pretending.

Besides that thing with Eric had been such a strange… What? Interaction? Occurrence? It was almost like something she had dreamed. And the more days that passed since that night, the more it seemed like it was just something she'd imagined.

She did, however, start locking her door at night.

She just added it to her nighttime routine. When Mother Greely called for lights out. Close book. Get out of bed. Turn off lights. *Push lock.* Run back to under the covers.

It was easy. And since Eric hadn't come back into her room since that night, she figured it had worked.

That's what she hadn't had at Janelle's. A lock on her door. That's all she really needed. Or thought she had needed.

But then things started *disappearing.*

Little things at first. Stuff she thought maybe she'd left somewhere else. A necklace. The book she'd been reading. Her Lakers sweatshirt.

But then it was stuff that Beegie couldn't think of a good reason for it to be missing at all. The little jewelry box that looked like a bunch of smiling fish that Beegie had put on her dresser. Erasers that looked like desserts that she'd gotten from a teacher for answering a question right. The headphones she used when the Greelys let her borrow their tablet, that Beegie remembered putting back in her top drawer, but weren't there the next time she opened it.

But still she didn't think anyone was stealing from her. She just thought maybe things weren't quite how she remembered them. Maybe she just needed to make sure she paid more attention.

A little voice inside her head wondered if that's how it started for her mother. Just forgetting. Thinking you'd done one thing when you'd done another.

But then her papers went missing.

And she knew.

The papers were mostly stupid stuff she'd put in an envelope. Christmas cards from people she didn't remember. A ticket with a picture of T-rex bones on it from a class trip. A test she'd gotten a hundred and ten percent on that her teacher had written "WOW" across the top.

But there were also two photographs. One of her mother. Not looking like Beegie remembered her, but pretty and young. Normal. And the other one. Of Jasmine. On the swings.

Beegie knew that no matter *what*, she wouldn't have lost that envelope. It was in her bedside drawer and it was too important. Even if she went crazy, she wouldn't forget how important it was.

So over dinner she asked Mrs. Greely if maybe she had taken it. Accidentally, she said. Maybe while she was cleaning. Maybe she didn't know it was important to Beegie because it didn't look important.

But it was.

Mother Greely sipped her soup and shook her head. *She would never.* She said, "I'll help you look for it after dinner, dear. Maybe you just forgot where you put it."

But even while they looked, Beegie knew. Even while Mrs. Greely shrugged her shoulders and said she'd keep an eye out for it.

Eric was sitting on her bed with the envelope when she got home the next day. He was usually at lacrosse after school, but he'd skipped it so he could be there when it was just her and no one else. Mr. and Mrs. still at work. Drew not dismissed yet.

"You know I almost pissed my pants last night watching you and Mom search in here. 'Did you look under the bed, my dear?'" His voice pitched in a breathy whine on this last part. A decent imitation of his mother.

Beegie just stood in the doorway. She didn't say anything. Didn't need to. She knew Eric would let her know what he wanted eventually.

"I've been thinking about that night. That we were together. The noises you made." He tapped the corner of the envelope in the cup of his hand. Beegie could hear the papers within it shift, each time it slammed against his hand. "You think you could make those noises again? Like the exact same ones. Those are the noises I think about when I think about you at night."

He paused here. Waiting for her to say something. Waiting for her reaction.

Beegie kept her face blank. But she felt sure he could see all the blood rushing to her face. The way the panic was coursing through her body.

When she didn't say anything, he continued. Disappointed she hadn't given him the satisfaction of fighting back. "You know how you're gonna get your stuff back, don't you? I'm going to give it back to you, one piece at a time."

Eric didn't say anything in response. Just dipped the glass in a dish of salt. The crystals stuck to the rim of the glass, like snow on flowers.

"Jesus, just give her her stuff, Eric," Drew shouted behind her.

The drunk girls startled at Drew's voice. The one on the floor yanked her hands from the dog like he'd bitten her. Until that moment they didn't even know there was something strange going on.

But now they were watching. Their eyes passing from Eric to Beegie to Drew. Trying to figure out the story between them.

"Okay, I got it," Eric admitted. His lips were smiling, but his eyes were not. "I'll give it to you, Beegie."

He held out one of the glasses. Tequila, salt, lime juice. "Drink."

Beegie glanced back at Drew. He shrugged.

They both knew she was going to have to do it. The only way Eric ever gave you anything was if you let him win first. If she didn't drink, he'd do something…underhanded, mean, *something*. It was who he was.

Beegie took the shot and downed it. The tequila was liquid sandpaper, scratching the walls of her throat as it burned its way down into her stomach.

She coughed. Her body folding over.

Eric and the girls laughed.

He waved her to follow him, "Come on, it's upstairs."

Beegie took a few steps. Then turned to look at Drew. "Come with."

Drew looked at his brother, who was waiting for her by the banister. The older boy threw up his hands. "Whatever. Fuck you, Beegie. You too, Drew."

10

Beegie *let him* four times.

That's how she thought of it. She *let him*.

And it wasn't just like before. Over quick. It was more.

He'd be in the house when she got home after school.
Call her from his parents' bedroom. His brother's room. His
mother's craft room.

They'd do it. *She'd let him*. And then Eric would go into
his room and come back with something. Her headphones.
Her jewelry box. Her book. Her sweatshirt. He'd throw it
on her bed, and without saying anything he would leave the
house again. Couldn't miss practice. He was always gone before Drew got there.

When she told Eric she wanted the envelope, he said, "Uh-
uh. That's special. You need to do something special for that."

Something special as it turned out was *letting* him put it in her. In the middle of the night. His parents and brother asleep in their rooms on either side.

The lock was a piece of shit. Always had been. Easy to pick. Just stick a pin in and it popped. She woke up when Eric opened the door. In his pajamas. The envelope in his hand.

Her hand made shushing sounds on the paper of the envelope while Eric did what she *let him*. She'd have to make sure everything was there when he was done.

He brushed the envelope out of her reach, "Make the noise or you don't get it."

So she did. Small whines. Like those girls in porn. She was pretending, but he didn't care. He didn't care about anything but her *letting him*.

There was a sound against the wall. A scrape that meant someone in Mr. and Mrs.'s room was up.

"Fuck," Eric whispered. He pushed against her shoulders as he turned to run from the room. Beegie only saw the ghosts of his feet by the time she turned to look. Her door left swinging open.

She heard someone moving through the hall as she climbed back under the covers. A creak on the floor. Low talking. Eric and *Mother Greely*. Whispering with each other. She wondered how he explained what he was doing up?

Beegie heard the sound of Eric's door shutting. Mrs. Greely walking down the hall. She shut her eyes, calming her breath so she would look like she was asleep. The woman stood there for a while. Watching her pretend to sleep. Minutes stretching long before Beegie heard the sound of her door being shut. The latch hooking closed.

Only later did she remember. Mrs. Greely *must* have seen it that night. The envelope she had helped Beegie look for, lying on her foster daughter's bed.

There was no way she couldn't have seen it.

Just like there was no way Mrs. Greely could not have smelled the scent in the room.

Climbing the stairs after Eric, Beegie wondered if she'd said something that first time if nothing that came after would have happened. Eric would have gotten in trouble, but everyone would have believed her. He wouldn't have been able to take her stuff. She wouldn't have felt like she had to give him what he'd asked for to get her stuff back. And he couldn't have reclaimed it all in one last power move when she was kicked out of the house.

But as Beegie crested the stairs, walking past the room that she had stayed in while she had lived there she thought, *Probably not.*

Everything would have played out exactly as it had. Her getting kicked out. Eric saying she was lying. Mrs. Greely using the word *consensual* and her having to ask Kate what that meant. And being embarrassed because Kate said it meant she thought what had happened with Eric was okay because she'd agreed to it.

Which wasn't true. She'd agreed to it, but it *wasn't okay.*

Beegie felt the tequila in her stomach. It didn't burn anymore…instead it was *warm.* The feeling spread into her arms, making her biceps feel loose and strange.

Eric opened the door to his room and stepped in, swinging the door back behind him. Beegie stuck her hand out and caught it before it closed. She didn't want him to have the chance to get rid of anything while she couldn't see him.

Eric looked back at her and Drew and shrugged. *So what.*

They stepped inside as Eric wheeled his desk chair to his closet. He opened the doors and pushed the chair against the clothes, before standing on it and reaching into the space above.

It looked like he had pushed his hand into the ceiling, his arm disappearing above the lip of the wall. Beegie stepped forward and saw that he had pushed aside a panel, opening a window into the attic.

"What was it you wanted again?" he asked. His smile broad, lips wet over his tiny teeth.

"Give her her stuff, Eric," Drew said behind her. Beegie looked back at him and realized he was almost as tall as his brother now. Skinnier still, but he'd almost caught up. Beegie wondered how long it would be until Drew couldn't be intimidated by his brother at all.

Unlike her. She would *never* catch up in her too-short little body. Never be big enough that anyone thought twice about bullying her.

Eric hooked something out of the recesses of the closet and winged it at her. Beegie's papers flew all over his room. Fluttering like snow onto his bedspread, blanketing the dark green carpet.

Beegie knelt down to scrape them up from the floor. Pulling them toward her until they were in a pile at her knees. The liquor already making her feel not like herself.

She found Jasmine. Little girl. Big smile. A pair of hands reached toward her out of the frame. Pushing her. Higher, higher.

Her old sweatshirt suddenly hit her in the face, zipper catching her lip. This was followed by her headphones, the earpiece crunching and folding against her forehead under the force of Eric's pitch. Her jewelry box bounced off the carpet next to her, the lid and bowl separating and cracking against the wall.

Drew stepped in, blocking Eric's next throw. His hands up, blocking Beegie's copy of *The Stand* from striking her in the face. The pages bent against Drew's fingers.

"You fucking cunt!" Eric yelled. "I didn't fucking *make you* do anything. That's what Mom said you told them. That I made you, for *this shit*? Who the fuck gives a blow job so she can get a fucking *book* back?"

Beegie started shoving everything she could into her purse. Every piece of paper. The cracked pieces of the box. Her sweatshirt.

"You did it because you wanted to, Beegie. Because you're a whore. That's what Mom said. Only a whore lets someone fuck her in order to get something."

Beegie stood and looked at the Greely brothers. Drew, his face still babyish, hand on his older brother's chest holding him back.

And Eric, breathless, still standing on the chair. *Did he really believe what he said? Did he really think he was the fucking victim in all this?*

Beegie left the room. And the brothers didn't follow her. She made her way down the stairs. Hand on the wall, 'cause the liquor was already making the world seem soft.

The girls in the kitchen greeted her with worried faces. They'd heard the shouting. "Is everything okay?" one of them asked. She held the tequila bottle, poised over the drinks prepared in Mrs. Greely's pretty glasses.

Beegie nodded. Then she picked up one of the glasses, drank its contents and *threw* it on the floor. Rooster yelped and ran out of the kitchen.

The girls shrieked and jumped away from the shattered glass.

Before they could say anything, Beegie was chucking all the remaining glasses at their feet. Every one of them still filled with liquor. One. Two. Three.

"Oh my God! Why would you do that?" one of the girls asked, her flip-flop-fitted feet sparked with tequila and broken glass.

Beegie just looked at her, face blank.

And then she pushed the monkey banana holder off of the counter. It struck the floor, cracking into a thousand wonderfully small pieces. Mother Greely would never be able to glue that back together.

'Cause fuck Mother Greely.

And then she walked out the front door.

All she had said to Kate was that she wanted to know if she could have a better lock on her door. Maybe one with a key, so she could make sure her stuff was okay while she was at school.

"Why are you worried about your things during the day, Beegie?"

Beegie shrugged. Kate had been really excited about placing her with the Greelys. Almost no fosters had fathers in the home, which made the Greelys special. Not that Mr. Greely ever said more than a word to Beegie. He grunted a lot. It was Mother Greely that spoke for the both of them.

"If I ask Mrs. Greely for this, she's going to want to know why you think you need it."

Beegie nodded. *Sure, sure.* "Can't you just say it's, I don't know, 'cause of some reason from my file."

"Are you happy there, Beegie?"

Beegie hesitated.

Then she said "Yeah," because mostly she *was*. She didn't like doing what Eric wanted, but it could be worse. Maybe it was just the price she had to pay.

Even though it made her sick to her stomach. Even though it made her want to spit and spit and spit. Brush her teeth until her gums started to bleed.

But otherwise…

No. She could make it work. She just needed a lock.

'Cause she didn't want to get all her stuff back, only to

have Eric break into her room and take it all over again. So he could make her *let him* all over again.

Actually, she just didn't want Eric in her room again. Ever.

She had thought it would be okay to ask. Kate wasn't new anymore. She'd been Beegie's caseworker since Tricia. Almost four years now. Long enough so that every time they met now, whether it was at school or in the resource center, Beegie expected there would be someone new at the meeting. Some soft-faced recent college graduate. *I have someone I'd like you to meet Beegie, she's going to be handling you from now on.* Kate would say, *This is Amber* or *Emily* or *Kelly.*

Usually when social workers are new they're jumpy. Everything's a crisis. But then after a few years they start…not to mellow, but to try to keep things the way they were. They try to make peace. Not to rock the boat.

Kate had been through it. She knew how it was. How it went.

Beegie knew Kate wanted her to stay at the Greelys'. If Beegie was at the Greelys' she was one of Kate's *success stories.*

"I just need a lock. Then everything will be fine."

Beegie slapped her metro card against the reader. The bus driver didn't even look at her, eyes forward. Just waiting for the chime.

She moved back to the middle of the bus. Didn't care where she was going anymore. Back to the old plan. Ride the bus until she got kicked off. Ride another bus. Be at Barb's house in the morning. Pretend this whole day didn't happen.

Her bag dug into her shoulder. Too heavy with all the stuff Eric had thrown at her. The tequila was now roaring through her body. How did Barb do this every night? She felt like was going to fly and fall at the same time. She stumbled, but to cover she sat down on one of the ugly fuzzy carpeted seats. Like that was where she'd been headed the whole time.

She started pulling her papers out of the dark corners of her bag. Stuffing them back into the envelope. Her heart flaring at the little things she remembered. A funny drawing she had liked. A pamphlet for some place called Glitter Gulch that she'd never been to, but had liked to look at the pictures.

She stopped when she got to the photographs.

Her mother had kept both taped to the mirror. No matter where they lived she put them up. Beegie didn't even remember her mother noticing them that much. She almost never talked about them. Never looked at them.

But no matter where they were, those photos ended up on the mirror. A picture of her mother back when she was pretty.

And a picture of *Jasmine.*

Beegie stared at the pair of hands behind the little girl. Wondered what the person attached to them looked like.

The bus shifted gears, and the sound of its engine switched pitches. Outside the Greelys' church rolled by, its message board lit up for the night. The Most Powerful Position Is On Your Knees.

Yeah, fuck the Greelys.

Beegie pictured the floor of Mother Greely's perfect kitchen. That stupid monkey in a thousand pieces on the floor. She thought about what kind of excuse the boys would have to make up to explain it. How so many of her precious things got shattered.

Whatever. She'd just believe whatever Eric told her.

The day after Eric had almost been caught in her room, Mrs. Greely was different with Beegie. Quieter. Like she would talk to everyone *but* Beegie. Her eyes sliding over her foster daughter. She answered Beegie's questions with *yes*'s and *no*'s but not much more.

That was until Kate called her. And Beegie's social worker must have said something, because when Beegie came home from school Mrs. Greely was *there*. With Eric.

At the kitchen table.

Eating cookies.

And Beegie noticed that Eric seemed cool about it. Like his mom hadn't been upset to find him home when he was supposed to be at practice. And when he left, she held her cheek out for him to kiss.

"Do you have something you want to tell me?" Mrs. Greely had said when he was finally gone.

Beegie shook her head.

"My boy was a good boy before you came here."

Beegie looked up into the older woman's face. All hard lines. "He told you?"

"He didn't need to." She puffed up at that. "I know everything that goes on in this house."

Beegie laughed at that. Couldn't help it. It was a little one. But it was a laugh.

Mrs. Greely narrowed her eyes. "You leave him alone."

Beegie laughed again. This time a big one. A *guffaw*. That was the word.

"He took my things. He *made me* do stuff to get it back. He *made me*."

"Not my boy," Mother Greely said.

"Every boy is somebody's boy," Beegie replied. "Why couldn't it be yours?"

The next day Kate was waiting for her. Everything Beegie owned in garbage bags by the curb.

Everything except the stuff she carried with her now.

Beegie had been right. Sometime between when Mother Greely talked to her and when she packed up her stuff, Eric had gone into her room and taken everything back. Which was why it wasn't in the bags of stuff Beegie unpacked when she got to Barb's.

'Cause if there was one thing she'd learned from scary movies, it was that the monster was predictable. He always popped up one last time. He always survived for the sequel.

"Well, well, well! If it isn't little pretty eyes!" said a man's voice.

And Beegie looked up. In the aisle stood the Busman, from before. He was grinning at her, holding the railing above and leaning in her direction. A can of beer still in his hand. A few more buttons on his shirt undone.

"Will you take one now?" He held the beer out.

Beegie smirked at him. Sure, why not. She wasn't going anywhere.

She took the beer from his hand and cracked it.

12 AM
DOWNTOWN

11

Away from the fires, the darkness had gotten unsettling. Dessa had used her flashlight for a few minutes, aiming it at the street so she didn't inflict further damage to her feet. But its bright glare drew eyes toward her...and she wasn't sure that was a good thing.

In fact, she was pretty sure it wasn't.

And so she had tucked the flashlight away. She could feel its heavy presence in her purse banging against her waist. She was sure she would find some store with shoes on this street quickly. Something that had been cracked open by the quake.

It was the light that drew her. The aquarium glow of the emergency lights. They hummed, faint and blue, casting the store in a sickly glow.

Zapatos y Ropas. Shoes and Clothes. A simple name for a business. To the point.

A trio of female mannequins dressed in bedazzled sports jerseys had tumbled through the broken window. More victims. Dessa stepped over them.

For some reason they made her think of her mother. She'd come to visit her about eight months after Dessa had made the move to L.A.—about five months before her diagnosis.

Dessa had taken off work to play tour guide, and had even taken her to Phillipe's for French dip sandwiches, hoping that her mother would appreciate the quaint little hats the servers kept pinned in their hair, the way the lemonade was still just fifty cents, the whole building like a time warp.

Instead her mother had been quiet, her eyes scanning everything. And as they stood in line waiting to order, she had looked down at Dessa's flip-flops.

"You look like a vagrant," her mother had said. "That is not how *we* dress."

That word. *Vagrant.* Dessa had heard her mother use it hundreds of times, never in the context of anything good. It meant low-class. Tacky. Uncontrolled.

Dessa's mother had considered class to be mainly a product of self-control rather than money. Her neighbors who did not bring their garbage cans in soon enough were low-class. As were women who allowed their underwear to peek out of their clothes. Loud phone conversations in public places. Visible intoxication.

And she made no exceptions for circumstance. People were poor because they were lazy. Addicts were not victims but criminals. She used the phrase "pulling themselves up by their bootstraps" a great deal while reading the news with Dessa's father.

As a little girl this painted the strangest picture in Dessa's mind. How was it possible to pull yourself up with something that's beneath you?

The interior of the store was flooded with boxes. Four tall shelves had tumbled, vomiting the store's entire stock of shoes onto the ground. Dessa waded her way through these, willing to take the first pair that was close to her size.

Finally she found some: pink and green. Horribly gaudy. But they fit. Wincing, she pulled the laces tight on her left foot. Securing her improvised bandage closer to her foot. It was not a tetanus shot, three stitches and a prescription for Vicodin. But it was worlds better than what she had had.

She decided she would leave money. Twenty-five. Thirty to be certain. She knew if she did not pay, it would bother her. That the shoes would somehow wear differently if she had stolen them, even out of necessity.

A vending machine had toppled and broken toward the rear of the store. Bottles littered the floor. Dessa could make out a few bottles of water among them. She had used the last of the water in her car, the small inch of backwash, to rinse off the bottom of her foot.

She had not had anything to drink since…since she had set her cocktail down at the bar and motioned to Gretchen that she was heading outside. Her mouth still tasted of cement dust and bile.

Dessa climbed over the fallen shelves, making her way toward the closest bottle. She leaned over to pick one up.

There was a sound, a rustling from the storeroom.

Then a muffled squeak.

Dessa stopped the questioning "hello" before it made its way to her mouth. Against instinct. She took a few steps more. Breath held.

On the floor of the storeroom sat a large black purse. Slouchy and worn. Someone had tied a red bandanna around its handle.

Something about it. Dessa was certain it had been set there *after* the quake. It was too neat. Too deliberate.

And then Dessa saw the movement on the floor…a few feet farther into the storeroom than the purse. She tried to make sense of it. A rhythmic swing. Back and forth.

It was the cuff of a pair of jeans, brushing gently against the floor, picking up dust with its hem. Dessa followed the line up to the point from which the jeans hung.

Because of her vantage Dessa had a hard time identifying it as an ankle at first. The jeans swinging, brush, brush. Suspended from a foot that hovered above the floor.

Another mannequin?

But then the foot kicked out, and all the pieces Dessa was truly seeing locked into place. Flesh. Movement. Violence.

Dessa covered her mouth. Holding in her yelp of horror. She held her repulsion cupped in her hand. She turned away from the violence.

Only to get a fuller view of it.

On the opposite wall, one of the store's three-way mirrors revealed the full truth of the scene. Two men. Hovering over a woman. One of them pressed the girl into a table. His hand over her mouth. Knife at her throat. While the other raped her.

That was the word. *Rape*. There was nothing about the encounter Dessa was witnessing that seemed even a small part consensual.

It was so quiet.

Horrifically quiet.

Just the sound of the table…squeak, squeak, squeaking… and the man's slightly labored breathing as he laid into the girl. The mirror framed them in a kind of sick tableau, the space beneath it affording Dessa a glimpse of her own horrified face.

They had been here *the whole time*. This violation unfolding in the back while she sifted through shoes in the front, debating the ethics of leaving money behind. Probably drawn here by the same lights she had been attracted to. Moths.

The girl moaned.

"Shut up, bitch, or we'll fucking kill you."

The man's voice was a brittle whisper. Which one had said it, Dessa didn't know, but it carried the weight of a promise.

A box tumbled over Dessa's shoulder. It landed at her feet, sending a shower of cheap plastic combs across the floor. Their cellophane sleeves rattling.

"What the fuck?" The man again. Not a whisper this time.

In the space of a breath, she was moving. Action before thought. Like the small mammal she was, her first defense to hide. Predators do not eat the prey they cannot see.

Dessa pressed herself into the skeleton of a collapsed ringed rack of clothing. Pushing through the curtain of cotton T-shirts that still clung to the arch of its spine. Willed herself breathless…no, breath free…soundless…inanimate.

There were steps on the floor. One of the men had left. Checking for the source of the noise.

But the squeaking continued.

Then the sound of *him* receding. Returning again to press his gravity on the girl, his weight and anger and power into her smaller body. The girl had been so quiet while all this unfolded, Dessa had thought at first she had been just a mannequin…and that's what she was to these men. A body to be acted upon.

And Dessa was hiding from it…just hoping it would not be her next…

As quietly as possible she pulled out her phone. Dialed a nine and two ones. Pressing her ear hard, hoping no sound would escape the space between flesh and glass.

A calm female voice greeted her, *"All our circuits are busy. Please wait and the next available—"*

There was a yowl of pain. One of the men. "Fucking cunt!" Dessa could not tell if it was the same man she had heard before.

And then the girl started screaming. Small impacts resounded. Fists against flesh. The squeal of rubber soles against the floor. Dessa bit her hand.

BANG!

Dessa jumped as something very heavy hit the floor of the storeroom. The girl was still screaming, but now the men were both yelling too.

"Jesus fucking Christ, just do it already."

"Then hold her the fuck down."

"I'm tryi—"

All at once the store came to life. Ranchero music blaring as the fluorescents burst on, flooding the disaster beneath them in bright light. Power restored.

Dessa could barely hear anything anymore. The shouts buried beneath the sunny horns of the music. Another bang. Metallic. Some shuffling. Quick motion, she thought, but she could not be sure.

"All of our circuits are busy. Please wait…"

Dessa slid the phone from her face. Help was a precious commodity.

The song finished and another started. A woman singing, her voice plaintive, though the music was still bright. More words Dessa recognized. *Triste*. Sad. *Llorando*. Crying.

Dessa was sure the men had left.

But she was not sure what they had left behind.

The woman on the speaker continued to sing. Dessa wasn't sure if the singer had been abandoned or was the one who had done the abandoning.

The shirts made a shushing sound as Dessa brushed past them. Her motion loosed them from their moorings, sending them on the slide to the floor. She crawled...somehow afraid to stand...afraid of what she would find in the back room.

In the mirror she saw the table. Collapsed to the floor. A few more boxes had joined the number on the ground. Evidence of the struggle she had heard.

But there was no body.

She had only stood by while someone was brutally raped. At least she was spared knowing she was so weak she would not have intervened in the woman's murder.

A well of self-loathing washed over Dessa.

She turned to face the storeroom. The black purse with the red bandanna was gone.

10 PM
DOWNTOWN

12

"This is Charlie," the Busman said, waving his hand at a man sitting across the aisle, "Say hi, Charlie."

"Name's not Charlie," said his friend. *Not-Charlie* was slumped forward. Face out. Like a baseball catcher. He grinned at Beegie.

"Fuck you. You're drinking my beer. Your name is Charlie if I say your name is Charlie," said the Busman. Not-Charlie barked a kind of wheezy laugh at this. An actual "Ha." Like when someone writes laughter down in a book. Usually people don't actually sound like that. *Ha ha ha ha.*

Beegie'd never thought of it before, but she realized most people sounded like *animals* when they laughed; Barb sounded like a donkey, brays with big deep breaths in between. And Eric sounded like a chimpanzee, kinda screaming and baring his teeth.

Beegie remembered her mom would barely make any sound at all when she laughed. She just froze, with her mouth open. Like all the air was being squeezed out of her by a giant hand. Beegie remembered being a little scared by this when it happened. That pause between her mother starting to laugh and finally making a sound again. A choke that turned out okay.

"Ha," said *Not-Charlie*. "Ha. Ha. Ha."

So strange.

The Busman grinned at her. "We need to give *you* a new name, Pretty Eyes…since you're drinking my beer."

"Tanisha!" shouted Not-Charlie.

"Fuck you, that's racist," said the Busman. Only he said *tha'sracis*.

Beegie knew a Tanisha. There had been one in her class when she was in sixth grade. That Tanisha was a bitch. She didn't want to be a Tanisha.

Beegie shook her head. She held the beer to her mouth, the bubbles sending small jets of liquid onto her lips through the opening.

"No… Elizabeth… *Queen* Elizabeth," said the Busman.

"Ha. Ha. Ha," said Not-Charlie.

Beegie took a sip. The beer sharp and warm in her mouth. She already had another name for herself. For the person she liked to pretend to be.

The Busman bowed. "Cheers, Your Majesty." He tapped his beer against hers.

It had been hours since Beegie had seen the man get on her bus that first time, headed in the opposite direction. Was he just riding it to pass the time, like she had planned? Where was the place *he* wasn't going? What confrontation was *he* putting off?

There weren't many people on the bus this time of night. Beegie wasn't sure, but it had to be almost ten. The sky all the way dark against the brightness of the storefronts as they rolled past.

The Busman offered one of the other passengers, an old Hispanic lady, a beer. "Cerveza? Huh-huh?" he said, and the woman shook her head, hard, without looking at him. Hugging her bag. When the bus reached a stop, Beegie thought she was getting up to climb off. But she actually just picked up her things and moved forward. As far away as she could get from the Busman and Not-Charlie.

And Beegie too.

She could tell the woman had lumped her in with the others. Since she was drinking with them.

The woman sat down again in the priority handicapped seats in the front of the bus. Right behind the bus driver. Beegie wondered why the driver was allowing them to drink. Why he hadn't called it in or kicked them off.

Probably because he was scared. Just like the old lady.

Beegie kinda liked the feeling that gave her. The idea that she was something worthy of being afraid of. Like her small-ass body could do any damage at all.

That was something else she thought was funny about scary movies. So many of them had these little girls that nobody would even think twice about...but in the stories the little girls are the bad guys. Regan. Samara. Carrie.

In one of those movies there's a priest that says that the devil makes young girls evil because the most horrific thing for an adult to see was corrupted innocence.

Beegie didn't think that was right.

She thought the reason it was horrific when a little girl became a monster was because it upset big people's whole way of thinking about the world. A little girl with the power to hurt someone bigger than her was frightening because it was the opposite of how they thought it should be. They thought little girls *should be powerless*.

"Hey, Your Majesty. Whatcha got there?" The Busman sat down next to her. Poking at the photos in her lap. His fingers grazed the top of her thigh, and the way he did it made Beegie wonder if it was accidental.

Outside a bunch of cars started laying on their horns. Like really laying on them. Beegie craned her neck, "What's going on?"

"Fucking L.A. that's what," said the Busman.

But Beegie didn't think so. Usually the horns stopped after a few seconds, 'cause whoever was making a left where they weren't supposed to got through or whoever was honking their horn made their point and everybody calmed down.

This was different though. Beegie could hear horns going off *everywhere*. From streets miles away to all the way to right on up next to the bus. Like every driver in the city had gotten into an accident all at the same time.

A fast tapping started up right next to her ear. The window next to her rattling, the metal frame and glass clack-clacking against each other. The sound got louder. Louder. Until every window in the bus was doing it, all at once.

The bus driver shouted something back at them. It was hard to hear over the horns and the rattling. Next to him the old lady started to pray. Crossing herself before clasping her hands and bowing her head.

"Holy shit." Busman was looking behind her, toward the sidewalk. Across from them was a restaurant, glowing yellow out onto the street. Inside, Beegie could see that the customers were panicking. Their faces wide with shock, tables toppling, chairs being knocked out of their way. The menu sign detached from the wall above the kitchen and dropped to the floor below.

"Earthquake," Beegie whispered.

Beegie could *feel* rather than hear the sound of the brakes. The bus driver slowing them to a stop. The vehicle *skipped*... That was the only way to describe it. *It skipped.* It's front half hop-scotching into traffic while its back tried to cling to the road.

The beer can leaped from Beegie's hand. Flying across the aisle until it struck the seat below Not-Charlie. The man's eyes were so fixed outside, he didn't even look down as it splashed his leg before setting into a spin. Beer poured out as it skid-ded, still spinning, wobbly to the back of the bus. Leaving a wake of yeasty, urine-colored liquid in its path.

And then the bus began rocking. Beegie pitched forward, the violent sway forcing her away from her seat. With her hands she flailed back, smacking the warm expanse of Bus-man's chest. He grabbed her then, keeping her from tumbling into the hard surface of the seats opposite.

Something hit the roof of the bus. Beegie could hear the impact above the roar of the windows and the blaring of the horns. Loud and heavy. There was another. This time coming from a few feet to the left of the first sound. Beegie looked up in time to see the ceiling dent inward, pushed closer to the inside of the bus.

Like a beer can. Crushed in its drinker's palm.

A hail of impacts started then. Raining down on the same spot. *Bambam. Bambambam.* The bus tilted toward the force of the blows. Like a seesaw, it pulled against them, then swung back, tipping farther and farther each time.

It was not going to last...

At the front of the bus the driver and the old woman were standing. She was helping him pull a lever attached to the dashboard. Hefting the doors into the open position. They needed to get off before...

Before...

They just needed to get off.

Beegie stood and was immediately thrown toward the ground. She braced herself, hands slapping the gritty wet surface of the floor. Inhaled the scent of her beer and the bottoms of hundreds of shoes before dropping to her elbows, acrid rubber and yeast.

She crawled. Her belly dragging, body rocking with the motion of the bus. *Bambambam.* She cleared the steps, sliding over them, their metal edges pulling at her shirt, dragging it toward her waistband.

She was almost to the front when the doors folded open. The driver clutched the old woman while they moved through the door. Their bodies slamming against the stair to the ground below.

Then everything happened at once.

Beegie was thrown sideways. Rolling and falling all at the same time. Her temple crashed against the metal support of the seats, before she folded down into the pocket beneath them.

It was dark down there. And quieter...though Beegie didn't know why all the noise had been replaced by the sound of ringing.

And then nothing.

What happened next Beegie couldn't quite piece together. There were dark spots in what happened after. Like her life was a movie she was watching, but the TV kept losing the picture. And each time the movie came back on, the story had jumped ahead, and Beegie had difficulty catching up. The scenes didn't make sense, and just when she felt like she was starting to understand, she would blink and the story would jump ahead again. She would be somewhere else. Doing something else. She would hear herself talking and understand the words, but not why she was saying them. She would see herself moving and not understand where she was going.

She really would have liked to have watched the whole thing. Because it felt like there was some essential piece of information she had missed. But there was no going back to get it, no rewind button. No one there to tell her what she had missed when the screen when dark.

But even though she was only seeing parts of the story, there was one thing she knew for sure.

The movie of her life she was watching was a horror film.

Beegie wakes to a world that has gone white. It smells like rubber and dust.

There is a tug on her shoe.

"You are one lucky bitch," says Not-Charlie.

She is drinking. There is liquid in her mouth and she almost chokes. A stinging liquor she hasn't had before and doesn't like. She coughs and spits.

Next to her the Busman laughs. He slaps her back, trying to help her clear the fluid. "That's a big girl," he says.

They are inside. But the lights are off, which is strange. The air is cool like the outside, not like the inside, which is also strange. She hears the sound of breaking glass and shouts far away.

Not-Charlie appears in front of them. He is wearing an enormous pink dress over his clothes. The kind you see in shop windows. It is sparkly and ruffly and very very pink. The Busman laughs at Not-Charlie while he dances.

Then Not-Charlie says that Queen Elizabeth should put one on, and that doesn't make sense until she realizes they are talking about her. And she says no, she doesn't like dresses and doesn't like the way Mother Greely looks at her when she's in them. And the Busman says, "You're talking strange, girl."

She is yelling at some people. Same as the Busman and Not-Charlie. They are yelling and telling these other people to fuck off. A man and three women. The people yell back but they are also walking away. One of the women lifts her dress and shows them her bare ass. She is not wearing panties. She slaps the exposed skin while she shouts something Beegie doesn't understand. The strikes leave marks on her bottom, a dark violent red.

The Busman throws an empty forty at the woman and it smashes on the sidewalk. The woman screams and drops her dress, running away in her heels. Click. Click. Click.

For some reason Beegie thinks of a monkey that used to hold bananas, but doesn't any longer. But she does not know why.

She is throwing up. Her hand is against a building and she is throwing up. She has been doing this for a while. She wonders if she has been doing this for so long that Busman and Not-Charlie have left her. Because she is no longer fun.

She smells barbecue. No. Not barbecue. Fire. Smoke but good smoke. The way the street outside of the last place she lived with her mother smelled like in July when their neighbors would set off fireworks. Tangy smoke. Smoke that made a taste like vinegar in the back of your mouth.

She hears more shouting, somewhere not very far from her.

Maybe it is the Fourth of July and I have forgotten, she thinks, but that doesn't make sense. She thinks she remembers sparklers in the backyard with the littles. Barb lighting the ends with her cigarette lighter. It could not be the Fourth of July then and also now.

She throws up again. Her fingers gripping the brick under her hand.

★ ★ ★

She is climbing over a body.

No, not a body.

She is climbing over a mannequin. She is laughing, and the Busman and Not-Charlie are with her again. They are laughing too. Not-Charlie grabs one of the other mannequins. He puts his hands up its shirt and pretends to feel her titties. He licks its face on the mouth. The dummy looks bored with all his attention and that is funny. The Busman laughs and so does she. They laugh harder when Not-Charlie leans over to lick the mannequin's tits.

She feels a hard squeeze on her own breast. She looks down and sees the Busman is holding it. His arm over her shoulder. But he is laughing. Not-Charlie is laughing.

But *she* is no longer laughing.

She moves his hand away. She says, "That hurts." But the Busman puts his hand back and squeezes her harder. And he laughs and Not-Charlie laughs.

"Stop it," she says.

"Be cool," says the Busman.

And she is no longer laughing.

She is on a table.

It is quiet.

Except for the table that squeaks beneath her, nothing else makes a sound.

They are no longer laughing.

1 AM
DOWNTOWN

13

Dessa has never been raped.

Once when she was a freshman, she had been on a night bus ride back from a choir competition. They had placed second, but it was enough to send them to the state competition, so the entire group had been filled with a giddy energy. They laughed and ignored the directions that they should stay in their seats, because, well, the choir teacher was ignoring it too. At one point a boy Dessa had a crush on had swung himself into the seat next to her. A senior. Out of Dessa's freshman reach. But he had talked to her like they had spoken before. Used her name. Before she was even aware of what was happening, his mouth was pressed hard to hers. Tongue trying to make its way past the barrier of her lips. Dessa was still trying to figure out the mechanics of this, the relaxation of her jaw and mouth, when she felt his hand wrap itself around her wrist. He placed her hand on the warm swell of his penis underneath his jeans. Realizing what it was she was feeling, Dessa had tried to pull it away, but he had tightened his grip on her. Holding her hand against his leg. Dessa froze under his mouth. Around them the other choir members were whooping and hollering. Eventually something someone tossed across the aisle knocked him in the head. He had turned from her, to yell at whoever had done it, his hand releasing hers.

On their way back, Dessa sat up front next to the director and the bus driver. The boy had smiled and winked at her as he made his way toward the back of the bus.

This had been Dessa's first introduction to the slippery line of consent. She knew there was something about what the boy had done that was wrong, but she shied at the word assault. Her mind jumped back from it, the same way her hands had when she had realized what he had placed them on. She had wanted the kiss. And though she had been young, she knew about the small negotiations of making out. *Is this okay? (Gentle brush). What about this? (Leaning in or moving away).* The *yes* was in the movement.

But then there were the times when she herself was not sure. Later with a college boyfriend, there had been a moment when she told him she was tired and wanted to stop. They had been fucking in the bathroom. Facing the mirror—his idea—bent over the counter, her breasts mashed against the Formica. It had been sexy until it wasn't. Until the backs of her knees had begun to ache and the edge of the countertop dug a line on her skin. She had asked to stop, but he continued, his weight pressing on her. For a moment she felt the true differential in their strengths. Her reliance upon his goodwill, because in fact there was nothing she could do to stop him.

But that had only been a collection of seconds. Moments before his hand had found her and she was enjoying it again.

Yes. No. Yes. Was it possible for sex to turn into rape for a moment, then back into sex? He never did it again. But then again, Dessa never volunteered for sex in the bathroom after that.

There were other times. A boss who always stood too close, who once put his hand on her neck, fingers curling gently over her throat. A friend, who had only *ever* been a friend, refusing to let her get out of his car when they had a disagreement— hitting the relock button every time she pulled the latch. A client who had waited for her in the parking garage, greeting her hours after their meeting, following her to her car.

Some of these were just boundaries that had been crossed. Unintentionally creepy. Others had been a kind of selfishness, a prioritizing their needs above hers. And still more had been momentary flares, flashes of their desire to remind her of their power, the things of which their bodies were capable. Forcing Dessa to confront the fact that the illusion of equality was just that, an *illusion*, dependent on *their* consent. Not *hers*.

These encounters had the flavor of *rape*. Just the tinge.

But they were not *rape*.

Dessa had never been raped.

But she had witnessed one.

She left the shoe store at a run. Disoriented and afraid. Tried Hailey and Joe a few more times, only to be greeted with that same stubborn beeping. She did not want to think what the failure to connect could mean.

The girl swam in her mind. The small sound she had made that had so angered the men. The pitch of her scream before the table fell. Had she bitten him? Scratched them? Certainly she had been braver than Dessa, fighting for herself when she was less capable of it than the woman hiding behind a rack of clothes had been.

Dessa replayed the scene. Looked for interventions she had missed. She could have thrown something at them. Drawn them away from the girl. Made them chase her into the street.

And then what? Where would her run have led her to? Safety? The city was feral.

She needed numbers. Groups of people. But she was lost. Somehow she had run off of the map of the city that she held in her mind. Couldn't orient herself to the freeways without their noise.

Eventually she heard voices. Women's voices over the lower rumble of men's. People walking. She joined the stream, heading in the same direction.

Dessa saw the corona of the lights first. The glow of the grocery store burned a halo in her eyes, so bright after the dark powerlessness of the city. A beacon. People streamed in and out of it, though Dessa was sure it was after store hours.

Looters.

But so different from the boys in the city.

There was almost an orderliness to it. Families rolling packed cartloads of canned foods and paper goods over the shattered remains of the entrance. Tired children seated in the front of the carts, teddy bears and blankies in their arms.

A police cruiser sat in the parking lot. Two cops standing next to it, their postures alert but relaxed. Watching the ongoing theft.

Dessa had heard of this. After disasters, sometimes the police were directed not to intervene with crime, but simply to make sure no one was assaulted in the commission.

"Help. Please. I need to report a rape."

The officer turned to look at Dessa, and for the first time she thought about what she must look like right now. Broken and slightly crazed. Blurred makeup. Bloody hands and knees. "Ma'am," he said after a moment. It was more a question than an address.

"In the Fashion District. After the quake. Two men. One had a knife." Her voice was traveling ahead of her, subjects arriving at their destination before their predicates, "I couldn't... I saw... They—"

Something in the man's eyes shifted. A decision. Funneling her in his mind down a trained pathway. He spoke again, this time his tone was softer. "Ma'am...you don't need to do this here. You can wait to make your report at the hospital... We have special people, trained."

Trained. He said it with a particular weight.

"I'm sorry?"

"There are people trained to take your story."

Dessa realized. He thought she had been the one on the table. Knife to *her* throat. *Her* jeans swinging on the floor.

"No." Her voice firm. Too firm to use with a cop but it was important. It had not been her. Crucial to insist upon this. The cop straightened. His armor back up. She demurred, "I saw it. A Black girl. Two men."

Dessa felt her own whiteness materialize before her as she said it. Yes, the girl was Black. And so was this police officer she was reporting the rape to. The man pursed his lips and looked away from her. A wince almost.

"She your friend?"

"No... I didn't even see her face. I couldn't... It was in this store...after the...after everything happened." She sounded insane. Sentences decoupling again. She had watched... Tonight she had watched so much. The building that swallowed Gretchen. The car that had swung out and carried the men away from her on the street. This girl.

And she had done nothing but watch.

The officer took out a notepad. "Look, I'll take your information. When things settle down we'll call you, but right now it's not safe."

Dessa made a sound like a laugh. A bray, somewhere between a guffaw and a cry. She had done nothing, *but she could do this.* She could tell the right people. "No! I need your help! I called 911 and I couldn't help her. I couldn't do anything... I just *saw.*"

Dessa watched the policeman shoot a glance at his partner. A pulse of communication between then. *Not dangerous. Crazy. Traumatized.* "Ma'am, do you know where the victim is."

A contradiction. When he first spoke, his statement sounded like a question. Now his question sounded like a statement.

"The electricity came back on and they ran away... I thought maybe they had... But she wasn't there... I need you to help me."

"Ma'am, right now you need to look after yourself."

"But what about her? *She* needs help." Her voice sounded childish, a whiny protest.

He sighed. Nodded in the direction of the people filing in and out of the grocery store. "There are currently ten million Angelenos in a state of distress. Everyone needs help. Without a body... I can't do more than get your name and take a statement."

Dessa felt something wilt within her. Of course. In a night of atrocities what did the ones Dessa had witnessed matter? Gretchen, Heidi, Laurel, the people in the club with them, the men on the street. They would just be more names in a count tomorrow. Listed among hundreds.

The only difference between those horrors and this one was Dessa's guilt. That she could have done something and didn't.

"You don't live near here." Another statement from the cop. This guy was good at them.

Dessa shook her head. "The Valley. I have a little girl..."

Those three impossible, stubborn beeps ringing in her mind. "I haven't been able to talk to her."

"We're organizing something. To get people home."

He gestured behind the cruiser. For the first time Dessa saw the collection of people huddled there. A few leaning on the car. Two women hunched on the pavement, one's head in the other's lap. Stroking her hair. A few yards off there were even more, watching them from the curb of the parking lot. Backs against a palm tree.

These were people like her. Who had come to the city for the night and survived the chaos. Whole, but not *intact*. Whose phones also would not connect them with the people they cared about.

"Have a seat." The officer was still looking at her. "We'll get you back to your girl."

14

There was a sense of resignation among the crowd. A uniform shrug of acceptance that they had climbed upon the bureaucratic trolley and were no longer masters of their own lives. Like the DMV, but spread out over the corner of a parking lot. Everyone feeling the limits of their patience, shifting their limbs restlessly, anxious for their number to be called.

Dessa made her way through them. A few eyes looked up, then away. She wasn't what they were looking for. She found a space on the curb, not too close or too far from anyone else. A radius of privacy within the circumference of an implied group.

The feel of the painted concrete under her thighs, the low voices of the other Valley refugees percolated around her. *"Soon,"* she heard someone say. *"I'm sure he's fine."* Another voice. Coos and soft reassurances. The wavered edge of voices controlled after a cry. Dessa closed her eyes. She pressed her forehead into the tips of her fingers, took a deep breath and let herself think about her daughter.

In particular, Dessa thought about fetching Ollie after her nap on the weekends. Sleep sweat made the curls on her head glossy and new, reverse bed head, steaming fresh ringlets into her hair. She would yell for "Momma" even after Dessa had converted her crib into a toddler bed and she could have climbed out by herself, and Dessa would find her still lying down, grumpy and crying. One half of her face stained red from the depth of her sleep. Dessa would lift her up and Ollie would give her all of her damp, lovely weight. Her head heavy on Momma's chest, digging between her breasts. Sometimes she would continue to cry even after Dessa had gotten her, not wanting to be asleep, not ready to be awake. These times Dessa would lie back down with her on the bigger bed. She would open her computer and let Ollie watch whatever she wanted, just appreciating the gravity of her daughter on her body.

Was Hailey letting Ollie sleep on her now?

Dessa could barely picture the woman she had left her daughter with. They had only spoken those few minutes. Vague blondeness, and white teeth. Dessa wasn't sure she could pick Hailey out of a lineup.

Had Olivia wrapped her small soft arms around Hailey's neck when the earthquake had hit? Had the woman whom Dessa couldn't visualize pressed Ollie's weight into her body as she ran for cover, the apartment shaking and grinding around them?

Ollie's body. The sine curve of her back covered in a soft, transparent almost fur that caught the light from their bedroom window. The parentheses of her belly, and rump. Shells of her ears. Delicate clever fingers.

A sharp sob curled itself out of Dessa's mouth.

Too far. She could not think of her daughter's body. It sat

too close to the *if*. Until she knew for certain, Olivia's body was both intact and broken. Her daughter's lungs both filled and didn't. Schrödinger's child.

Dessa considered calling again. She would have pressed that redial button again and again and again, if it had not occurred to her that the distress of her failed calls would be made even worse by a dead battery. Better to ration it. Better to be able to seek out connection sporadically than to not be able to seek it out at all.

"What's taking so long?"

Dessa opened her eyes. A woman sat next to her, a few feet down the curb. Dessa had not heard her approach, but she felt certain this woman had sought her out. The moviegoer who sits directly behind you in a completely empty theater.

The woman made an impatient noise. Dramatic. Clearly trying for Dessa's attention.

She was, Dessa guessed, in her midfifties. In the long, flowy clothes worn by a type of woman of that age, the kind meant to disguise figure flaws but actually ended up making women's bodies look like a kind of fuzzy geometry. Vague triangles and blurry squares wearing chunky jewelry and sipping white wine at the club social.

Dessa's mother had loved those clothes.

"Jan," the woman blurted.

"Excuse me?"

"Jan," the woman repeated. "I'm Jan." There was a mild offense to her tone. Like she couldn't believe Dessa could have possibly misunderstood the single syllable she had barked at her without context.

"Dessa."

"Nice to meet you, Dessa." The woman was smiling again. Practiced. She held out her hand and Dessa took it, struck by the absurdity of the exchange. The two of them shaking hands like they were meeting for the first time at a book club, rather than after a major natural disaster.

Jan reminded Dessa of the women who had stopped by when she flew back home to visit her mother after she got sick. Her mother's friends who had seemed to have appeared out of nowhere. Well-dressed women with lipstick smiles, whose names her mother had never mentioned, but who had so much to say about *her.* "Your mother just loves you so much." Or "She's so strong. She's going through so much, and you would never know it."

But it had seemed to Dessa that of course everyone knew what her mother was going through because she would *tell* them about it. Her mother was her own best publicist.

Ever since Dessa had gone to college, her mother had begun every phone call with a declaration that she was miserable, but that she didn't want to talk about it...which Dessa understood to mean that *it* was what she *most* wanted to talk about. Dessa was trained to ask, "No, what's wrong, Mom?" And then her mother would fill the better part of an hour with complaints. The job she wanted to retire from. Dessa's father's work hours and the messes he left around the house. The neighbors' property lines. And always, *always*, there was a litany of unspecified health scares. Her mother loved the word *procedure* with its vague clinical flavor. But when Dessa demanded to know what *kinds* of procedures, her mother would get slippery. "I haven't even told your father," she would whisper dramatically. "I can't tell you until I tell him."

When her mom finally *did* get sick, Dessa had expected more of the same. But her mother grew quiet. The performance she had been rehearsing played out differently when the stakes were higher than just a plea for attention.

Late stage lung cancer, discovered in her mother, who had

not smoked a cigarette in her life. Dessa could tell she was embarrassed by this. She considered lung cancer low-class, reserved for plebeians who could not abstain from things that were so obviously bad for them.

Dessa had expected her mother to say that she had known it all along. That all those mystery *procedures* had missed what she had known intrinsically was growing inside her. But she never mentioned them.

Instead she blamed Dessa's father.

"It was taking care of *him*. The stress of it, when he died. That's what gave me cancer."

Dessa had left her after that. Red fury blurring at the edges of her vision. It would not have been appropriate to punch a woman in hospice.

"Do you live in The Valley?" Jan asked. Coffee-cake casual.

Dessa nodded. She wondered about the calculus the woman had done to decide to sit next to her. What social signals she was sending out that caused this woman to decide they belonged together.

The easy one. Skin tone. Handshake tribalism. *Of course. Nothing like casual racism as a form of social sorting*, Dessa thought.

But there were probably a few others. Her dress. Purse. Jewelry. Social cues.

"I'm from Encino," Jan offered when Dessa didn't reciprocate fast enough.

"Van Nuys," Dessa said, and she sensed the small shift in the woman as she tried to reconcile Dessa's appearance with her address. She covered it well though. Polite if nothing else.

"This is taking forever."

Dessa nodded again. A lesson she had learned as her mother's daughter. It is easier simply to agree when that's what people want, rather than point out the flaws in their statements.

Dessa could mention the fact that the earthquake was more than a minor inconvenience for millions of people right now. But to what end? Jan didn't look like it had done much more than ruin an evening out.

"I met this guy. He said he could get me home. To The Valley. No waiting."

Dessa looked at her. Her voice had changed at this last statement. Almost like that of a different woman. This was not small talk.

Dessa felt a tendril of something curl around the box with her daughter inside. *Hope.*

"How?"

"He said he knew a way around the freeways that fell. But that it'd cost a grand."

"Jesus—" A thousand dollars. Highway robbery. Or rather robbery to avoid the highways.

"I told him I'd get it…but the ATM would only give me five hundred."

"Do you think I could go with you?" Dessa asked. Jan considered her. It was an act, Dessa knew. This had been why she had sat down next to her. Why she had selected Dessa out of the crowd.

"Do you have the money?"

Dessa calculated. Yes. No. Yes. The number was in her checking account. Yes. But calculated to the penny. Rent. Power. Insurance. Groceries. Gas. Every cent already assigned.

Were they conscious? Trapped? Burned by a fire? Had Hailey known the songs to sing to calm her? Had Ollie screamed for her mother while it happened? Was she still?

Anything that would get her to her daughter faster. To close the gap between the *might be* and the *was*. All other claims to her money were void.

"I can get it."

★ ★ ★

Jan led her to an ATM a few blocks away. She had been suddenly quiet on the walk. Her face clouded over with worry, hands clasped in front of her.

The change was so profound that Dessa had reassessed her initial opinion of the woman. It was unfair of her to assume that just because Jan had been so self-consciously polite that she was somehow oblivious to the pain of others. Dessa hated it when she could tell people were making assumptions about her...and yet she'd done the same thing to Jan.

She felt like an asshole. Some people just lean on courtesy in times of crisis. Making sure they say please and thank you as the paramedics wheel them through the doors. *Thank you for saving my life. Sorry that some of my blood got on you.*

The parking lot of the bank was empty. Naturally, since it had been after hours when the earthquake hit. Dessa had worried that the ATM wouldn't have power, but the blue and red logo of the bank glowed brightly over the kiosk.

Dessa put her card in and punched her pin.

"Where did he say we should meet him?"

Jan's gaze was directed outward. Searching the street. "He said he would come back to the police car."

Dessa was suddenly struck by the stupidity of trusting a total stranger. This person who had volunteered as guide... he was an unknown. "I don't think we should give him all the money up front."

Jan turned her attention back on her. "He said I had to."

"He could rip us off... Or just take the money and leave us in the middle of nowhere." Dessa was nodding at the wisdom of this while she scrolled through the prompts. "We should show him we have it. But only give him half. The other half when we get there."

The machine beeped. A minor tone.

"Shit. My limit is three hundred." Dessa rarely took out more than sixty, so she'd never explored her account's upper limit.

"That's fine." Jan's voice was clipped again. Her eyes outward.

"You think we can talk him down?"

"Sure."

Dessa hit Accept and the cash shuffled out into the tray. She watched the bills collect. A paltry fifteen. She collected them. Three hundred dollars. Making eight with Jan's five. So much. But not enough.

How do you barter with a man who takes advantage of people in need? Profiteers. Their guide had decided on a price because that's what he thought he could get. But if they got as close to his price as possible, Dessa thought they might have a chance of swaying him. She opened her purse, "I think I have a little bit more—"

Jan ripped the stack from Dessa's hand. She was already running before Dessa even realized that she had been robbed.

Dessa took off after her. "Stop!"

But of course Jan didn't. This had always been part of the plan. Some badly played short con Dessa had been foolish enough to fall for.

Dessa caught up easily. Jan's was not a body built for running anymore, and their difference in years more than made up for her head start.

"Stop!" Dessa screamed, grabbing the older woman's arm. She clawed at the money in her hand, fingernails scrabbling at the edges. The bills tumbled from Jan's fist and scattered, cartwheeling across the parking lot.

She turned on Dessa, her arms swinging wild. The flat plane of her fist connected with the cartilage of the younger woman's throat. Dessa heard a meaty click inside her head as her esophagus strained against the blow.

And then she dropped.

It was as if Jan had robbed the world of air. Dessa gasped and rolled onto her side. Fighting for breath. Fighting to stay conscious.

She was vaguely aware of Jan near her. The older woman scrabbling on her hands and knees. Collecting the scattered bills as quickly as possible, before some vagrant wind blew them away.

And then she was leaning over Dessa. Still coughing, immobilized on the ground. She put a hand on her shoulder, and in a motherly voice she said, "I'm sorry…but I need this more than you," before she disappeared into the dark.

15

Shaking, Dessa gently set the tips of her fingers on the skin of her throat. White pain pulsed within her, but she couldn't feel that anything had been broken. Her throat ached, but she could breathe. Pull air past the corridor of her mouth and into her body.

Dessa rolled to her back. Her fingers continuing their tender journey down the slope of her neck. They stopped at the notch where her chest met her clavicle. The lazy U where Joe had rested his index finger the first time he gave himself permission to kiss her.

He had touched the same spot the night she told him she was pregnant. The two of them in his car. He had hidden his face behind his hands for a long minute…but then he had looked at her and reached across the space between them. His fingertip soft on the vulnerable hollow of her neck.

She swallowed, wincing. And willed herself to move.

★ ★ ★

Dessa was getting sick of the sound of her feet. The uneven skid of her injured foot on the pavement, just a fraction of a second longer than the other. *Shh-shhh. Shh-shhh.* Just off the standard syncopation enough to unsettle her, though it was unsettling enough to be able to hear your own footsteps in Los Angeles.

But if she got back to the parking lot, she would not need to hear them anymore. Surely whatever the cop had promised, the "thing" he had said they were working on to get them home, would have wheels. And seats.

Or at the very least enough people that Dessa could not distinguish the sound of her own stuttering footsteps among the many.

She reversed the track that Jan had led her on. Weaving a path backward through her own goddamned stupidity. Her suppression of instinct. Her assumption of trust.

She turned finally onto the street where the grocery store sat.

They were gone.

"Oh my God," Dessa heard herself say as suddenly her feet picked up pace. Pointlessly running to the spot where they were *supposed* to be. Where they had been.

The police car. The cops. Her fellow refugees.

Whatever transport they had been waiting for had appeared and whisked them all away in the time it had taken Jan to rob and assault her. In the time it had taken her to recover and limp her way back here.

"So…fucking…stupid!" Dessa reached the now-empty spot and lashed out at its only remaining occupant. A lone shopping cart. She screamed while she kicked it. Metallic splashes reflecting from her impacts.

She was angry.

So *fucking* angry.

The cart rolled away from her, escaping her fury, and she screamed again. Letting the anger swell through her. Fury at herself and Jan and missing her ride out of here. Fury at not knowing if Joe and Olivia were okay. Fury at the fact that she had stood by and done nothing while a woman had been raped. That she had watched her best friend get crushed and there was absolutely nothing she could do about it.

Fury that she had been through all this and that this… night…experience…whatever it was, *was not yet over.*

Dessa screamed again.

The anger felt so much better than the fear and loss and the speculation of loss that had been stewing inside her.

"Fuck this! Fuck *you!*" She said this, though she did not know to whom.

Across the lot the cart ran into a pole, a bright cymbal's crash of metal on metal. Dessa sat, out of breath. Her eyes fixed the cart while she pulled herself in. Just breathing and watching until the cart and the pole it had run into became shapes in the backs of her eyes. The kind of gaze her dad would call a "case of the stares." Waving his hands in front of her face whenever she got lost in thought.

"Welcome back," he would say to her when she finally pulled her eyes from whatever they had fixed on.

Of course, later he had also gotten the "stares." They had been the first symptom that something was wrong.

Thoughts of her father jolted her out of her reverie.

Anger was good, but only if it kept her moving,

It was a street sign. The pole that the cart had hit. Dessa followed the line of it up to the green tags cantilevered out over the street. She did not recognize the names.

Her father. Again. Fingers on a map. Orienteering. Yellow dotted with blue. Lakes and trails. Campsites.

"Before you can know where you're going, you have to know where you are," he had said. "Where are we?"

Thirteen-year-old Dessa had tried to reconcile the topography of the shoreline with the lines on the paper. Was that peninsula the one they had passed or was it another one? How many hours had they paddled? What did that mean in miles?

"We are here," she had said. She tapped the spot. Not quite sure, but almost.

"Good. Now find our destination."

Dessa's eyes swept the map. Another tap. Thumb where they were. Index where they were going. About five inches and four hours paddling. Dad had nodded.

Now, how do we get there?

The light fixtures dangled from the vaulted ceiling of the store. Some of these had lost their chain supports, swaying, in a powerless reach for the floor. But most were still attached. Shedding antiseptic light on the clutter below.

Dessa imagined what they must have looked like during the quake. How they must have rocked. Swinging in time with one another.

The looters had disappeared because most of the goods had as well. Not much had been spared. Meat, Frozen, Dairy. Dry goods, canned. Bottles of condiments. Toilet paper and toothpicks. As she made her way through the store, Dessa could only tell what was supposed to be on the bare metal shelves because of the tags that were attached beneath them. *Bumble Bee Tuna 3 for 1. Supplies are limited.* Ha.

The floor of the liquor aisle was awash in a fragrant bath of wine and glass. Dessa's eyes stung as she considered it, the fumes tickling at her nose. If any bottle had survived the tumble, it had not outlived the subsequent supermarket sweep.

Dessa understood. The past few hours had made her want to drink too.

She reached the magazine and paper goods aisle. Even here had not been spared. Someone had cleaned out the cards and wrapping paper section. Dessa wondered at the kind of person who would steal hundreds upon hundreds of greeting cards hours after the whole city had crumbled.

A thought bubbled up as a dark laugh. Gretchen would. She loved shit like that. Gretchen was definitely the type of person who would give someone a greeting card after an earthquake.

Congratulations! You Survived!

Balloons. Bright glittery letters.

Or a sympathy card.

Sorry your best friend died...that was kinda a shitty thing for me to do.

With a flood of relief Dessa saw that most of the books and magazine had been spared...though she couldn't be sure if this was because of the reading tastes of the looters or because all of it had fallen to the floor.

Dessa didn't know if they made what she needed anymore. She kneeled, the magazines slick against her legs, and began digging. An amateur archeologist looking for a remnant of the recent past. Dessa hoped against hope that the ubiquity of GPS had not run them out of business. Or caused the market to stop stocking them.

Somewhere under the pile, the edge of a magazine sliced her finger. She flinched. Putting the finger in her mouth.

Another imaginary card from Gretchen. Cutesy girl in pig-tails. Holding out a Band-Aid on her finger.

Heard you got a boo-boo! I'd switch places with you if I could.

And then written in Gretchen's scrawl on the inside.

Stop being such a fucking pussy.

Love, Me.

This earned another dark laugh from Dessa. Some of the magazines slid from the pile, revealing a thick stack of bound paper. She fished it out. *The Thomas Guide: Los Angeles and Orange Counties.* A map.

Dessa pulled herself up and headed back toward the entrance. She knew where she was going; she just needed to find where she was. The book was thick, wire bound and floppy. The grid of neighborhoods stretching out across its pages. Dessa reached a checkout stand and laid the book open on the conveyor belt. Tracing the edge of the index of street names.

There was crunching. Shoes against broken glass by the entrance. Dessa looked up to see a group of looters entering, these with crowbars and bandannas wrapped around their faces.

She startled as she saw them. Frozen. Braced to run. But the figures looked surprised to see her there. One of their number pulled down her bandanna.

They were women. Girls. Teenagers, mostly.

Sizing her up as no threat, the looters broke out of their stasis, the rubber of their shoes squeaking as they made their way to the cash registers. Crowbars angled under to pry them up.

Dessa located herself on the map. Her thumb making the little arrow. YOU ARE HERE. She swung her index finger to Van Nuys.

Her palm spanned the length of the map. Twenty miles. "Damn..."

Dessa looked up. One of the girls had moved to the register next to her. She eyed the page. Admiring the distance between Dessa's finger and thumb. She whistled. "You need to start walking."

The doctors had prescribed walks for her father. Said it was therapeutic. As long as he was accompanied, it was fine. The summer between Dessa's sophomore and junior year of college was spent walking with him. Making different zigzaggy paths through the various housing developments. She mapped their paths in her mind. Winchester Hills was blocky, right turns. Buckingham Green was loopy, all curves. The houses were neocolonial, so similar she couldn't tell them apart—and she wasn't the one with problems with her memory.

Dad had seemed fine though. Mostly himself. Mom's phone calls had been all gloom and drama, but when Dad had gotten on the phone, he had seemed normal. He was the one who told her not to come home until break. That he loved her but he wasn't going anywhere.

Dessa's mother had greeted her return like the arrival of much-needed reinforcements. "I'm so tired, doing all of this myself." Her voice a show of exhaustion. Dessa had looked at her father when she said this. He had been making himself a sandwich at the time. She had rolled her eyes and he shrugged. *"What are you going to do."*

Yes, he had decided to "retire" from his job. An up-and-comer had been found, someone willing to pay for the business as long as Dad helped with the transition. Neither of her parents had said it directly, but Dessa heard hints that he had mistaken one of his clients for his long-dead sister in the middle of a meeting, upsetting both her and her husband.

"It's fine," Dad had said when she asked him about it. "It's not like I lived for my job." He ruffled her hair, "I live for you and Mom."

So rather than get a summer job, Dessa babysat her dad. In the morning they would have breakfast while Mom clucked around them, issuing directives while getting ready for work. They'd watch the news. Go for a walk. Have lunch. Go for a walk. Nap. Walk.

Once Dessa had suggested they go to the pool. Dad had

agreed and they headed out. Dessa had changed into her suit quickly and found two lounge chairs by the deep end. She waited. Ten minutes. Twenty. Finally she went to door of the men's locker room and called inside, "Dad, are you okay?"

There had been no answer, but Dessa heard something that sent chills down her back. A grunt. Her father.

"I'm coming in!" she yelled. "Woman inside!" And she entered the cement confines of the room, the sound of her bare soles slapping the wet concrete echoing.

He had wet his pants.

Somewhere between pulling up his trunks and grabbing his towel, her father had lost himself. He stood by the lockers, his eyes not vacant but scared. He had been crying.

"I'm sorry," he said.

"It's okay, Daddy." Dessa put her hand on his bare back. "Let's go home."

She did not take him swimming again. Instead, they walked.

Dessa found Wilshire. L.A.'s arterial vein, it passed through all the maps on this side of the hills.

She was not the only one. There were pockets of pedestrians all around her. Lit by moonlight, on foot. Everyone was tired. *A million miles before I sleep.*

Dessa walked behind a family. Mother, father, two little girls. Hispanic. Salvadoran, she guessed, but she couldn't know.

She hung back but kept pace with them. They were safe. Their presence made her less of a target until she needed to turn off the main road.

Dessa wasn't quite sure of the path she would take yet. She took out her flashlight and directed its light onto the map.

When Dessa had taken her mother on her driving tour of Los Angeles, she had been careful to avoid the places she knew her mother would find *dangerous* looking. But to her mother's suburban eye all the streets in L.A. looked dangerous.

"Is that graffiti?" she would ask. And yes, it was. But that didn't mean it was a bad neighborhood, Dessa explained. There was graffiti all over the map.

Her mother crossed her arms. "The problem with maps is they don't tell you what streets you shouldn't be driving on."

Dessa considered her options. The avenues forking off of Wilshire. She hated anything that made her feel like her mother…but she did wish the map would tell her which street she *shouldn't* pick.

She tucked the map back into her purse and looked up.

The street ahead of her was flooded with water.

"El lago," said the father. The lake. He pointed.

MacArthur Park. A works progress beauty, known for its man-made lake and more recently for its frequent daytime gang related shootings.

The earthquake had ripped the concrete bowl of the lake. A gentle flow of water poured over the sidewalk onto Wilshire. The moon rippled on its surface. The family in front of Dessa hesitated for a moment. Then each parent picked up a child and pressed on. Socks, shoes. The water wicking up the legs of their pants.

Dessa followed. The water was bright cold, the kind that promised you could get used to it. Within a few steps it was at her knees, a gentle current tug-tugging at her shoes on the pavement. A continuous tide. She wobbled as it pulled at her.

Dessa tucked the map into her purse and looped the strap around her neck. It rested on her chest, awkward, but less likely to throw her off-balance. She kept the flashlight out though, the tail of its beam cutting through the water in front of her.

The little girl in the father's arms was watching her. Eyes curious about the stranger who followed her. Her face placid.

Dessa smiled at her, trying to get her to smile back.

The little girl stuck out her tongue. Playful.

Dessa stuck out hers back. A game. She did this with Ollie.

The water kept rising, almost to their waists now. The sequins of her dress lifted under the water, catching the light. Dessa could see the edge of this little river though...the dry shore of the other side of the road.

The mother glanced back at Dessa, her eyes nervous. She spoke in a hushed tone to her husband. The man nodded and they began to move diagonally, away from Dessa.

Dessa swallowed and stayed her course; she didn't want to make them nervous by following.

The little girl stuck her tongue out again. Trying to regain Dessa's attention. Just like Olivia. Dessa swung the flashlight so that it angled up into her face. Light and shadows drawing a ghostly face on top of her own.

"Boo," she said, taking a step.

And then the earth was no longer there.

16

There had been ground. And then there wasn't.

There had been air. And then there wasn't.

Dessa had blinked and she was under. Somehow falling and being pulled at the same time. She clawed at the surface, green, receding moonlight but it was gone too quickly…and instead her free hand connected with the ribbed surface of steps.

An escalator.

The subway, she realized. The lake was draining into the giant underground cavity that was the Westlake metro station, and here she was just another unwelcome spider in the bathtub. Flailing against the drain.

The flashlight in her hand connected with the side of the stairs, a dull thud threaded through the sound of the rushing water. It slipped and she tightened her grip on the metal cylinder that was miraculously somehow still working. Slicing light through the water, affording her glimpses of her new world as it passed. Tiled wall. Commissioned public art piece. Ticket kiosks. Turnstiles. All underwater.

The current changed direction and Dessa was swept toward the westbound platform. Santa Monica bound. Down, down. Another ladder of stairs, pointlessly sweeping by below her.

The fingers of her free hand caught the rail and for a moment she hung horizontal in the water. Frozen in flight.

And then the current pushed her handbag around the hinge of her neck. It floated upward, like a balloon...its handle strangling her.

Dessa brought the flashlight-burdened hand to her face, trying to free herself without letting go of either her handhold or her light. The current pulled the straps farther up her neck, darkness seeping in the corners of her eyes. Cutting off her brain's supply of already-oxygen-starved blood...

She let go.

The pressure of the water pulled her away, slamming her body into a concrete support and jolting the flashlight out of her hand. Dessa's mouth opened in shock at the blow, releasing a bubble of precious air. Her lungs ached. Burned. Screamed for oxygen.

The current was slower here. Ripples reflected above. She kicked up...and hoped.

Dessa gasped as her head broke the surface. A pocket of air between two ceiling joists. The sound of her breathing reverberated between the supports, her head the sole occupant of a long-empty ballroom. She trod water, bobbing in the half-light. Like night swimming. Something she'd done once with Gretchen in Lake Tahoe and once with Joe in a hotel pool, after hours.

Dessa bobbed and listened to her breath. The quiet splashes

of her waving hands reflecting back at her. Imagined Gretchen
or Joe next to her.

Joe would have kissed her. Pressed his body against hers
and pulled them both to the side of the pool. Wet tongues,
wet bodies, wet hands.

And Gretchen? What would Gretchen say? What *had* she
said that night in Nevada? Floating in the calm, skin sleek and
pale under the water.

Not bad.

And for tonight? What would Gretchen say?

Shittiest night ever.

Dessa laughed. Almost a bark. A release of the pressure. The
sound echoed but it was definitely shorter than it had been.
Bouncing around a smaller space than it had a minute ago.

The water was rising, rapidly closing the pocket she had
found for herself.

Dessa spotted a light far below. Small yellow. Her flashlight. Still lit.

There was something else down there. A bluer clearer light
that was throwing the shadows up here. Something farther
in the murk.

If she lost her ability to see down here, she'd never find a
way out. She needed that light. Dessa wrapped her purse strap
around a pipe and dived. Pushing her way back down.

A slow current pushed her sideways as she pulled herself
downward. The bluish light grew stronger, until Dessa could
see its source.

A train car. Submerged. Inside dim shapes knocked against
the glass. Bodies.

Dessa recoiled. Twisting away. She clawed the flashlight
from the ground and pushed upward. She surfaced with a gasp.

Those poor people. What kind of shitty luck do you have
to have to drown during an earthquake?

Somewhere in her mind Dessa could hear Gretchen laughing. *Your kind.*

Dessa reached out for her handbag...but it wasn't there. She had come up between a different set of joists.

She swung the flashlight over the water. Something caught her eye.

Maybe her luck wasn't so shitty after all. The edges of a ladder at the end of the joists, just above the rising surface. Twenty feet away. The kind they attached to exhaust fans, or cooling systems...it did not matter what, just that it could be the kind that could take her up. And out.

Dessa swam toward the end of the joists. Her arms pressing an odd stew of cigarette butts and paper wrappers out of the way. A Dodgers hat. Soda bottles. A scum of irretrievable detritus finally lifted up from where it had fallen next to the third rail.

She dropped under the surface. An access panel. She swung it open and shined her light inside. Another ladder led to a vent above. The way out.

Elation filled her as she began to climb. And then she heard it.

A familiar ring. Her phone.

Olivia.

She turned.

Plunging back into the water, Dessa recognized the stupidity of her actions. Going back for her phone. If she died now it would be Darwin worthy.

But the ringing... If it was her... If it was Hailey and Olivia or Joe and Olivia...as long as it was Olivia... In her mind the phone and her daughter, they were the same.

The light from her flashlight caught a dark mass floating in the joists above her. She kicked up toward it. Only just as she was about to crest did she catch a small motion…or rather a thousand small motions.

Dessa burst through the water right next to a scrabbling cluster of rats. The animals were squeaking. Panicked. Clawing at each other to climb aboard some larger piece of floating trash. One on top of the other. An island of terrified rodents.

And then they were swimming toward *her*. Squeaking. Claws biting into her hair.

She screamed and dropped under. Shaking her head in the water. She kicked away and she felt the rats let go, searching for their companions. Dessa came up in another section…her phone was still ringing…not here…but closer.

She dropped again. Ducking into the next section. Again. Again. The phone still ringing… But the water was still rising, each time she emerged higher and higher… To her neck. Her chin. Her lower lip.

She came up again. Her breath small…only inches from the ceiling. The ringing had stopped. Dessa's daughter slipped away. *Please. Please.*

She turned, reorienting. Something moved against her neck. A slither against the pulse of her throat. She beat at it, her hands wild birds attacking. The animal gave no fight… It chimed at her. A voice message.

She had swum *up* through the ring of strap, looping it around her neck. Dessa fought the desire to check her voice message. *Darwin award*, Gretchen said in her head. She could wait to do that when she was on dry land.

Dessa lay on the sidewalk next to grate she had pushed her way through. Marking the sidewalk with a wet stamp of her limbs, her torso, her hair. Her body burned…she should be cold, she knew. She was shivering but her skin felt like it was on fire. In her hand she held her cell.

One of Olivia's first words was *phone.*

Dessa had heard this was pretty common now. Parents holding their devices constantly made them totems. Before she could walk, Ollie could scroll... Searching out the pictures Dessa kept of her on the phone.

For a while Dessa worried that she was creating a little narcissist. Obsessed with looking at pictures with herself. But as she saw the way Ollie giggled and responded to videos of herself, she realized it was more of a game. The same as she had done as a little girl in the mirror. Just a second or two behind.

Ollie was responsible for Dessa having a waterproof phone. There had been a near miss. Dessa running a bath before bedtime stories. Loading some toys into the tub, Ollie helping. Little boat. Little dolphin. Little mermaid.

The phone dropped just below the surface before Dessa snatched it up. Ollie did not discriminate between her toys and Mommy's.

Typically, Dessa had panicked. Overreacted. And yelled a great big scary "No" at her daughter. Ollie recoiled, crying. Not sure what she had done wrong.

The store had been able to recover everything.

"Even the voice mails?" Dessa had asked, and the clerk had nodded.

Dessa had started shaking with relief. Holding down insurgent tears right there in the store. So unlike her. The blue-shirted clerks and her daughter as witnesses.

The waterproof phone case had been extra but it was insurance. Against bathtubs and accidental splashes from the sink. Spilled glasses of water on the bedside.

She had never imagined it going swimming.

But it had, and it—and she—had survived.

Dessa stared at the phone in her hand. A voice mail message. Unknown caller. She pressed Listen. It was two seconds.

Empty sound. Then it cut off. She hit it again. Pressed it in her ear. Silence. Was it possible it was Hailey? Was there anything else in those seconds? Some hope to hold on to. The sound of Ollie breathing?

Nothing.

Dessa scrolled to bottom of the list of voice mails. Two listed the same date, even though they had been left at different times. The date of the phone's recovery. She pressed Listen on the first.

Her father's voice. Thick and distant. Like he was pulling the words up from under a swamp. "My Dessa. Hello. Strong girl. My strong girl. Mom. Love."

Left three days before he killed himself.

Dessa had wondered what he had meant. Was she the strong girl? Or Mom? Had he known this was going to be his last message? Rationing his little bits of reality before he had taken a handgun into the stand of trees behind their backyard.

Or had he not known? Had it been an accident as her mother so desperately wanted to believe. Had he been playing a tape of his younger days, hunting with his father.

Dessa pressed Listen again.

"My Dessa. Hello. Strong girl. My strong girl." She stopped it before he said anything else. Played it again. "My Dessa. Hello. Strong girl. My strong girl."

1 AM
WESTLAKE

17

Beegie thought she would hopscotch ahead again. *After.* The way she was doing before. She kept expecting to blink and then be somewhere else. Seeing something else.

But the world kept spooling itself out right in front of her now. No more jumps. Like what happened in the back of the store *forced* her life to thread together again. Someone smacking the player to make it work.

There had been an earthquake.

A big one.

A big motherfucker of an earthquake.

This she remembered. Sort of. The bus shimmying under her belly. All the horns blaring outside.

There were other pieces of her time with Busman and Not-Charlie that made more sense now. Pieces to that puzzle. All the broken buildings. A fire. Beegie remembered she had seen someone crying, but she didn't remember who.

For a moment she considered herself. That she was the one who had cried.

But that thought didn't...*wouldn't* make sense.

Beegie didn't know where she was, but she kept moving anyway. Eventually she would find something. A familiar name or building. A bus stop with a map that she could use to figure out where she was.

The inside of the bus she had been in flashed into her mind. Caved in and broken. The buses probably weren't running now. Current circumstances and all.

She was limping but she was trying hard not to. "Don't let them see you when you're weak," her mother had said. During one of the good times. The times when she looked most like the woman in the picture Beegie carried. Different but close enough.

Beegie wondered if Jasmine's family would have said anything like that.

Probably not...

She forced herself to push those thoughts down. Mother thoughts. Other thoughts.

Instead, she thought of possessed little girls.

She wondered about the spaces *in between* the stuff she remembered.

Maybe she had been *possessed.*

She doubted it. But that didn't mean she couldn't *like* the idea. Her with supernatural powers. Throwing people down staircases. Tossing them into walls. Anybody that crossed her.

Maybe she had even caused the earthquake. Or not her, but the angry thing that *possessed* her. That's how the horror movie would start. The earth opened up and it released a demon and it found a nice comfortable home in Beegie.

Until it *left*.

Beegie decided she should find a *gun*.

This strange thought flew into her head. It hovered over her want for a *possession* in her brain. The two ideas related somehow. If she could not have a demon to make her strong and scary, she could have a *gun*.

Her brain sent her pictures of what it would feel like in her hand. Heavy. And *cold*. It would feel like power. It would feel like no one would ever fuck with her ever again. Like it didn't matter that she was small, that if she had a gun no one could touch her ever again.

That's what she wanted.

Never to be touched.

The right to tell people not to touch her and have them *have to* listen to her. Because they were afraid.

The idea of the gun grew large in her mind. *Bang* she would shoot the Busman. *Bang* Not-Charlie. *Bang Bang* for Eric, but not for Mrs. Greely because she had never touched her. Even though she was a bitch.

And even though Beegie *knew* she wouldn't really do those things, she thought about them while she walked. Because it felt better. Better to be angry than in pain. Anger felt like power.

She looked around. Dark buildings. Black storefronts and parking lots. Houses with flickering lights on inside. Candles lit by the people who lived there. The neighborhoods had changed without her noticing.

There were people here. Beegie could hear them. Fires in the front yards. A woman crying.

Beegie steered clear.

She pushed her way up the darkest street. No people meant no problems.

This was why she did not see them until she was almost

BRIDGET FOLEY

right upon them. A man and a woman arguing. He had her arm in his hand, and she was *shrinking*. Like she was trying to make herself smaller to make him happy.

Neither of them noticed her watching. She didn't even bother to duck behind the car she was next to. She just stood there.

Their talking got quiet. Beegie couldn't make out their words before, but now it sounded like they were barely speaking. But the woman was scared... Her eyes open and wide as she looked at the man's face.

Like every part of her body was begging. *Please.*

And then the woman twisted, pulling against his arm. The man grabbed her. And it was *so easy for him*. He started dragging the woman toward the yard. And the woman was still begging. Like the outcome of this whole thing wasn't already decided. Like there was anything that could be done to prevent it.

Beegie's eyes caught on a spilled river of brick that lay across a lawn. Cousins to the ones from the bus. All set free by the earthquake.

She slipped her bag from her shoulder before she picked one up. It was heavier than she thought it would be. But still it flew. It struck the man and jarred his hands away from the woman. Both of them were stunned for a moment. Both of them not sure where it had come from.

The next throw was better. Striking his neck. He stumbled then and Beegie *gasped*. Riding the train of this moment. *Letting herself* instead of someone else. The next one smashed him in the back of the head. He fell.

But monsters always get back up.

The woman was staring at her now. Her body still stiff with panic...with the same *please* it had before. Beegie fixed

168

her hands on a chunk of concrete and lifted it. Heavy. Arms shaking.

And then the woman knocked it out of her hands. "Don't," she shouted. Like the man under Beegie's arms had anything good planned for her in the dark behind the house.

Idiot. Bitch.

Beegie felt the woman's eyes on her while she searched the man's clothes. Feeling his waistband. Around his legs. He looked like the type who would have what she wanted.

But he didn't.

Maybe it was all an act.

Or maybe he had just left his at home.

She wasn't going to find what she needed here.

18

As she walked, Dessa's skin flared hot and cold. Heat ema-
nated, then abandoned her, leaving trails of gooseflesh in its
wake. Chilling her.

Shock, maybe. Dessa wasn't sure. Didn't want to think about
the things she'd been swimming around in. What she might
have been exposed to.

Her hair and clothes were beginning to dry, though her
shoes were still sodden…the ones she put on her feet while in
the back of the store…

Dessa pictured the hem of the girl's jeans swinging.

A flare of guilt and horror welled within her.

Dessa put it away. She willed herself into the moment she
could effect. *Concentrate on each step.* On her feet. On moving
herself forward.

Her shoes were damp. But it did not matter why. It did

not matter when or where she had gotten them or what was happening while she was putting them on. It did not matter that they were not the shoes she had started her night with or what had happened to make her lose the others.

All that mattered was now. Her feet. Moving forward.

Just. Get. Home.

Dessa could feel the makeshift bandage she had fashioned on the sole of her foot. Warm damp clinging. An injury from a lifetime ago.

It had been an evening of lifetimes.

Disaster clusters. That was how Dessa thought of them. One disaster opening doors into others. A husband has a heart attack while his wife is in surgery. A single car accident wipes out two generations at a family reunion.

That was what was probably happening all over this city. Millions of families tallying their share of the disaster. Counting the disparate losses of the earthquake. The children that did not make it home. The houses that were not there to make it home to.

Dessa pressed Call again. The three long beeps sounded. Again.

Her phone had connected with someone in the bowels of the subway station. But outside, it refused.

But it *was* capable of connection. Dessa kept hitting that button. Like a meditation. *Beepbeepbeep.* Like the rosary her aunt had led them through, first at her father's funeral and then at her mother's. Each press a prayer. Each step bringing her closer. She noticed the neighborhood around her in between the beeps. Rusted cars. *Beepbeepbeep.* Chain-link fences. *Beepbeepbeep.* People standing outside their homes. *Beepbeepbeep.* A tag marking this as some gang's territory. *Beepbeepbeep.*

Just. Get. Home.

Dessa almost didn't understand when suddenly her cell made a different sound. A long trill. Connection.

"Mrs. Reilly? Hello?"

Dessa almost dropped the phone. Fumbling. Bringing it closer to her face. "Hailey? Hailey? Can you hear me?"

The babysitter's voice was shaky. "We're all right, Mrs. Reilly. Olivia is all right."

Something broke free in Dessa. A hope so big she did not know she had been holding it. "Oh God... Oh thank you." *Thank God. Thank Hailey. Thank the phone company. The person who invented satellites. All of them.*

"But we can't get out."

"What do you mean?"

"The door won't open." Hailey cracked into tears, and suddenly Dessa could imagine her face perfectly. It was incredible to her that she had ever had difficulty. "I keep waiting for someone to come. No one is coming!"

In the background Dessa could hear Ollie. A whimper.

"Hailey. I need you to stay calm."

Up ahead Dessa could see that her raised voice had drawn attention. A group of young men stood around a fire that had been constructed on one of the front lawns. Shaved heads. Long shorts.

Dessa tucked her head to the phone. She felt their eyes on her as she crossed the street. She lowered her voice. "Joe was almost there when..." God, that had been hours ago. Dessa pushed the thought of what could have happened to him away. "He will be there."

The men around the fire had stopped talking. They were openly staring at her as she passed.

"Can you put Olivia on?" Dessa asked. There was a rustle and then:

"Momma?"

Dessa felt an actual rush of pleasure run up her at the sound of her daughter's voice. "Hi, sweetie." *Her head. Her hands. The shells of her ears.*

"I want you."

"I know, honey. I'm coming."

"Lady... Hey, *lady.*" This voice not from inside her phone. One of the men. He had broken off from the crowd. He was following her on the opposite side. Dessa picked up her pace. Trying to ignore him.

"Momma's coming. Just like the Runaway Bunny. Remember?"

"I'm the tree?"

"Yes... Yes. Honey, you are the tree I will come home to."

Three long beeps. The call had dropped. Olivia was gone.

"Hey...why'd you cross the street?" He was still behind her, but in the street now. Dessa sped up. So did he. "I said, why'd you cross the street?" His voice laced with anger.

The street was darker and quieter here. They were well away from his friends now, though Dessa wasn't sure if that was a good thing or a bad thing. He moved so that he was parallel to her in the middle of the street. Matching her pace.

"You know, we're out trying to help our community, and some white lady comes in and treats us like fucking criminals." He was so angry, though Dessa could not be sure if it was at her or something else. But it didn't matter. He was angry and she was the one who was here.

She broke into a run.

Barely made it to a yard before he cut her off. Stepping on the sidewalk in front of her. "I just want to talk to you!" he yelled.

She stopped short of him... Her head turned away. Terrified to engage. Trapped.

"Fucking look at me. Look at me!"

Dessa forced her eyes to connect with his. Taking in the details of him. Simultaneously noticing that he had beautiful eyes while also noticing the fact that he was at least seven inches taller than her. Noticing that his clothes were clean and well tended while also taking in the rage on his face. Everything in an instant. His right to his anger and his complete and unquestioned ability to overpower her.

"I have a fucking news flash for you. In this neighborhood, brown people are on both sides of the street."

"I'm… I didn't mean to offend you."

He grinned for a second. And Dessa could then tell that he was also drunk. "You didn't mean to offend me? To offend me?" He played with the word. Elongating the vowels. *Ooofeeend.* "Everything about you fucking offends me. The way you walk, the way you talk, your fucking rich whore dress."

"I'm sorry." Dessa's voice sounded so small.

"Fucking white bitch out slumming downtown. But we don't have any twenty-dollar martinis in this neighborhood, do we? Looks a little different when you're not looking at it from the highway?"

Dessa could reconcile his rage. His characterization of her. This was in fact who she was. Downtown with friends. Their drinks *had* been expensive. She *had* only ever seen his neighborhood from her car. This was true.

Dessa wondered what would have happened if she had simply *not* crossed the street. If by not signaling to this man that she was afraid of him, she would not have so enraged him that she felt he was something to fear.

"I'm sorry," she repeated.

He was quiet for a moment. He rocked on his feet, looking at her. His energy changed. "Yeah, you look like you got it nice."

Dessa put her head back down. Hoping their exchange was over. He stepped back, opening a path for her to make her way past his.

"Thank you," she whispered as she moved to make her way past him. Not sure if that was the right thing to say, but she was too afraid of him to say nothing.

And then his hand was on her arm. "Do you? Got it nice?" A whisper. But forceful. "Got the AC. Leather seats. Some bitch take care of you…buy you shit. You give him head on Saturdays?" Questions he didn't *want* the answers to.

Dessa pulled her arm away from him, but he just increased his grip. "You know what me and my *brown* friends are doing?"

Dessa shook her head. This close she could smell the tang of alcohol on his breath.

"We've been pulling bodies out of houses. Babies…" This last word came out a cry. His voice edged with pain. The transition so fast Dessa wasn't sure what had happened. He sniffed. "No firemen coming to help." And then it was gone and the anger was back. "You think the firemen came to your neighborhood?"

"I just want to get home," Dessa whispered.

"Fuck you, bitch!" His voice jolting her. "You know it. You know they come to your neighborhood. They only come here when somebody gets killed." He stared at her for a beat. "I could kill you. Then they'd come."

Dessa stared at him a moment. His beautiful eyes. He did not seem to be threatening her. Just deciding. For a moment. The two of them deciding if he was serious.

And then Dessa started to move. Her elbow breaking free from his grip. Twisting away from him.

But he was faster. Bending down. Contact slap on her arms. Wide grip on her wrists. Dessa dropped. Desperately pulling all of her weight away.

"Please don't."

But he wasn't looking at her anymore. He was dragging her, his face turned toward the nearest house. A toppled chimney lying across the yard. Darkness farther back.

Dessa pivoted, trying to get her feet under her, but he was too fast. The pavement turned to brown grass beneath her.

"You call 911." His voice was crazed. Almost like this was a conspiracy between them. "In your white lady voice, you tell them some banger gonna kill you."

"Please!" Dessa was desperate now. She did not want to disappear into that darkness with him. Did not want to know what was on the other side of it.

"They'll come for you and we'll make them stay. Make them hel—"

There was sudden motion by his head. For a moment Dessa thought it was a bird flying toward him. But it was followed by a cracking sound. A muffled bone crunch as something heavy connected with the side of his face.

Dessa identified the "bird" as it tumbled down from his shoulder. A chunk of brick.

The man stopped moving and let go of her wrists. His hand reached up and touched the temple of his forehead. A rose of blood already blooming there.

And then another brick flew toward him. This one connected with his neck, bigger than the last. A small surprised sound emerged from him…smaller than Dessa would have expected. An *oof*. A little girl's expression. Strange from such a large man.

The force of the blow drove him sideways, and his knees hit the ground. Dessa dodged as the brick tumbled down the slide of his body. She turned, looking for the source.

In the darkness Dessa could barely make out a dark figure on the sidewalk. A silhouette, dark shape limned by the light of the moon. It bent over and picked something up...a chunk from the corpse of the fallen chimney.

"What the fuck?" The man twisted, trying to get up.

And then the third brick hit him. Its impact pushing him down onto his side. He collapsed. Face forward into the ground.

The figure stalked toward them. Dessa had the odd sensation that the figure was getting smaller as it got closer. Proximity making it shrink rather than grow as it approached... no, as *she* approached.

The woman kneeled over the fallen man. For a second Dessa thought she was praying, her body still with concentration. And then she raised a jagged chunk of concrete from the plane of her lap. Her arms shaking with the effort, readying to drop it on the man's skull.

"No! Don't!"

Dessa leaped forward, her hands pushing the concrete out of the figure's grip. "It's enough! He's down! It's enough!" The rock fell with a dull thud a few feet from the man's head, burying itself in the ground. There was no doubt it would have killed him.

Dessa sat back. Out of breath. The girl stared at her. Willful.

Because she was *a girl*. No more than fifteen, Dessa figured. Black. Petite. Pretty.

The girl looked away from Dessa and immediately began searching the man's clothes. Hands fumbling at his pants, diving into his pockets and waist of his shorts. She turned him over, sweeping his back.

"Fuck."

She rose, disappointed. Dessa could not imagine that the girl had saved her just to facilitate a mugging. She turned, watching the girl make her way back to the sidewalk.

She needed to say something.

"Th…thank you," Dessa managed lamely.

The girl made a small sound. A cluck. But she did not look at Dessa.

Instead she pulled her bag from where she had placed it on the sidewalk. Dessa recognized it as the girl hefted it onto her shoulder. Black leather with a red bandanna around its strap.

It was the girl from the store.

19

Sometimes Los Angeles did this. Shuffled a cast of recurring characters through the various backdrops of one's life. It was why it was sometimes hard for Dessa to believe that ten million people lived there, when she would see the same people over and over in disparate parts of city. They could not all be her neighbors, but seeing them again and again made L.A. feel like a small town.

It reminded Dessa of a book Olivia sometimes pulled from her small shelf. *Where's Waldo*. At the end there was a list of other characters to be found after you had already found the striped-shirted wanderer on every page. This was how Dessa thought of these familiar strangers. Dapper old man with cane. Woman in turban. Suspenders mustache guy. She would spot them all over town. And it gave her a little thrill each time.

There you are. Hello, friend. She would think, though she had never spoken to any of them in her life.

There was one in particular, a woman she had spoken to but was certain would not remember her. A tall woman, Jamaican with long hair and a soft voice.

It was she who had run Dessa through her preliminary questions at the women's clinic. Before she told Joe. When there had still seemed to be options. Dessa saw this woman everywhere. Getting coffee at the kiosk near her work. On the pier at Santa Monica. In line at the CVS by Gretchen's house.

Dessa would see her and the context would take her a moment. Then a jolt of recognition and the memory of her lilting voice saying, "We can schedule a D and C this weekend, if you like." This last word especially lovely. *Lai-ke.*

Dessa always wondered what it meant, this recurring coincidence. Why did she see this woman so often? There was no way she would remember her.

And yet, each time Dessa saw her, she fought an impulse to say hello. To tell her about the daughter whose existence, or more importantly lack of existence, she had once discussed with her. But she never did.

And here the city had churned up another coincidence.

Another person. Another choice Dessa had made.

She had not seen the girl's face in the store. Just her shoes and her jeans. And in the mirror, the bare expanse of her thigh bracketing the man's body. Her neck beneath the knife the second man had held.

But it was her.

Dessa had been saved by the girl she herself had done nothing to save.

The girl swung the bag onto her shoulder and began walking away.

Dessa was up on her feet and jogging to catch up with her

before she even knew why she was doing it. The image of the woman from the health clinic flying into her mind, a potential lifetime of running into this girl and never saying anything. Just constantly confronting the deficiency of her bravery.

"Hey… Hey, wait."

The girl stopped. Turned to look at Dessa. A shrug. *What?*

Dessa still didn't know what to say. "Sorry…"

The wrong kind of apology. *Sorry I'm holding you up. Sorry I'm inconveniencing you.* There were no words for the real apology she owed this girl.

"Uh… I'm… Thank you."

"You said that already." The girl waved her hand and moved on. Her steps big for someone her size. Dessa thought she might be five-one or five-two. Three or four inches shorter than her…though she was still so young. It was possible she was still growing.

"I wasn't trying to help you." The girl didn't look over at her as she walked, "I thought he might have something I needed."

"What?"

"A gun."

Dessa could tell she was trying to shock her. To get her to go away.

But she couldn't. Couldn't resolve this tough talk with this young face. Couldn't leave this opportunity that had somehow presented itself to…what? Redeem herself? Was that even possible?

"How old are you?"

"Fuck you, how old am I?" The girl rounded on her, angry. "Old e-fucking-nough to know you don't go walking through this neighborhood in a hoochie dress after a fucking earthquake." She turned and picked up her pace. "Stop following me, girl. What, did I adopt you or something?"

Dessa was struggling. Why was she doing this? Pursuing this? But she persisted. "Where are you going? We could... I think we could be safer if we were traveling together."

"I'd be a lot safer without your conspicuous white ass tailing me."

"Do you really believe that?"

The girl thought about it. The features on her face softening. Seeing the wisdom of it. "Shit... I'm going to East Hollywood."

Hollywood, Dessa knew. West Hollywood. North. But East? "I don't know where that is?"

"The shitty part of Los Feliz."

Dessa nodded, despite herself. "I know that part."

"Where you going?"

"Van Nuys."

The girl looked her up and down. Dessa could barely imagine what she looked like right now. "Uh-uh. That bag? That rock? That's not some Van Nuy's piece of shit, that's fucking Calabasas. Beverly Hills or something."

"Why would I lie about that?"

"Okay. You live there. But you're not from there."

Dessa thought about the subdivisions where she grew up. Cut green lawns. College degrees. Kids who got hand-me-down cars on their sixteenth birthdays.

No, the place where she was from was nothing like Van Nuys. The girl made her feel like an imposter. A cultural tourist in the place she was raising her daughter. "Gimme your earrings."

Dessa hesitated.

"Fuck you. I'm not trying to rob you." She reached into her bag and pulled a large purple sweatshirt from its recesses. "You don't get rolled if you don't look like you have anything worth taking."

That's what Jan had seen in her. And the man whose unconscious body they had left down the street. Something worth taking. And this girl's word for it, *rolled*...that was precisely how they had made Dessa feel. Like something had rolled over her. Flattened her.

She handed the girl her earrings and watched as she pinned them to the inside of the pocket of the sweatshirt. "You put your money and your jewelry in different places. You wearing a bra?"

Dessa nodded.

"Put your ring in there. Anyone sees your titties you got bigger problems."

Dessa rocked the ring off her finger and followed her instructions. The diamond felt hard and cold next to her skin. The girl handed her the sweatshirt and she zipped it on, pushing the sleeves up. She was swimming in it. Dessa wondered why a girl even smaller than her would be carrying something so big until she realized what it did.

It hid her. Swallowing her body in a swathe of shapeless terry cloth. The hem of her dress peeked out, but barely. If she had a pair of baggy jeans and a baseball hat, there would be little to even mark her as female.

"Be better if your chicken legs weren't sticking out. But... least you don't look like a disco ball anymore."

They walked. Quiet in the dark. The small scuffing of the girl's shoes on the pavement a counter point to Dessa's uneven patter.

But it did not feel like they were *together*. Dessa was struck by a familiar sensation of crowded pathways. On visits to New York City or on the street, when she would accidentally step into the rhythm of a stranger. Keeping pace with someone for a little too long was *unsettling*. There was always a pulse in these situations, a herd sense that one should slow down while the other broke ahead.

Dessa always thought it was funny how uncomfortable it made her. The relief she felt when the unintended bond was broken. What strange little panicky creatures humans are.

Walking with the girl felt just like that. As though they had accidentally fallen into sync with one another, and to avoid embarrassment one of them would do best to fall away. Because they did not belong together.

Dessa imagined what they must look like. Her "conspicuous white ass" next to this hard-faced black teenager. Less an odd couple now that she had the sweatshirt on, but still…

Dessa searched for a way to bridge the gap between them. Conversation prompts. They all seemed ridiculous. *Where are you from? What brings you to this part of town?*

There was a more natural one. *Where were you when the earthquake struck? What happened to you? How did you survive?* But those questions sat too close to the truth that Dessa already knew about this girl. What she had survived.

So they walked through the dark neighborhood in silence. Quietly weaving out of the way of clumps of people. Avoiding the bubbling voices in the dark.

They slowed as they approached a highway underpass, both of them sensing the wrongness of it at the same time. A dark shape hulked down from the line of the road above, throwing the tunnel into darkness.

Dessa swept her flashlight across it.

Through a breath of gray dust they could make out the bridge's supports. The cement cylinders had buckled onto themselves, ribs of metal supports poking through their concrete skin, dropping the tunnel clearance to just above Dessa's head.

"Fuck," the girl whispered.

Dessa stepped closer to the tunnel and the light sliced farther onto the carpet of rubble on the ground.

"I think it's open."

Dessa clicked her flashlight off and squinted, willing the dust and the darkness away. Slowly she was able to make out the other side of the pass. Dim light reflecting off the road about fifty feet away.

The tunnel moaned. A dying thing.

They couldn't go through. The bridge may not have collapsed yet but it was collapsing. The slowness of the process didn't take away from the fact that it was inevitable.

Dessa took out her map. The surrounding streets made bent-pipe U-turns at the hard cliff of the highway. She traced her finger, looking for the nearest way through to the other side.

"The next underpass is ten blocks west. We'll have to double back."

The girl made a sound in her throat. The slight catch of exasperation. It was the first thing the girl had done that revealed her youth. Dessa's mother had called it the teenager sound.

"It'll take us an extra hour."

Dessa knew she was right. Ten blocks west, then ten back. And that was presuming the next underpass was open.

"Shit." The girl sighed. She turned. Dessa watched her. The moon drawing a line on her body, resting on her shoulders as she walked away.

No one is coming.

Dessa heard Hailey's voice. In her mind but as clearly as if it had just hit her ears. The tone and timbre of it. The desperation.

The door won't open.

I keep waiting for someone to come.

No one is coming.

Those were the words she had said. Dessa did not know which door she had meant. Which one it was that would not open. How many doors were there in her apartment? Which of those was her daughter trapped behind? Dessa flipped through the options. Her daughter hunched next to the babysitter in the bedroom. In the bathroom. In the linen closet. The pantry.

It was only fifty feet.

Dessa could not say that it was a conscious decision. It did not feel like it. It felt like she thought of Olivia and then she was inside the collapsing tunnel, dark ceiling pressing down toward her, feet searching for balance among the debris.

Her shallow breaths brought with them the dust, coating the insides of her mouth and nose with the tastes and smells of destruction. A paste of saliva and grit forming on her tongue. Dessa closed her mouth and swallowed, mineral tang of concrete left a trail on the walls of her throat.

"Hey!"

The girl's shout bounced around Dessa, and she stopped. Her heart's beat the only motion. If a yodel could bring down an avalanche, what could a shout do in here?

The echo died and Dessa stood for a moment. She was maybe fifteen feet in. Ten more to halfway.

A clink behind her told her the girl was following. Her careful steps echoed, china cup kisses amplified. Dessa listened to her cautious approach without turning toward it.

And then something brushed the back of Dessa's hand. A brief warmth. The girl's hand. Momentary fingertips touching. Letting Dessa know she was there. For an instant Dessa wondered if the girl would take her hand, but then it was gone. She turned, seeing only the shadow of the girl next to her. The faint sound of her breathing.

They moved. They crouched, making their bodies smaller.

Necks bent, fingers poised to brace them against the rocks if they fell. The scrape of the rubble against their feet.

Clink.

Clink.

Clink.

It could barely have been a minute...but each second was stretched, doubled, tripled by their awareness of the gravity of the weight above them.

They reached the halfway point, as distant from where they were going as they were from where they began. Dessa tried not to think about the roadway above them. What essential last piece of it was keeping it up?

Every camel's back has its straw.

For some reason she pictured a glass of water. Filled to the brim, liquid impossibly bulging from its top. A kindergarten-simple concept. Surface tension. The atoms of the water held improbably, but not *impossibly* in *balance.* One could add drops of water to the bubble, infinitesimal amounts that would be absorbed—

Until a single drop broke the whole improbable spell of the surface tension and water would spill everywhere.

Dessa imagined there must be a precipice, a tipping point where if a drop contained a single atom less that it would allow the bubble to hold. A precise and measurable line marking the moment between balance and chaos.

The tunnel shuddered. A leviathan's complaint. Deep and loud from within the belly of the beast.

A fresh rain of dust broke onto their heads. Dessa saw the girl look up just as a wrenching sound cracked above them. The back of the beast was breaking.

They ran. Dessa pushed herself forward, her hands touching the rubble in front of her.

They reached the other side, clean air sweeping their limbs

as they kept running. They were nearly half a block from the tunnel before their feet slappped a slower beat until they stopped. Bodies bent and breath hard.

Dessa lifted her head looked back toward the tunnel.

It had not collapsed.

It taunted them, still open, other side still visible. A schoolyard "made-you-flinch" moment.

Dessa started laughing. Huge rollicking laughs. Her body still roiling with flight endorphins. A roller coaster high.

The girl stared at her. Eyes wide.

"You…are…crazy."

Of course, that made Dessa laugh even harder. She snorted, like she had on that night so long ago with Gretchen. Her need for air and her need for release fighting.

The girl shook her head. "What the hell were you thinking?"

Dessa panted, her breath still not caught. "I was thinking I didn't want to walk another twenty blocks."

At this, the girl finally smiled at her. A slow revelation of white teeth, curling back into the soft curves of her cheeks. Everything about her softened into the grin, making her seem even younger than Dessa was sure she was. She shook her head. "That was fucked-up."

Dessa stood up, the laughter within her petering out. She pressed her mouth into her hands, ironing the tension away. "I need to get home…soon."

"You got somebody?"

Dessa nodded. "A little girl."

"Well that was some crazy mom shit. Going under a jacked up bridge…" They were quiet for a moment and Dessa thought about whether she really *had* her daughter. It was the way people said it. But motherhood had seemed like a series of lessons derived to teach her that she did not *have* her daughter, but that her daughter in fact *had her.*

The girl grinned. "I heard some moms can lift up cars when their kids are in trouble."

"I heard that too."

"What's her name?" The girl's voice was sweet. Soft.

"Olivia. She's two."

"My sister is two." The girl pulled something from her bag. It took Dessa a moment to identify it as a manila envelope. Its edges frowsy and worn. Stained with thumbprints. It was stuffed full. Dessa could make out the corners of greeting cards and brochures trying to escape its confines.

The girl rifled through it for a moment before producing a photo.

She did not hand the picture to Dessa, but instead stood close enough so she could see. Her thumb tight on the corner. The toddler in the picture was grinning wildly, her fists wrapped tightly around the chains of a swing. She was caught in motion, eyes wide and happy. Pigtails lifted by the wind.

"She's beautiful," said Dessa. Because she was.

"Her name is Jasmine."

"I'm Dessa."

The girl took the photograph back and looked up at her. As if she had been wandering around a decision and finally decided to arrive at it.

"Beegie."

"Nice to meet you, Beegie." Dessa held out her hand.

The girl took it.

20

The white lady looked like a social worker.

Or a Barbie. Somewhere in between.

Dessa. That's what she said her name was. Weird name for someone who looked like her.

When she was in her sparkly dress that's probably what made Beegie think of the Barbie dolls. In her sweatshirt Dessa now looked less like a Barbie. But the way she talked. *Nice to meet you, Beegie.* Like on the television. She talked like she had money. Or used to. People with money don't live in Van Nuys.

She had a voice like the new caseworkers, the ones who were trying to make "the world a better place" but who had no idea what they were getting into.

But Dessa had surprised her.

Beegie couldn't imagine one of her old new social workers going under a fallen down bridge like Dessa had. The way her face had looked so angry, but *not*. *Determined* was the word. She looked *determined* while she made her way through. Then she'd laughed like crazy when the whole thing didn't fall on them, but Beegie knew she wasn't really crazy. Beegie knew what real crazy looked like.

So maybe Dessa was different. Even though she sounded like social workers and looked like a doll.

She also didn't talk to Beegie just to make noise the way they did.

As they walked into Silver Lake, that's what she expected. The usual questions she got whenever she was around someone who sounded like Dessa. *"So how are you doing?"* and if they were new, *"You used to be a very good student. I'm concerned about your grades."*

Chitchat.

But Dessa was quiet.

Beegie could tell the woman was looking at her sometimes. Eyes over, sneaking a peek. But she didn't force Beegie into conversation.

The houses here looked drunk. Canted and wobbly in the front, but otherwise intact. There was a row whose porch supports had slipped, making the roofs hang like jaunty hats over the face of the houses. Like children putting on a show.

Beegie wondered where the people who belonged to them were. The neighborhood was so quiet, like it was abandoned, but of course it couldn't be. There must be people here, inside these jaunty houses, waiting for the sun to come up and show them the damage that had been done.

It's what she would do. Hide.

A heavy perfume smell found them, wrapping itself around Beegie and Dessa, folding them into its sweetness. White star-shaped flowers speckled across dark bushes. A whole long line of them, spanning the fronts of the houses.

"Does your sister bloom at night too?" The woman spoke, but Beegie didn't understand her. She thought maybe she'd misheard. It happened sometimes when she was thinking hard. Someone would say something and it wouldn't make sense at first...then she'd hear it again a few times in her brain and the words would sort themselves out, slotting themselves the way they were supposed to be.

But what the lady said didn't do that. Each time she heard it in her head, what Dessa had said sounded more and more like what she'd heard the first time and the less sense it made. Sisters blooming? Beegie pictured a daisy bursting out of a little girl's head.

"Your sister." Dessa nodded at the bushes, sensing Beegie's confusion. "The flowers. They're night blooming jasmine."

Beegie looked again at the bushes, seeing them differently this time.

"I thought jasmine was purple."

"It smells purple, doesn't it?"

It was a strange thing for her to say. Not that Beegie was wrong. Not that the flower was obviously white. But that some part of Beegie was correct.

Beegie inhaled the color of the flowers again. They *did* smell purple, even as she was looking at their white bodies, letting her fingers touch their cool petals. Their scent was too high and round for white.

It occurred to her that there were other things like that. But that she hadn't ever thought about it until Dessa had said it. That sometimes the smell of a thing and its shape don't agree. That a white flower can smell purple. Peanut butter and stale smoke can smell like love. Men's deodorant and cardboard can smell like pain.

The insides of Beegie's legs ached. Tendons like they had been pulled to snapping then let go.

Something else occurred to her. She tried saying it.

"They also smell loud. Purple and loud."

Of course what she meant was *strong*. She knew that's what she was supposed to say, but *strong* wasn't the right word for how much of the jasmine was in the air. It came in through her mouth and sat on her tongue like a taste. It was more than a scent, it had volume and color.

Dessa nodded. Loud purple scents surrounded them.

They fell quiet again. Walking.

The flashlight in Dessa's hand died. Its small pale beam growing yellow then flickering out. Without a word, she put it in her bag.

The drunken houses gave way to the dim shapes of apartment buildings. Beegie could make out the horizontal lines of their balconies, small dark squares of potted plants. Vague shadows of bicycles and lawn chairs.

A thin sound curled into their ears. A high keening.

It could be a dog. It didn't sound quite human.

But then, it didn't sound like a dog either.

An animal wail. Wounded.

Dessa's breathing became shallow. Her arms tense.

Ahead of them there was a darkness smeared across the street. It broke across the line of parked cars, smothering the ones Beegie imagined should be there, in a spiky hulking mass.

It was an apartment building. Or rather, half of an apartment building. Ripped off and vomited onto the street. Its other half was still standing, giving them a dollhouse view of people's lives. Living rooms and kitchens. A table stood right at the edge of the break. A chair still pulled up to its side.

The mass consumed their path, reaching the other side of the street. They made their way around it, pulling closer to the jasmine-clad fence on the opposite side. Cracked wood and plaster littered the sidewalk. Without a word Dessa hopped the fence to find a clearer way and Beegie followed.

She pushed her hands into the flowers to find the wire fence beneath. The ugly thing hidden by the beautiful. The purple scent everywhere.

"God."

It was Dessa who said it. Though Beegie had thought it.

Up ahead three more apartment buildings had collapsed upon themselves. Their contorted shapes unnatural, stucco and wood jutting blue with moonlight. Sick bouquets of destruction.

The wail grew louder. More hollow.

They could hear other smaller sounds underneath it now. Stuttering cries and moans. Leaking out from the rubble.

Asking for help.

This was a haunted place...populated by ghosts that had not yet finished their dying.

How many people were in there? Where were the trucks? The firemen? How torn was the city that no one was in this place, helping these people?

Dessa stopped walking. Her eyes shifting from building to building.

Beegie picked up her pace. "Fuck 'em."

"But..."

"Don't listen."

"Somebody should be helping them."

"What are you going to do? Dig through every one of those busted ass buildings?" The white woman stared at her. Beegie put on her street face. The one that made her jaw hard and her teeth ache. "Keep walking. They would."

Beegie believed that. Those moans and wails belonged to people who, if their places were switched, would move past. They might feel bad. It might bother them later. But everybody put themselves first. Prioritized their own selves over others.

Beegie could be in one of those building right now. She'd screamed before. No one had helped her.

"Beegie."

She was mad. The flat of her hands hungry for hurting something. The world. The way it was. For what it did to her. For what it made her do. "It's fucking shitty luck, but it's their shitty luck. I got my own shitty luck."

A hysterical scream picked up in one of the houses. Threading its way above them all. A woman. Over and over.

"Jesus."

"I thought you had a girl to get back to."

Beegie didn't wait for Dessa to say anything else. She just went. Her face felt heavy and hot. The screams picked up in tempo. Somewhere in the destruction someone had become untethered. Drifted away from sanity and floated on the edge of their voice.

There was nothing they could do.

Beegie felt warmth gather at the edges of her eyes. Wet weakness leaking. She blinked hard to clear it.

Dessa appeared next to her. The woman's elbows were up, tucked close to her body. Hands at the sides of her face. Her face was soft but she was moving. Doing what she needed to.

Like Dessa, Beegie put her fingers in her ears. The screams were muffled then, barely audible under the scent of all that loud purple.

21

Sunset Junction shone like a street fair.

Its glow made Beegie's eyes ache. She had gotten used to the violet darkness, with its shadows and gray shade.

Now that she was looking at the light, she was glad for the dim they had been walking through. It meant she didn't have to see things fully. She wouldn't have to remember anything but their general shapes. Broken buildings and lives buried under dust and dark.

But as they made their way, up at the top of the hill, Silverlake was alight.

"How do they have power?" Dessa whispered as they made their way toward the collection of buildings.

Words flew into Beegie's head.

Capricious. A phrase she had seen written on one of her reports. She knew what it meant. That she changed her mind and her mood a lot, which was bullshit, it was all the other shit in her life that was changing…and her mood and her mind changed right along with it. New house, new foster mom, new shit to deal with. Sometimes better but never for long. More times worse.

Fuck yeah, she was capricious.

The earthquake had been capricious.

Beegie thought it sounded like a rapper name. Someone Eric would listen to. A fast-talking spitter lady with blond hair and a big ass. Talking hard and sexy.

She thought *that* was how this neighborhood had power when all the others they'd been walking through didn't. Capricious Nature had been walking through with her mood swings all night. This house, she likes. She'd leave this house alone. But right next to it, she'd smash one all the fuck up. That house pissed her off.

Sometimes luck was just about real estate. Where you are when Capricious Nature decides to look your way. Beegie imagined her in a video, a giantess with big fake lashes stepping over the neighborhood they were walking in. Liking the way the lights below shined up her skirt.

Ahead, someone was playing music.

No, not just music. Party music.

"What the hell…" Dessa's jaw hinged open. There were hundreds of people here, dumped out from the bars and restaurants. It was like a block party. A street fair of hipsters. Young white people in old hats taking pulls from cans of beer. A few places people had even taken out folding chairs and set up hibachi grills.

"Say 'Earthquake.'"

Beegie turned to see a group of girls taking a group selfie. They wrapped their arms around one another and smiled, their fingers forming peace signs.

"What the fuck is wrong with these people?"

Dessa shook her head as she pushed her way into the crowd. The smell of barbecued meat wafted past them. "You think they don't know how bad it is?"

They did. At least some of them. Here and there Beegie could see pale, shell-shocked faces in the crowd. Their friends rubbing their backs. Forcing bottles into their hands.

There was a desperation even among the revelers. *Eat, Drink and Be Merry for tomorrow we die.* They had said that in one of the movies she had seen.

There was a sense among them that no one knew how to act. This was what they had been doing when the quake struck and they were waiting for the grown-ups to arrive to tell them what to do. Some of the bars were still selling drinks, but the crowds radiating out were all centered around the electrical outlets near the ground. Their hands cupped their phones nervously, glancing from the screens to people who had claimed the plugs.

"I got it!" a young man yelled and there was a cheer. He held a power strip over his head and the people cleared the way for him to make his way to the wall. He plugged it in and they pressed toward him again, their voices raised. Each insisting they had been there first. Each insisting their need for power was the greater one.

Dessa whispered as they walked past. "Do you see how no one is actually getting through? They all just keep checking and checking. But no one's texting or talking to anyone. Everything is down."

She was right. But that didn't keep them from looking every five seconds. Panicking that they were disconnected and untethered from their digital worlds.

"Odessa Reilly?"

A man with a camera stood in their path, staring at them. Or really staring at Dessa.

And then before she could say anything he was pulling Dessa toward his body. Beegie felt her hands fly up, ready to claw her away from him, his sudden movement alarming.

But then he was pressing Dessa against his body. A hug.

"Oh my God. It is you!"

Beegie couldn't see Dessa's face, but she could tell from the way she was holding her body that she was confused. Tentative.

The man's lips pulled back in a grin over a set of huge, almost impossibly perfect teeth. Beegie sensed that he was one of those people who had the volume turned up in their souls. He was good-looking...not like a movie star, but like a movie character. Brash and full of it. He winked at Beegie, watching them over Dessa's shoulder.

"I can't believe I'm running into you here! I heard you had a baby. Did you have a baby?"

Dessa stumbled back from his sudden intimacy. She nodded.

"That's awesome! I always thought you would be an amazing mom. You've got one lucky kid."

He was chewing gum. At what point in the night had he decided he needed fresher breath? Beegie didn't know what time it was, but she knew it had been hours since the earthquake. Had this dude had that same wad of gum in his mouth since then? Had he held it between his teeth while the earth moved under him?

He turned his big smile onto her. "Hello."

Dessa finally said something. "Zach. This is Beegie. Beegie, this is Zach."

"Odessa and I used to be together."

"In college," Dessa added quickly. Her body had gone tense,

like he was making her just as uncomfortable as he was making Beegie. But Zach wasn't picking up on it.

He swung his camera around. "Oh! You have to see some of the shots I got." He started scrolling through the display screen. "I got this shot of a homeless guy on Fountain. A wall fell on him. The lighting on it is incredible." He turned it so Dessa could see. A glow cast on her somber face. Whatever she was seeing, Beegie did not think she would describe it as *incredible.*

"It's so weird running into you like this. I live in Brooklyn now but I'm in L.A. for work… I just feel so lucky I'm here."

"Zach, we have to go." Dessa backed away from him, her hand gently touching Beegie's shoulder.

Zach's mouth made a big O shape. "Oh my God… I'm such an asshole! Where are you guys coming from?"

"Downtown."

"That must have been intense! I can't wait for sunrise…the pictures are going to be amazing… Hey, you gotta come to my friend's place. Well not really my friend…but the guy I'm out here to work with. He told me he might have internet… which I'm interested in because, you know, whoever gets the first pics out of this thing is going to make a mint."

Zach chattered at them while he led them up the street. Something about proto-gonzo journalism. Dessa nodded, but Beegie didn't understand anything he was talking about.

Beegie didn't like him. She didn't think Dessa did either, but still they had gone with him to his friend's place. Dessa didn't say it but she probably thought she could get in touch with her people if they went there. Her girl, Olivia.

A green plus sign glowed over the street. In its shadow stood a big bearded dude, cherry glow from a blunt between his lips.

"Wade, my brother!" Zach reached out his hand in some white boy trying to be black handshake. "DSL up yet?"

"Nope." Wade exhaled a cloud.

"Damn it! Damn it! Why does this shit always happen to me?"

Zach actually stomped his foot. Like a cartoon girl who wasn't getting candy.

Beegie caught Dessa's eye. *We should go.*

"I'm sorry. I'm just a little upset at the situation." Zach saw the look pass between them. "That wasn't cool."

"We're fine, Zach. It was good seeing you." Dessa was polite.

"No, no wait! Do you need anything? Maybe Wade can hook you up."

"We don't need any pot." Dessa was firm, but Beegie knew better than to pass this up.

"What else you got?"

It was the first thing she'd said since they'd run into this asshole, and she could tell that her speaking had caused both men to see her differently. Like she hadn't really been there until that moment. Or like she'd just been one of Dessa's accessories, something that was supposed to stay quiet, like her purse or her shoes.

Wade stepped out from the dark and for the first time Beegie saw that he had a shotgun braced on his shoulder. He smiled at her.

"Come on inside, little girl."

Beegie hadn't ever been in a pot store. But she had been in a Starbucks and that's what this place looked like. Well, like that but fancier. It was all finished woods and glass display cabinets with lights beneath them. There were bongs that looked like statues rich people would put in their bathrooms.

"Looks like a Chihuly, doesn't it?" Zach was talking to Dessa. "It's not but Wade's in talks with his people. He's at the forefront of the whole upscale bud franchise things. That's why I'm out covering him. He's trying to do for marijuana what Screaming Eagle did for cabernet."

Beegie didn't know what that meant but was pretty sure that whatever Screaming Eagle did to its wine, it made it expensive.

Wade set his shotgun on the counter. Beegie knew better than to look at it. Like black eyes and split lips, you're never supposed to acknowledge guns when you see them. You and the holder both know they're there, you both know they mean power, either yours or someone else's, but talking about it makes everybody uncomfortable.

An impulse told her to grab it. Wrap her hand around the barrel and run toward the door. Then she'd have what she'd been looking for before she met Dessa.

She shook it off. Never work.

But there was something practical they needed.

Beegie made her face hard. "Batteries. We need batteries."

"Size?"

Beegie looked at Dessa. The woman took a moment to realize what it was they needed them for. She fumbled with her purse for a moment, pulling the flashlight from its depths. She unscrewed the cap. "Ds. We need Ds."

Wade pulled a leather case from under the counter. The word SUNDRIES stamped on it. It opened like an accordion, with a black velvet interior: Condoms, individual packets of aspirin, breath mints, chocolate. He pulled a package of batteries out and slapped it down.

"Hundred."

"I'm sorry?" Dessa said, even though she meant something else.

"Ds are a hundred."

"Jeez, bro, can't you give them a discount?" Zach asked.

"That *is* a discount. Batteries are going to be at a premium."

Dessa shook her head. "I don't have it."

Wade slid the pack of batteries back toward himself. Beegie was mad.

"Fuck it. Everybody else is just stealing shit right now. We'll just get them somewhere else. For free." She headed for the door.

"Beegie, wait…just…wait." Dessa was quiet a moment, thinking. "Would you take something else?"

Wade seemed interested. "Like what?"

Dessa exhaled. Placed her purse on the counter in front of him. He glanced at it.

"Is it real?"

Dessa nodded, and Wade put his hands on either side of the bag. Inspecting it. "Gold fittings. Stitching doesn't cross the logo." He lifted his eyebrow, "You bought this?"

"It was a gift."

"Nice gift. It's a little…damp."

"If you know what it is, you know it's worth way more than a hundred dollars…even wet."

Wade flipped it over again and inspected the bottom. His fingers trailing the seams and the little brass nubs on the underside.

Finally he nodded and slid the batteries back toward Beegie.

"I'll need a bag to put my stuff in."

Wade headed into the back of the store. Beegie leaned into Dessa, whispering. "This is fucking crazy, giving Moses there your purse, when everybody is just taking what they want."

"Not everybody…" Dessa's eyes met hers. "Not us."

The way she said it made Beegie feel like she was drawing a circle around the two of them. Joining them together. An *us*.

Suddenly Beegie felt the edges of several emotions at once.

Lodged inside of her like bullets or birth control implants. Anger pressing into the back of her throat. Hope tickling in her chest. She wanted to punch this woman and hug her at the same time. Because she had said *us*.

"We doing this?" Wade had returned with a plastic grocery sack.

"Yes." Dessa began pulling out the contents of her purse. Flashlight. Wallet. Sunglasses. Phone.

She paused as she pulled out a folded yellow page.

"Gretchen," she whispered. Her hands shook slightly as she carefully unfolded the paper. Rows of numbers with serious looking script next to it. All businessy.

"Everything okay?" Wade tilted his head. Something about her had left the room.

"Yeah. I just found something I didn't expect."

There was a chime as the front door opened. Three men with bandannas wrapped around their faces crowded the door. Their eyes widened as Wade racked the shotgun.

"We're closed," he said, aiming it. "Move along."

22

Dessa imagined how Gretchen must have gotten that folded sheet of numbers into her purse. When they had hugged, surely. Her taller friend had pressed her lips into her hair and slipped it in, assuming it would be discovered later. Opened and reconsidered. A small push in the direction of common sense...though Dessa's relationship with Joe had never had much of that.

Dessa had met Joe at Gretchen's office Christmas party.

This was why Gretchen felt responsible.

But all Gretchen had done was take pity on her sorry, grieving friend. Asking her along for a night of coworkers pretending to make merry together. Stuffy lawyers and free booze in one of the higher-up's incredible homes on the Hill. All windows and caterers, she promised. "I can't get drunk, but you can."

Dessa thought that if Gretchen was responsible for her relationship with Joe, then so was her mother, who had had the bad taste to die before the holidays, leaving Dessa without a reason to travel back to Pennsylvania for the first time in her life. Even a cold mother had been better than none at all.

Or maybe it was her father's fault. For having a way of turning his head away when he laughed...a familiar gesture that had faded along with his personality. But Dessa knew that if fault was to be assigned for her life getting sidelined, it belonged to no one but herself.

"I'm not looking to date right now."

Joe had blurted it after they had only been speaking for a few minutes. Awkward. Assuming a chemistry between them before she had even recognized it herself.

But she had been charmed by the way he had blushed when he had said it.

"I mean... I like you...but I'm not...you know."

Dessa had shrugged. "You're too old for me anyway."

"How old are you?"

"Twenty-four."

"How old do you think I am?"

"Not twenty-four."

He had smiled at that. "That is a very good answer... I'm thirty-seven."

"See...just like I said...not twenty-four."

And then he had laughed. Turning his head away from her. For a moment so like her father.

Dessa liked him. The fact that this powerful lawyer could still be awkward, embarrassed even, it was charming.

"You know, Joe..." Gretchen had told her in the car on their way home that night.

Dessa had stopped her. "Don't worry," she said. "He's not interested."

But when he called her after the new year, the sound of his voice on her phone had made her chest flush red and put a hitch in her breath. She spent the entire call trying not to sound like she had been running, trying to disguise the odd little pant he had called up in her. She noted that perhaps the reason she was no good at this was that she had never had any practice. Until this moment she had only ever been asked out via text message. *Boys text*, she thought, *Men call*. Joe was a man.

And even though he said it was not a date, they both knew it was.

Dessa slipped her hand into the plastic sack that now held the contents of the extravagantly expensive purse Joe had given her. Her fingertips found the damp corner of the sheet of paper with Gretchen's handwriting on it. Her friend's last nudge. Only hours now but so much had happened...

Beegie was thoughtful next to her as they walked. Lips closed, mind working.

There was too much. Too many events. Too many memories laying themselves over them. And worries. She felt like her thoughts were falling through space, interjecting themselves at odd moments. Memories of Joe and Dad and Zach. The feeling of Olivia's forehead pressed beneath her lips, of Gretchen's breath as she whispered in her ear, the sensation of the clothes hangers beneath her while hopelessly watching Beegie get raped...though she hadn't been Beegie then, she had just been yet another person experiencing this surreal nightmare of a night.

The image of melting clocks and Dali's mustache flew into her mind. Another inappropriate thought.

Her mind couldn't quite keep hold of anything. The real world had broken, and this was a new reality. A surreality.

Dessa shook her head and tried to lock her thoughts down. Discipline them into boxes again.

Her second grade teacher, Miss Applegate, entered her mind. Standing in front of the classroom. "When you have a large task to do, try not to think of everything all at once. Instead break it into smaller pieces. Every big thing is made of many little things."

The thought set sail across Dessa's mind. A building is a big thing made of rooms. A room is made of walls. Walls are made of sheet rock, wood, plaster and nails. These are the small things that make up the big things that can crush a body beneath them.

"Your friends are fucked-up."

Beegie's voice brought her mind back. For a moment she wondered how Beegie knew Gretchen. Why she thought she was fucked-up. Then she realized, she meant Zach and Wade.

"They're not my friends."

Beegie pursed her lips together. "Pretty boy said…"

"We lived together. In college. I would say he was different then…but I'm starting to think maybe I was the one who was different. We all have things we regret."

The girl shook her head. "Not me. Everything I ever did, had to be done."

"Really?" Dessa watched her. The girl's eyes scanned the street ahead of them.

"Yeah." Beegie was quiet for a beat. "Now, the shit other people did to me…that stuff I regret."

Dessa's thoughts slipped again. Reconciling the first time she'd seen this girl with the second. Their evening together. The secret she had carried with her since the moment she recognized her. The pain Beegie must be carrying herself.

"That's not regret Beegie…that's…something else."

Something bright floating in the street ahead caught her

eye. Primary-colored figures flashing, floating in the interior
of a minivan. It was a movie. A video screen had been lowered
and was playing a Pixar film before an audience of children,
their small heads silhouetted in the cabin below.

"This is a good scene," Beegie said. Through the windows
Dessa could make out Joy in the darkness. Bing Bong ad-
dressed her from a red wagon.

A woman carrying pillows and blankets approached the
car, swinging the door open and handing them to the children inside.

"Everybody still okay?" she asked, her voice forced brightness. Small sounds responded. Sleepy children.

The woman saw them watching. Beegie and Dessa. She
smiled, a gentle hand waving.

"I think we have room for one more," she said, her eyes on
Beegie. "Your mom can come back for you…"

It took them a moment to understand what she had said,
the offer she was making, the assumption she had made. Based
on their being together and Beegie's size relative to Dessa.

Beegie exhaled, her head shaking. "No, thank you."

The woman nodded. Looked at Dessa. "It's just… Do you
know the Hans, in the red house on the corner? Jackie? Their
daughter Elizabeth might be at your bus stop."

The woman clearly thought they were neighbors. Must
have mistaken them for some local family with mismatched
skin tones.

"Anyway, their house got hit pretty bad. We're trying to
help…but Joe's on the front lawn." And then she whispered,
"You might not want her to see…"

Beegie snorted softly and Dessa caught her meaning. *That
particular cat was out of the bag.* "It's okay," the girl said for them
both, pushing her way past the woman.

On the corner, they saw him. Joe Han in his pajamas. Sitting on the front lawn. In his lap lay the broken body of his wife. A spill of red hair threading through his fingers while he wept and wept.

Inside the black remnants of their house, the beams of flashlights threaded through the dark. Joe and Jackie's neighbors inside, calling out for Elizabeth.

Beegie and Dessa pressed on.

The girl stopped walking.

"This is my street." Beegie pulled her bag closer to her body, glancing down the block of darkened houses. The red bandanna brushed the top of her hand as it squeezed the strap. *Small disparate steps. Things within one's control.*

"I'll go with you."

"What about Olivia?"

Dessa thought about regrets. Hers. Beegie's. The things that were not regrets but something else. This was something she *could* do.

"It'll take two minutes." A tricycle lay on its side in the worn-out yard. Sun-sapped children's toys littered the patches of dirt and grass, cartoon stickered eyes faded and bubbling.

Beegie stopped with her hand on the gate. She turned her head, a small glottal stop escaping her lips, the beginning of saying something…but nothing followed. Instead the girl sighed quietly and lifted the latch. Beyond the paint-peeled front porch Dessa could make out a flickering glow behind the drawn shades. Someone was up.

"I don't have a key," Beegie whispered. Her head hanging. Her knuckles rapped softly on the door.

A groan emitted from inside. Followed by the sound of movement. The door opened, revealing a sour-faced white woman with a small boy on her hip. She eyed Beegie.

"You *would* come back now."

Dessa felt Beegie shrink beside her.

The warm acrid scent of gin reached across the space between them. Without a word the woman ran her eyes across Dessa but did not greet her. Instead she readjusted the toddler on her hip and turned back toward her living room.

"Didn't think you were coming back this time... Leesi wet the bed during the earthquake. I couldn't find a clean sheet so I put her in your room. You can sleep on the floor."

Dessa followed Beegie inside, getting a better look at what she could only assume was her *foster* home. A sagging couch. A pair of cracking plastic high chairs. Crayon on the walls.

"What about the couch?" Beegie's voice was quiet.

Her foster mother sat. "The couch is taken."

A pulse passed between them. The older blonde woman challenging Beegie to challenge her.

But Beegie was diminished. Dessa could barely reconcile this cowed girl from the savvy bold young woman she had spent the last few hours with. This was what Beegie had wanted to tell her at the door. Why she had given her an out from coming with her to her...place...place was the right word because this certainly wasn't Beegie's *home*.

Beegie's foster mother leaned forward to pull a cigarette from a pack on the table. She lit it with one of the candles, staring Beegie down the whole time. Daring her to say something.

But Beegie just stared. Mouth closed to anything she might have said.

The woman exhaled. "You miss me that much you need to memorize me? You know where the blankets are."

Beegie left, disappearing into the dark recesses of the house.

The toddler stared at Dessa. For the first time Dessa noticed he had a Band-Aid on his forehead. SpongeBob's maniacal grin hovering just over the boy's quiet eyes.

The woman ran her fingers through his hair. Took a drag of her cigarette.

"Where'd she find you?"

It was the first she had acknowledged her.

"We were downtown. During." Her voice creaked.

The woman flicked ashes into an empty Coke can on the end table.

Dessa considered how she had imagined this exchange would go. A worried black woman answering the door when Beegie knocked on it. Pulling her daughter into her body. Blanketing her with kisses.

Maybe Beegie would cry with relief. Melt and confess the horrible thing that had happened to her this evening. She would be transformed, not because she was cowed but she was finally safe and loved and within reach of comfort.

But that was not going to happen with this woman.

Instead, Beegie would fold even further into herself. There would be no confession. No comfort.

But this woman was who Beegie had. This was the place she had chosen to retreat to.

"You need to get Beegie to a doctor." Dessa pitched her voice low.

"Yeah, that's at the top of my list."

"She was raped tonight...she needs medical treatment. A rape kit. Anti-virals. Plan B."

"You a nurse?" The woman raised her eyebrows.

"No."

"Then why are you telling me what she needs?" The woman looked at her for a beat. "You don't know her... *I know her.* And whatever she said, I wouldn't trust it."

Dessa couldn't believe this woman. "She was *raped.*"

The woman shook her head. Incredulous. "That's what she *told you*...but she lies. All the time. Probably just wanted you to feel bad for her... Maybe some john didn't pay up or somebody stole her money."

"She was *raped*," Dessa repeated but the woman just barreled right through her.

"Maybe *something* happened...but if it did, I gotta tell you, I don't feel too bad for her. What she got's been coming to her for a long time."

Dessa didn't know what to say. She couldn't imagine telling this woman that she had *witnessed* the crime. That there was no doubting it. The woman glared at her, her hand still buried in the boy's hair.

Footsteps signaled Beegie's return.

"You should go," she said softly, appearing at Dessa's elbow. She held a flat pillow and a threadbare blanket.

Anger welled within Dessa. A bubble of rage rising from the pit of her stomach.

"Where's Jasmine?" She looked at Beegie.

"Who's Jasmine?" The woman was confused, looking from Dessa to her charge.

"Beegie's little sister. Is she here with you or is she somewhere else?"

The woman laughed. Short and sharp. A bark almost. She sat up. A mean smile spread across her face. "She doesn't have a sister."

"Yes, she does. She showed me her picture."

Beegie looked stricken. Her eyes closed off.

"I don't care what she said. I told you, *she lies*. She doesn't have any sister. She doesn't have anyone."

Dessa looked at Beegie and saw that what she had merely thought of as a family resemblance had in fact been an identical one. Shame made Beegie look even younger, but Dessa wondered how she could have missed it before.

"Do you want to be here?" Dessa whispered, canting herself toward the teenager.

Beegie shook her head, ironing her eye with the edge of her palm.

"Let's go." Dessa wrapped a hand around hers.

The two of them moved to the door and suddenly the woman's mouth was agape. Realizing what was happening. She stood, indignant.

"You can't take her! It's illegal. She has to stay with me! Do you think that if you take her the state will send *you* my money? I'll tell them you kidnapped her. They'll arrest you. The cops'll fucking arrest you!"

Dessa looked back at her. "They'll have to find me first."

And then she slammed the door.

23

As she chased after Dessa, Beegie kept hearing the words in her mind.

"They'll have to find me first."

It looped with the sound of her slamming of the door. Cycling faster and faster until the sounds ran together in her mind.

Have to find me first. BANG. To find me first. BANG. Find me first. BANG.

Beegie had slammed doors before. Heard her own words refracting though her own mind. Angry shouts repeated endlessly until something else entered her brain to knock them away.

But no one had ever been angry *for* her.

Slammed the door for her.

That's what the caseworkers assigned to her were supposed

to do. To listen when she told them that it wasn't important *why* she needed a lock. That everything would be just fine as long as she had it.

They'll have to find me first. BANG.

Barb had told Dessa about the picture. About the lie she'd told about having a sister. And even then, Dessa'd been angry for the way Barb had talked to Beegie.

It felt good.

Even if it wasn't real. Even if it didn't last. Beegie knew better than to think it would. But just to hear someone else's voice angry *for* her, not *at* her.

Dessa was mumbling under her breath as she walked, "At least I have a couch. Jesus. That woman should not be anywhere near children."

Beegie wanted to explain. Before the anger Dessa felt toward Barb subsided. "Dessa...the picture..."

Dessa's face softened, "It's fine."

"No...it's not—"

"I don't care about the picture, Beegie. I'm just glad you don't have a little sister living with that monster."

Beegie didn't know how to explain. The picture. The lie. The story behind it. Being happy and sad all at once. Going from one home to another. The way her mother had talked about the family like they'd tried to steal Beegie from her when she'd thought all they wanted to do was to love her. About her confusion at feeling warm about them even when Momma said they were bad.

Momma said they had sent her that picture of Beegie, thinking they were doing her a favor. They had told her they were going to call her Jasmine, because she deserved a real name not just the one given to her by the hospital.

And hearing that had made Momma fight harder. Which

was good because Beegie loved her mother and was glad they were together.

But it didn't keep Beegie from staring at the photo when her mother was at work. Or from wondering about the person behind the camera and the other one whose face was out of frame. She had long-ago memories of a house that smelled like soup and a staircase that creaked when you climbed it, of pill bugs and sandboxes, but none of it seemed quite…real.

When she fell asleep at night, Beegie used to think about what her life would have been like if she had been Jasmine. Did a different name mean a different life? Or did people with different lives just get different names?

And when she went back into foster care…well it had been years since that family that had wanted her. Probably they had moved on. Didn't care anymore. She was too old. Not cute anymore.

It was a strange impulse that had driven her to start showing people the picture and telling them it was her little sister. She'd started it at Tricia's, her first placement. "Isn't my little sister cute?" she say, showing the picture to adults when they came by.

"Oh yes. Very," they'd respond.

"Her name is Jasmine," Beegie would tell them.

"Pretty," they'd say.

Beegie didn't do it for too long. She had stopped doing it by the time she was at Janelle's. Too many people knew the truth, she could tell. She knew too many people were just playing along.

But when Dessa had said her daughter was almost three, Beegie had the photo in her hands almost instantly. The old lie she used to tell. Fishing for compliments. Maybe it was because she had gotten it back so recently…or maybe it was because of the events that had unspooled in the hours between

the earthquake and meeting Dessa. But there she was again...
trying to fill some hole in herself with a stranger's polite praise.

Beegie stumbled on the words, trying to explain without
giving up too much of herself. "I don't have a lot of people
saying nice things about me. But people...if I show them the
picture...they tell me my little sister is cute... I know that's
fucked-up."

Dessa stopped walking. She shook her head. "I don't think
it's fucked-up...what's fucked-up is that no one says nice things
to you."

They had moved a few blocks north toward Los Feliz Bou-
levard. The street was filled with cars. None of them moving.
Dessa's face looked orange in the reflection of the brake lights.
A dark hulking shape loomed on the horizon. The upward
slope of Griffith Park.

Beegie shuffled. She didn't want to look into Dessa's eyes.
"I like people to know I wasn't always like this."

"Like what, Beegie? You were a cute kid." She paused.
"You still are."

Men's voices rang out, reaching toward them. Angry shouts.
Thumps. Followed by a chorus of car horns.

Beegie stepped out toward the curb to find the source.

A gas station. At least thirty cars in a snarl under the working lights. People on their way somewhere else, or at least *in
hope* of heading somewhere else.

Two cars were parked pushing in toward the same pump.

A man with a beard, his long hair held up in a bun, held
another man over the hood of a BMW. He drove punches
downward, into the other man's face.

The man stopped, suddenly allowing his victim to slide
to the ground. Then the attacker pulled the handle from the
pump and selected the grade of gas he wanted for his Prius.

The man he had been hitting rolled over. His bloody hands leaving stamps of themselves all along the white paint job. He used the car to support himself, leaning against it as he made his way to the driver's side door. His hands slipped on the handle, barely lurching it open, before leaning inside.

"Do you think he's okay?" Dessa said just as the man swung back out of the car.

He had a gun in his hand.

"Fuck you, you hipster douche." The man with the Prius stared at him, his mouth agape.

Beegie pulled Dessa down into a crouch. She pushed her into the street, running low past the bumpers of the idling cars.

Tires screamed against pavement. Beegie looked up in time to see the Prius pulling away, launching over the sidewalk to get away. The pump handle separated from his tank and dropped. Gasoline fountained outward, a clear arc through the air as it fell to the ground.

"Everyone's gone crazy," Dessa was panting next to her, still in a crouch as they reached the opposite side of the street.

And then the ground moved beneath them.

It was a jolt. Hard, sharp shake. Violent spasms.

An aftershock.

A terrier earthquake. Smaller than the last one, but just as mean.

That's how it felt.

Beegie thought about the Greelys' dog, Rooster. The way he would wait by the tree in their backyard for hours. Eyes up on the leaves. Just watching. Waiting.

Once Beegie saw him catch a squirrel.

Or actually she didn't see the catch, she heard it. The squeak squeak scream drew her to the window where she was just in time to see the snap. A small gray body in Rooster's mouth as the dog shook it and shook it long after the squeaking had stopped.

That was how it felt. She and Dessa fell to the ground, their hands on the cement. She saw them as two limp squirrels, gray and brown, caught in the mouth of an ugly dog. Whipping the fight out of them.

Beegie could swear she could hear growling. Inside the rumbles. Beneath the shaking and the breaking. A thousand million earthquake dogs. Growling through their teeth while they shook, shook, shook the world.

There was a bright flash down the street as an electrical wire was set free from its pole. The gas station and all behind it plummeted into darkness. The wire skittered. A snake spitting blue sparks, it danced on the street.

A small ringing bubbled up through the sound. Beegie watched as Dessa pulled her phone from the plastic sack. Thumbing it to answer.

"Hailey?"

A sound leaked from the phone pressed to her ear. A child crying. Short frightened whines.

"Ollie! Ollie!" Dessa shouted over the growling of the world.

Three fast beeps sounded. Dessa pulled the phone away from her ear, hands shaking. Desperately trying to get her daughter back. She hit the redial button.

"Jesus Christ. Please…"

No good. The beeps sounded again.

Dessa turned into the car. Her head pressed against the door. For a second Beegie thought she was praying. The older woman was whispering to herself.

The shaking had stopped. Beegie thought of Rooster finally walking away from the body of the squirrel. Its broken body, fur dark with the dog's saliva. The way the dog trotted to Eric when he called. So pleased with himself.

"Just get home," Dessa whispered.

Yells rose from the darkness where the gas station was. Beegie could see silhouettes of people running, their legs flashing in the headlights.

Pop, pop! Bright flashes sparked the darkness. Gunfire. Followed by a scream.

Beegie dropped next to Dessa again and said, "People are the problem. We need to get the fuck away from people."

24

The first time Dessa went to the Los Angeles Zoo she got lost in Griffith Park. She had decided that they would go see the animals and packed Ollie into her car seat, still blobbish and sleepy at eight weeks. It was ill-advised. An end run around the guilt and maternal horror she felt as the days of her leave dwindled and she faced the reality of heading back to work.

The park's roads are a snarl of loops, conjoining lanes and confusing five-way stops. Though there are patches of green, much of its acreage has reverted to Los Angeles's natural state of desert...velvet hills of brown scrub, dusty green leaves. Even the trees have taken on a sun-bleached hue, like fading photographs they stand in gangs by the roadside. The park is huge, blanketing the mountain between Los Feliz and Burbank. Dessa missed the sign for the zoo and lost her bearings, turning and turning, always to the left it seemed, up and up, but never reaching the top. Ollie woke up and began to cry, new baby squall. Dessa tried to settle her with her voice. *It's okay, sweetie. It's okay.* But as she passed the museums and playgrounds, the carousel and runners' paths, she began to cry too. She and her daughter were lost in this strange jungle in the city.

She pulled over by the side of the road and climbed into the back. She pulled Ollie out of her car seat and calmed her, bouncing and shushing. Dessa tried to still her thoughts too. She worried her tension and fear would soak through her skin and infect Ollie with her mother's maladies.

Eventually there had been a knock on the window. A park ranger. The woman had said she wanted to make sure everything was all right, but Dessa sensed that she had planned to say something else before she saw the look on Dessa's face.

The ranger led Dessa down the turn she had missed. After she had parked, the woman had handed Dessa a fistful of free zoo passes. "Take care of yourself," she had said, touching the rim of her hat. "And that baby."

An hour later, pushing the stroller up the zoo's steep hill, damp with sweat and lonely, Dessa wondered what the whole point of it had been anyway. Ollie's new eyes could just barely make out her mother leaning over her, much less the dusty zebras and bored emus thirty yards away. She had done it so that she could tell herself that she had done *something*. A box ticked off for when she dropped Ollie off at day care that first time. A prophylactic against her future guilt.

It was only after she had gone back to work that she realized how pointless that day had been. There is no elixir to cure you of wanting to be with someone you love.

But that day had shaped her life in the most mundane of ways. The fistful of free passes meant that she continued to go to the zoo with Ollie on weekends. Dessa used them regularly, even after they expired, when she learned that no one at the zoo checked the dates on these things.

Since Ollie had become a toddler, Dessa had found herself at the park nearly every weekend. Proximity to both sides of the hill, plus the added bonus of most of its attractions being free or cheap made it an easy way of keeping Ollie busy; Birthday parties at Travel Town, playdates at the Shane's Inspiration, ice cream by the carousel.

Dessa could not imagine getting lost here now. Even in the dark, walking Crystal Springs Road with Beegie next to her, it seemed a benevolent place. Through the trees to the east she could make out the parking lot of taillights drawing a red line up the I-5 freeway. A river of humanity seeking safety but going nowhere. Distant voices reached them through the dark. Impotence rising to frustration before becoming anger. They were too far to make out the words, but Dessa knew their meaning without the shape of syllables.

The road drew them away from the highway and the voices dissipated. Now trees flanked both sides of the street. Clumps of tall pine stretching against stars that were usually impossible to see.

"It says the park is closed." Beegie waved the flashlight over a sign that read *Park Hours Sunrise to Sunset.*

"That's why we're going in. No people. No buildings that can fall on us."

Beegie eyed the trees. Unsure.

"It'll be just like going on a hike. Or going camping." Dessa tried to make herself sound reassuring.

"You know only white people camp, right?"

"What?"

"Camping, hiking…all that is a white thing. Black people, Mexicans, Latinos, whatever, we don't do shit like that."

Dessa laughed in spite of herself. The glow from the flashlight splashed up on Beegie's face and she could tell the girl was smiling. "Okay, I'll bite. How is it a white thing?"

"It's rich people pretending to be poor. Sleeping outside. Eating on the ground and shit. Only white people are crazy enough to play homeless for fun. All 'getting in touch with nature.' Brown people, uh-uh. We don't pretend. We don't get in touch with nothing. Our relationship is good the way it is. Out of touch."

Dessa shook her head, smiling. She opened her mouth to say something, but then couldn't quite figure out how to say it.

Beegie got there first. "I bet you know a black guy who likes to camp."

"I do."

"We're gonna take his card." Beegie winked and Dessa snorted.

"Well, this white person hated camping. My dad used to take me. Being dirty and cold and the bugs...ugh. But then I realized that my mom hated it too. And I didn't want to be anything like her. So I decided to love camping."

"You don't like your mom?"

Beegie's question was light, tentative. And Dessa realized who she had just said that to. A foster kid. Who knew what was in Beegie's past?

Dessa answered slowly. Careful, "No. I didn't... She's dead now, but I think that's why I can finally say that. I couldn't admit I didn't like her until she was gone."

"But you loved her."

"Yeah. I did. Sometimes I wish I didn't though. It would have been easier not to like her if I hadn't."

Beegie was quiet for a beat. "Moms are hard," she said, finally.

"Yeah," Dessa agreed.

"I gotta pee."

Beegie stepped off the road, dried leaves crunching under her feet. Dessa watched as she scrambled down the embankment toward the open expanse of the golf course.

She took out her phone. The stuck stutter cry she had heard during the aftershock. Ollie's open mouth. A vowel sound. Ahh. Before it was taken away. Swept away by the movements of the earth, the vagaries of her cellular network and those three little mind-fucking beeps.

She was alive.

Or she had been.

But she had been screaming. Scared.

First letter. Long vowel. Ahhh.

The carrier name appeared on the screen of the phone. Like magic.

And a single reception bar.

Dessa called Hailey first. There was a busy signal before the call dropped.

She tried Joe. His voice mail came on the line. "I'm not available right now."

The question was *why* he was not available right now. They had been speaking when the quake struck, but since then… Dessa took a deep breath. "Um… I know I don't usually leave these things. But I think tonight…" She stopped herself. Another breath, another thought. "I need you to be alive, Joe. I need you to be alive and to be with Olivia. I don't…" She wasn't sure of the words she needed to say to him, she had avoided saying them for so long. The words were atrophied. Weak from disuse. They failed to find their way to her tongue.

She heard Beegie returning and she quickly hung up. Joe would understand. She didn't want to record a goodbye.

"It's weird peeing outside," Beegie said as she pulled herself up to the level of the street. Dessa held out her hand to help Beegie get upright. She winced as Dessa pulled her up the embankment, reminding Dessa of the particular nature of Beegie's trauma.

"You got a picture of your baby on that thing?" she asked as she dusted off her knees.

Dessa nodded. Called up an album of pictures of Ollie. She handed the phone over and Beegie began to scroll through. "Aww, she's cute."

She stopped at a picture of Ollie with Joe. "This is her daddy?"

"Yup."

"Not bad. She looks like you though." She handed back the phone. Dessa took it. Afforded herself one last look at Joe and Ollie before clicking it off.

"Is there anywhere we could get something to eat? I just saw a pinecone that looked good."

Dessa nodded. She knew just the place.

The roof of the carousel threw the bodies of the painted horses into shadow. From the vantage of the picnic table, their muscular forms floated, suspended at different heights, though it was impossible to make out the poles that held them.

Dessa pried the wrapper off yet another melting bar of ice cream, the paper slowly releasing the softened cookie sandwich. Beegie licked her thumb. A pile of wrapper carcasses on the table in front of her.

They had been lucky. Whoever had chained up the small retractable metal shutter. Dessa had been able to pull the shutter up just enough to squeeze through across the counter. The freezers she found inside the small building were off, hundreds of dollars' worth of SpongeBob and Spiderman Popsicles melting within. She had grabbed the least melted of these and passed them to Beegie. The inventory was a total loss for the owner anyway…whatever she and Beegie ate would not have to be cleaned up tomorrow.

Dessa led them to the same picnic table where she sat with Ollie when they came to ride the carousel. She found herself eating bar after bar of the same chocolate-chocolate Häagen-Dasz bar she'd buy for herself. The forces of habit. It would have felt strange to have sat anywhere else. Though it was possible the familiarity of the view of the carousel and the taste of the ice cream made the moment even stranger. Parallel sensations. An inverse moment. Night for day. This larger child licking her hands in place of her own small one doing the same.

A scraping sound pulled Dessa from her thoughts. "What was that?"

Images of predators flew through her head. Plausible scenarios. *Someone had seen them go into the park and followed them. Or someone had hidden here and was waiting out the chaos. Opportunists.*

Beegie swung the flashlight out over the ice cream stand then the surrounding bushes. The beam pushed farther up the path toward the carousel, its light diffusing to almost nothing at the foot of the ride.

"Go back!" Dessa pointed just off of the path.

There was a milky shape on the grass. Two dark spots blinked at them.

"Is that a goat?" Beegie laughed.

The animal took a tentative step in their direction. It watched them, head cocked. Confused by the light and their voices, but not running away. It stepped forward, its hooves making a clapping sound as it stepped onto the pavement.

Dessa squinted. "Actually, I think it's a urial."

"What's a urial?"

"Just…a goat. They have them at the zoo."

In fact, Dessa was sure it was a urial. The high-climbing

goats were a favorite of Ollie's. She would insist upon being taken out of her stroller and held so she could watch their bow-bellied forms perch impossibly on the small ledges of their enclosure.

"They have goats at the zoo? Like a real zoo or like a petting zoo?"

"The real one."

"Where's that?"

"Just down the road a little. I take Ollie there all the time."

"I've never been." Beegie was watching the goat. Fascinated.

Dessa thought about how sad this was. Beegie's house wasn't even five miles from the zoo. It wasn't right.

"You should come with us some time."

Beegie looked at her, features bland and passive. Unreadable in response to this spontaneous invitation. It made Dessa uncomfortable, like she had crossed a boundary she hadn't realized was there until she was over it.

The goat bleated.

The sound broke the strange moment. Dessa was glad to have an excuse to look away.

"You're a long way from home, little one." Dessa grabbed an ice cream sandwich and lobbed it gently toward the feet of the animal. The urial leaned down toward the treat and licked it.

"I shouldn't have done that. She'll probably get diarrhea now."

Beegie chuckled at that. Her face relaxed again. That strange studied passivity gone as quickly as it had appeared. She smiled and looked at Dessa.

"Your boy called you *Odessa*."

"My boy?"

"Asshole with the camera."

"Zach is not *my boy*." Dessa wanted to be clear on that.

"But still he called you *Oh*-Dessa…with an *o*."

Dessa sighed. "That's my name."

"Weird name."

"Okay, *Beegie*."

The girl laughed at this. Her grin making Dessa feel like she had won a prize.

"Odessa was my mom's name. And her mom's name. And probably hers before that. I don't remember when I realized that we all had the same name, but I remember being really angry about it. So when I went into kindergarten, apparently I refused to answer to anything but Dessa. I would just ignore the teacher until she dropped the *o*. I wouldn't write it at the top of my papers. Nothing."

"How'd your mom feel about that?"

"Angry. She was the only one who kept calling me Odessa after I was five… Well, her and Zach, who thought it was cute to push my buttons… What's really funny about it is that it's pretty much what Odessa means.*"

"What's that?"

"Full of wrath…so basically my mom named me Pissed Off Reilly. I was just living up to my potential."

Beegie cracked up.

"Okay, your turn… Is Beegie short for something?"

The girl shrugged. "It took my mom a while to give me a name, so people just called me Baby Girl."

Dessa remembered Beegie's foster mother. *Let me tell you about Baby Girl.* The name clicked into place.

"Baby Girl… Bee. Gee."

She nodded. "It's better than the name my mom said she would have given me though."

"What's that?"

"LaNinja…it means '*the ninja.*'" Beegie karate chopped the air, "I'm still waiting to live up to *my* potential."

Dessa laughed as Beegie executed a number of *hi-ya* moves. She looked like any normal goofy teenager, her hands flying through the air, teeth shining in the moonlight. The girl was such a strange combination of too much experience and too little.

Dessa sighed. "We should go," she said and instinctively began collecting wrappers. She crunched them into a soggy pile and headed for the trash can.

"Hey, where's our friend?"

Beegie stood, the flashlight in her hand. She shone a pool of light on the ice cream bar Dessa had gifted the urial. It lay abandoned, melting where she had thrown it.

"Here, little goatie, goatie." Beegie swung the light out over the grass. "Maybe he wasn't in the mood for ice cream."

Finally the beam found it. About forty feet away.

The goat's body lay on the grass, bright red gashes across the white of its coat. It took Dessa a moment to realize that the creature's throat and belly had been ripped open, blurring the curve of its body under the red.

"Dessa?" Beegie squeaked.

A low feline *rumble* emerged from the darkness of the carousel. They were not alone.

25

It didn't sound real. The cat sound. Like a purr but not. A low clicky, click rumble echoing inside a giant furry chest. To Beegie it was like a sound effect, something you heard on a TV show or at the beginning of a rap song about how hard the singer was.

But no beats were about to start. This wasn't the radio.

And it wasn't Capricious Nature that took those bites out of the goat.

Dessa was still. "Beegie, don't move."

No shit, she thought. But it was like her body wouldn't listen because suddenly it was shaking. Quivering like it was cold even though she wasn't. The flashlight trembled in her hand, making the blood on the dead animal's coat flash and jump.

Shaking with fear. Beegie'd always thought it was just a figure of speech. Something people said.

But here she was doing it.

The rumbling stopped. But it was followed by a series of smaller sounds coming from the darkness of the merry-go-round. Footsteps. Soft pads with tiny clicks buried within. *Claws.*

Beegie angled the flashlight toward the source. Desperate to give a shape to the sound.

"Don't." Dessa's voice stopped the motion of her hand. The end of the beam shook at the foot of the ride, exaggerating the small involuntary motion of Beegie's grip.

Dessa continued, her tone one of enforced calm, "Have you ever seen a cat play with a mouse?"

Beegie nodded. This wasn't a YouTube compilation of kittens sticking their rumps in the air and pouncing on laser dots on the ground, but she understood. Waiting and watching was part of the game. Stalking.

And it would be over the second whatever it was that was making the sound knew that *they knew* it was there.

The low rumble started again.

A sound lodged itself in the back of her throat. Riding on the shaking exhalations of her breath. Involuntary squeaks. Like the mouse that she was.

"Listen to me." Dessa's voice was firm. Beegie fixed her eyes on her shape by the trash can. The falling moon struck half of her face, her eyes unreadable black pools. "*Slowly* walk toward the ice cream stand. Do not run."

"It's…it's gonna eat me." The words came out. The mouse in the back of her throat speaking the words before they even made their way into her brain. Her thighs twitched, begging to move…anywhere as long as it was *away*.

"If you run, it will chase you."

Everything that was her was shaking. Lips, body, feet, breath, voice. She felt sure that if she moved…if she *let* herself move even an inch…that her feet would decide their speed on their own. The mouse inside her would run no matter what she wanted.

"Just walk. Like you don't know it's there."

"I don't think I can."

The ice cream shack seemed impossibly far away. Even more impossible was that to get there she would have to turn her back on the carousel. That did not seem like a good idea.

"What's your favorite number?"

Beegie turned back to Dessa. *What?*

"Mine's the number one. Don't you think it's funny that people don't usually pick it as their favorite?"

The form of Dessa's body was moving. Slow but deliberate. Working her way toward the small building. "You would think more people would. Since it's…you know…number one. But they don't… So, what's yours?"

Why the hell was she talking about numbers?

A creaking sound emerged from the ride. Her eyes picked up a movement in the darkness between the hovering legs of the wooden creatures.

"Jesus!"

"A number, Beegie." Dessa's voice was insistent. Like this was the most important thing in the world.

Beegie forced the word past the fear.

"E…eight."

"Now take a step and tell me why."

Her brain cast wide to find a reason. *Why had she said eight?* Simply to say something… Or was it—

"The loops… I like to make the loops."

The press of the pencil between her fingertips. Rows of eights. Stacked circles on top of each other. Like reflections in a lake of themselves.

Her feet were moving finally. Slow jerky steps, each one

pulling her closer to the dark gray bulk of the shack. Dessa had reached it and was wrapping her hand around the handle of the retractable shutter.

"I like the loops too. Like infinity, right?"

She was almost halfway there. "Yeah. Circle of life."

The shutter screeched as Dessa pushed it upward. An ugly protest.

In answer, the creature in the carousel *growled*.

Beegie froze again...all thoughts of numbers erased by the sound.

Closer to Dessa, she could now see how hard the woman was working to keep her voice calm. Her face was pale, dark lines drawn on the outside of her nose and mouth. Dessa cupped her hand toward her. Gently, "Come on."

It was then that her eyes slipped from Beegie's face to the merry-go-round, growing wide.

Beegie turned.

A distinct feline shape dropped down from the platform of the ride. Impossibly large.

"Run. Now. Run." Dessa was no longer trying to hide the panic in her voice.

And then Beegie was flying. Feet biting into the ground.

The flashlight clattered against the lip of the serving bar as she reached it. Dessa was already pulling herself inside, her head and shoulders wedged under the retractable grate.

Beegie pulled herself up, hand reaching across and finding the other edge of the counter. She levered herself, dropping her arms down and using gravity to fall forward. She hit the rubber mats of the floor with the top of her head and her body curled after, feet hitting the opposite wall as she fell.

"Beegie!"

Dessa was stuck, the door caught somehow on the fabric of her dress.

The soles of Beegie's sneakers squealed against the wall as she twisted her body upward. Dessa was flailing, trying desperately to pull herself free, but she couldn't reach. The door flexed, rattling as Beegie's palms connected with its corrugated surface. She gripped the bottom edge and pushed up hard.

Dessa screamed with effort, her arms straining. The door bounced as its connection finally snapped. The contraption moaned, sliding a few inches downward as her body fell to the floor.

Beneath the sound of their relieved panting, Beegie heard a strange scratching. Like rock against pavement.

And then the whole building shook. Beegie jumped as the door inches from her flexed, metal popping. Something pierced the space next to her, punching its way inside through the remaining opening. She screamed and fell back as the paw swiped at the space where she had been, the wind from its motion kissing her face.

The creature pulled away and suddenly the shutter was alive, its slats beating out a rhythmic screech as it dragged its claws across the grooves. Again and again, the door shook, its metal popping and resisting. Threatening to give way.

Beegie felt a warm presence against her arm. Dessa's hand. She must have fallen on top of her. She could feel the older woman's chest moving against her back, the way she was trying to gain control of her breaths. They were drawn out. Long and shallow.

A paw swiped out into the space above them. Trying again to extract them. Beegie felt Dessa's breath stop, then begin again as the beast resumed dragging its claws down the length of the window. If it was hitting the shutter, at least it wasn't actively trying to slice into them.

She tried to time her breaths to Dessa's. To start when the older woman started so their chests would rise at the same time.

Eyes closed, she imagined Dessa's breath as a road she was riding. Rising and falling onto the gentle slopes made by waves of air.

A frustrated yowl broke her concentration. Beegie didn't know how long it had been but suddenly the rattling stopped. Beneath her Dessa moved, her chest moving away from its contact with Beegie's shoulder.

A chuff sounded outside the shack. Followed by that rumbling purr, moving away from the window. Dessa leaped to her feet. The metal gate whined quietly as she pulled it closed, dropping the small space into even more darkness.

Beegie's eyes turned, seeking out the remaining glow. Under the side door, a shadow cut through the bleeding light.

Sniffing. Then a loud *snort.*

The shadow moved away, leaving the blue light to fan across the floor unobstructed.

Beegie whispered, "Is it gone?"

They listened.

A quiet *thump, thump…*and then—

The roof of the shack *flexed.*

"Oh my God."

It was above them. Whatever it was. Huge and deadly. Hungry. A rain of dust scattered down from the cheap plaster ceiling as the *thing* walked in a circle. Small scrapes against the flashing of the roof, followed by the sound of something heavy being set down on one end of the shack…and then the other.

They waited.

A hollow shooshing sound reverberated through the shack's interior. Amplified by the metal of its walls.

Its breath. It was waiting for them to leave.

26

When Beegie was little, and she still lived with her mother, she knew her momma was gonna be leaving for work whenever she saw her kneeling by the door. Beegie'd be lying on the couch, Dora on the television, and she'd look over and see Momma, her hand on the skinny little screwdriver that she kept on top of the refrigerator. Couple of twists to loosen the screw.

"You be good, baby," Momma'd say.

"Peanut butter in the fridge," Momma'd say.

"Swiper, no swiping," Dora would say.

This was after she had almost been "Jasmine," after her mother had gotten her "act together," and the judge said Beegie could come back to live with her. Beegie's memories of this time were stronger, realer than her earlier ones.

Beegie knew that she wasn't supposed to tell anyone about

her mother leaving her alone and that was fine. It felt like something special, a secret between the two of them. And Momma taking the doorknob off the door was only so Beegie would stay inside and stay safe. She only did it so she could work because she needed to take care of her little girl.

Beegie was proud of the way she could take care of herself while Mommy was making money. She would climb on the counter and get the bread and the plates. Make herself a sandwich and pour herself drinks. Clean it all up in the sink. She'd brush her own teeth and put herself to bed.

Most times she'd wake up when Momma was crawling into bed next to her. Almost morning. They'd sleep together for a while, but not for too long before Momma was getting her up for school. Brushing her hair and dropping her off outside the doors. "See you in the afternoon," she'd say.

But other times Momma wouldn't climb in and go to sleep with her. Sometimes her mother would wake her up and they would have a party, even though it was too early and all their neighbors were still sleeping. Momma would turn the music up really loud and they would do a crazy dance and when the neighbors hit their walls to tell them to stop, Beegie's mother would tell them to "Shut the fuck up!" Her mother's eyes would glow like fire, and she would tell Beegie all sorts of wonderful things that they were going to do together, all the businesses that she was going to start and the houses that they were going to live in.

Once in a while Beegie would wake up and her mother would be sad. Crying in the bathroom. Or rolled up in a ball on the couch.

On those days Beegie took herself to school. It didn't happen too often and it never lasted too long. She was glad for that.

It was almost like Beegie had three mothers instead of just

the one, and she never knew which one was gonna come home from work. The tired one who would sleep all day, the fun one who would laugh without making a noise and talk and talk and talk, or the sad one who would sometimes forget that Beegie was even there.

Maternal history of bipolar disorder.

Beegie had seen it on one of her forms when she got older. Looked up what it meant along with *capricious*. It meant that her mother had a broken brain. One that either spun or stopped, instead of chugging along the way it was supposed to. The way most people's brains do.

Bipolar disorder was the nice way of saying it.

Crazy bitch was another way.

That's what the cops who came to get her called her mom. *"Crazy fucking bitch…with a kid locked up at home…"*

This was after they had to beat the door down because Beegie couldn't open it, and wouldn't have even if it had a knob because she was pretending she wasn't there. Hiding behind the couch because her mother had told her she shouldn't answer the door for anyone. Listening to their knocks and then their kicks as they forced the door off its hinges to get to her.

Beegie didn't remember anyone telling her that her mother was dead after that. They must have though, because she knew it now. And before you can know something you have to be told. So someone *must* have told her, even though she couldn't remember, and maybe that was a good thing.

Years later, at the Greelys', she had seen an ad on the television for some medicine. For "the treatment of patients suffering from bipolar disorder," the commercial had said. The ad showed people riding bikes and going hiking. White people, Black people, Asians, Hispanics. Beegie remembered watching the commercial and thinking, "those people are like my mom was." Broken brains, spinning and stopping.

Except then she realized they weren't.

The people in the commercial were rich. They were sad and mad in houses with nice kitchens and fancy pillows on the couches.

And Momma was the opposite of rich.

Beegie wondered what would have been different if her Momma had been rich enough to afford not to have a broken brain.

But then she stopped.

Because it was stupid to imagine that money would have just changed that *one thing* about her mother's life…because money would've changed just about *everything* about her mother's life.

Maybe even having money would have kept her mother's brain from being broken in the first place.

When the cops started to break the door down, Beegie was sure it was a monster come to get her. Even though she was eight and she'd stopped believing in monsters…mostly. While she hid she imagined something huge with long sharp claws, breaking down her door to eat her. She had screamed and screamed when the door burst open. Screamed when the policeman picked her up and carried her out. Screamed while they put her in the back of their car. Screamed even when they offered her a teddy bear.

That's what she was reminded of when the tiger or panther or *whatever the fuck it was* was beating at the shack. The way she felt when Dessa'd been trying to keep her calm even though she was sure she was going to die.

It was memory of her mother *not coming home* and instead a monster coming to break down her door.

"I am the stupidest person," Dessa whispered. Beegie could barely see her, just a vague shape in the dark. Dim and quiet on the floor of the shack.

Beegie thought of the way Dessa had gotten her to walk. The way she'd gotten through Beegie's panic. *What's your favorite number?* The fact that she'd gotten them in here when Beegie could barely think, could barely *move*...

Beegie didn't think Dessa was stupid.

But the woman didn't stop to let her say so. Instead Dessa just barreled right though. "*I* made us go into the park! I took us past the *fucking zoo!* I saw that goat and I didn't think *any-thing!* And now, we are stuck here and—" Dessa's leg shot out, "No! One! Is! Coming!" Her leg struck the freezer with each word, the metal flexing beneath it.

A low rumble reverberated from the ceiling above. The creature's reply.

The older woman kept going, her pitch high. Touching crazy, reaching broken. "That *thing* is going to stay there and *wait.* No one is going to come and rescue us because they are all too busy looking out for themselves! No one is going to help Olivia. No one helps anyone! I am so fucking stupid!"

And then she started crying.

Beegie couldn't really see it but she could hear it. Wet snuffling. Quiet gasps. Dessa letting a wave of self-pity wash over her.

Beegie understood why Dessa was crying. But something about the way she was doing it...made Beegie *angry.* She hated the dance this woman was sending her on. Making her shuffle back and forth between thinking she was good and smart and then thinking she was a weak bitch. She couldn't decide if she should feel the way she'd felt about her when she was whiny crying with that gang banger but then she turned it around by the way she'd talked to Barb.

Shit, she'd saved her facing down a mother-fucking lion. She had been cool *then*, but here where they were out of danger, she was melting like the ice cream in the freezers.

242

Beegie wanted to shake her.

"Fuck you," Beegie said.

The sound of Dessa's crying stopped. Hiccuped into silence.

Beegie continued, "Do you want me to feel sorry for you? Do you need me to say 'oh there, there, you were only doing your best'?" Beegie let that hang in the silence for a moment, "Because fuck you. I'm here too. I'm here because you brought me here and I don't feel like listening to your shit."

Beegie heard the sound of Dessa swallowing in the dark. Her exhale. "I'm sorry, Beegie," she whispered.

"Fuck. Your. Sorry." Beegie stood but there was nowhere to go. She felt the wall right next to her, only five steps to the other side. A bigger person could probably touch both ends of this shack with arms extended.

Above them the creature rumbled, lungs filling. Beegie's hand brushed a canister to her left and suddenly she was throwing it at the ceiling. There was a big metallic clash and then a rain of plastic, hitting the surfaces and the floor of the shack. *Straws.*

They were quiet for a moment. The sound of their breathing in the dark.

"You know I don't have one person in the world right now that gives a shit that I'm here."

"Beegie…"

"Fuck you, *listen*… If I get out of here or if I don't, the only person who will really give a shit is *me*. You don't get to cry in front of me, Odessa Reilly, because *you have* people who give a shit about you…there is nobody in the world who thought of me when that earthquake happened. Nobody who's wondering where I am and why I'm not home…"

Dessa started to say something then, but Beegie cut her off, "Don't tell me that's not true because you don't know my shit. You don't know me, you don't know what I've been through and you may feel sorry for me but don't lie and say that I've got someone who cares about me who isn't paid to do it."

There was silence, then—

"I care."

"Then you're right... You *are* fucking stupid...'cause I'm *nobody* to you. I'm just some bitch who saved you from walking through the wrong neighborhood. We would *never know each other in real life*...and it's fucking weak to give a shit about someone you barely know."

"No, it's not, Beegie," said Dessa, trying to put on her grown-up in-charge voice again. "It's not weak to care."

"You walked past all those broken houses, same as me. You put your hands in your ears and you said I don't care about those other strangers' pain."

"It's different."

"Why? I'm a stranger, same as them. Don't tell me you give a shit about me. I'm too fucking smart to believe you."

"I couldn't help them!"

"You haven't helped me!" Beegie sent her voice high and mocking, *"Oh where would I be if the well-meaning white lady hadn't helped me? At fucking Barb's and not trapped by a fuck-ing lion."*

Above them the weight of the animal shifted, the sound of its fur shushing against the roof.

Beegie let herself slide back to the floor, all of her energy suddenly abandoning her. She thought of her mother. Of the sensation of her mother slipping up against her back when she joined her after work, wrapping her hands around her and holding her. She remembered trying to match her breathing with her mother's. Wild when she was wild. Calm when she was calm. Riding her mother's breaths, matching them in time so that they were breathing as one.

Dessa had grown quiet. Sitting up in the dark and silent.

Beegie could feel the warmth of her legs across the small space from her. Something occurred to her that she wanted to say. She wasn't sure if she meant it as a kindness or a barb...but she needed to say it. So she whispered.

"Olivia needs you. Right now she's got someone. She's got you. Even if she's dead, she needs you. Even the dead need someone to care."

If Dessa heard her, she didn't say anything back.

27

Somehow they fell asleep, though Dessa did not remember closing her eyes. Or lying down. But exhaustion had won, and the sound of the creature's breath was soothing, a white noise roar that became less disturbing when you forgot what it was. What it meant.

When she woke, her eyes searched the darkness for the shape of Olivia's bed, a sluggish mind falling into the well-worn path of routine. The confirmation that accompanied her daily rise into consciousness. *I am here. My baby is there.*

It took a moment. Split-second disorientation before she remembered where she was. Who she was with. The realization of her circumstances confirming itself with her waking senses. The faint outline of Beegie's sleeping body limned in the light from under the door. The way the floor mats she had fallen asleep upon had pressed shapes into her face. The cramping of her arms and legs. A throbbing in her foot. An ache in her soul.

She had dreamed of Gretchen. Of the morning she had picked her up to drive her to the abortion Dessa had scheduled. The one Dessa had canceled, calling from the parking lot of the clinic, because she had realized that the small clump of cells inside her was not just related to Joe, but also to her father... *Her father*, who she missed so much and wanted so desperately to talk to about this horrible situation she had gotten herself into.

They had driven up the coast after she canceled. Gretchen glaring into the rising dawn. Eventually they stopped and got fish tacos on the beach. They said almost nothing to each other, choosing instead to squint into the too-bright ocean.

In the dream, Olivia was on the beach as well. Dancing in the surf. Visiting them for bites of fish. Her thin legs speckled with wet sand. "Watch!" She yelled at them over the roar of the waves as she bent her body forward. Attempting a somersault. "Watch me, Momma!"

Gretchen had looked at her. "It's not too late," she said and Dessa wasn't sure what she meant. Was she advocating for the end of Olivia's existence, the way she really had that day on the beach, clinical, lawyerly?

Or was it the other meaning? Not too late to save the daughter that came from Dessa's resistance to her arguments. The girl on whose belly Gretchen planted kisses every time she saw her. The person she loved, whose existence she had once argued against.

Dessa winced. Rolled the tips of her thumbs across her fingers. Waking herself up.

She no longer heard the sound of the big cat's breathing. It had moved on or at the very least left its rooftop perch.

Beegie snored softly across from her. Asleep she looked even younger. A child still. Song sweet.

Dessa remembered the words she had spit at her. *She's got someone. She's got you. Even if she's dead she needs you. Even the dead need someone to care.*

Dessa did not know how to mother a dead child. Did not want to learn.

A buzzing sounded somewhere in the shack. Her phone. Dessa got to her knees, hands patting the ground searching the darkness for the sack that held her belongings. The screen was lit up. *UNKNOWN.*

Hope blew into Dessa's body. Sometimes when Joe called from work or home instead of his cell it would show up this way. She answered, voice bright. "Joe? Joe?"

"Dessa?"

Not Joe. A woman's voice. "It's Amanda."

Dessa was silent. Not Joe. Not Hailey. Not Olivia.

"Amanda Sampson."

Dessa's mind finally brought forth a fuzzy memory of the face that belonged to the voice. Her sophomore year roommate— she of the sister at whose party she met Gretchen. Never close, but cordial. Their exchanges reserved to hearting and liking each other's posts for years now. Posting of birthday wishes but no calls.

"I'm in New York. I just woke up and oh my God, Dessa… it's all over the news. It's so awful. I remembered that you lived in the Van Nuys. They're saying it got hit pretty hard. I just wanted to see if you were okay…"

The East Coast was waking up. The footage Zach was so desperate to get out finally making its way onto their screens. *Am I okay?* She didn't know how to answer.

Amanda marinated in the silence. "I got your number from an old email you sent me. I hope you don't mind…"

What was the news showing of Van Nuys? Could Amanda have seen her apartment building on her screen? Would Dessa want to know if she had?

"I can't really talk right now."

"I know this is weird since we haven't actually talked in six years...but let me know if there is anything I can do..."

Dessa shook her head, mumbled a quiet *no*. Amanda had called on impulse, but now actually hearing the pain in Dessa's voice her morbid curiosity had waned. They both knew there was nothing she could actually do.

It was Dessa's responsibility to let her off the hook.

Except...

"Wait, sorry, yes. There are numbers. I need you to call them... As much as you can until you get through. My phone is almost dead and the circuits have been jammed since last night."

"Who?"

"One is for my babysitter. She was with my daughter when it happened. I talked to her after...but there have been aftershocks."

"Oh my God, Dessa."

Dessa ignored pity in Amanda's voice. She didn't have time for it. "I also need you to call my daughter's father. His name is Joe. He may be with her." She swallowed...trying to control the waver in her voice. "If you reach them...let me know... if everyone is okay."

They waited until they heard the birds. Penny-bright chirps leaking into the darkness of the shack. Signaling that the sun was on its way.

It seemed off. The birdsong. Dessa felt she should have heard a difference in their voices. That the sound of their chirps should reflect the change that had happened in the world.

But they sang the same this morning as they likely had yes-terday. Like they would tomorrow. Like the earth wasn't up-ended. Of course, Dessa supposed, the ground didn't matter to creatures who could hold themselves above it.

Dessa had been looking out the crack beneath the roll-up shutter when she felt the girl's presence next to her.

"Do you think its still out there?"

Dessa shook her head. Beegie looked up at her, bruise-colored light across her face. They stared at each other for a moment.

Then Beegie slammed her fist into the rolling door. It crashed against itself. Jarring and loud. Outside the birds squawked and flew, the sound of their wings beating cold morning air.

But no growl. No flexing of the ceiling. Their friend had slipped away while they were sleeping.

They opened the side door. Eyes searching the violet-stained clearing for movement. The goat's body was gone from where it had lain the night before. A dark stain on the grass in its place.

Dessa hesitated.

There were no guarantees the *thing* was gone.

Or that it was the only animal that had gotten out of its cage.

They could wait here for days, and their odds would never be any better than they were at this moment.

She tightened her grip on the bag straps and stepped out into the pavement. Heard the sound of Beegie's shoes, scuff-ing behind her. Then a whoosh as the door swung itself closed behind them, metallic click locking them out into the world again.

Just. Get. Home.

They walked. Grass painting their legs wet. Eyes search-ing the trees.

They reached the main road as the sun crested, painting the park in an orange glow. They moved north. They moved quietly. They moved as quickly as their tired bodies would let them.

Just before they reached the park exit, Beegie pointed to something on the ridge. Dessa turned and gasped when she saw them. Three giraffes on the hill, two adults and a juvenile. The sun beating against the slope of their backs, making their bodies dark, almost prehistoric. Behind them the sky blushed.

28

Beegie watched the traffic light cycle between green and red as they mounted the on-ramp. Regulating an imaginary morning rush. The light flashing green as they walked past it, giving them the go-ahead to merge.

The road was empty. Like a message had been sent to every driver in Los Angeles.

Roads closed. Bridge is out.

Which one?

Too many to number.

And so all the commuters were all tucked safely in their homes.

Or under them. Beegie thought, the purple smell threading through her mind. Echoes of what she had said to Dessa the night before.

Beegie glanced at the other woman. Shadows of lines traced her mouth, eyes pinched, lips pressed thin. Her face looked strange. Not just tired, *old*…like she had aged decades since they had met.

Dessa had not said anything since they had left the shack. Even the decision to take the highway had been a silent one. A pause at the turnoff, a glance at the trees and houses of the surface streets. Beegie had followed her gaze and seen the same thing…places where predators could hide.

An open expanse of road was an easy choice after that.

It felt strange to be walking on the open ribbon of concrete, unprotected by a car. The road stretched out wide and quiet before them. Dessa stuck to the side of the highway. Eyes forward in her young/old face. Thoughts elsewhere.

Beegie floated into the lane beside her. She made a game of taking steps so that the toes of her shoes kissed the yellow lines. Lengthening her stride so that it hit the stripe just right each time. It was stupid. And childish, she knew. But she kept doing it anyway, just staring at the ground and the repetitive lines under her moving shoes. Happy if she got it right. Pissed if she got it wrong.

They kept walking, and soon it became as if the game was her whole reason for being on the road at all. An illicit joy of being somewhere that she was not supposed to be. Like the taste of spoonfuls of grape jelly eaten straight from the jar… something that was better because you were *not* supposed to being doing it.

Beegie pushed into that feeling. The good feeling. The young feeling. Her feet looked small on the pavement, and maybe for a minute she could pretend she was small too. Like she was eight and at Tricia's house. Or ten and at Janelle's. Or younger on the good days with her mom or the fuzzy-faced family, even if she wasn't sure any of those memories were real. Even if none of it had really happened they were still hers, she could still have them.

The game was almost like hopscotch. Or jump rope. Without realizing it, she began humming Miss Mary Mack... *All dressed in black, black, black.* Each painted line beneath her foot became a button on the black dress of the road. Beegie imagined threading them back through the fabric of the concrete with her jumps. Pushing it down, revealing the nakedness underneath.

Thinking of buttons was a mistake...

Beegie's stomach lurched at that last thought. Miss Mary Mack's naked spine was gone, replaced by the thoughts of her own buttons and the Busman's hands. The sensation of his knuckles against the skin of her belly. Tucked into her pants. Fumbling with the waistband of her jeans. Threading the button through the hole. His hands dipping into her panties for a moment, before pulling it all down. A violent yank, skinning the pants from her legs. But only one side. Only one shoe off. He left the other side dangling. The other shoe still on.

Beegie shook her head. Fuck that. She didn't want to think about that.

She tried to recapture the game she had been playing. Head down, focused. Foot touching the painted edge of the line. *Play the game and it is possible to forget.*

But what had happed to her last night had infected this moment. Stained the brief forgetting she had found.

Another flash. Another moment she had stared at her shoes. Walking...after the earthquake. An arm around her shoulder, maybe two arms... A hand on the small of her back. She says something to them...she doesn't remember what. Not Charlie's laugh in her ear.

She stumbled. Then in her memory, and now on the highway. "Are you okay?"

Beegie looked up at Dessa by the side of the road. The woman had stopped moving and was staring at her. Beegie shuddered. All at once she realized she was cold. Freezing actually. The sun was starting to heat up the concrete but she was shivering nonetheless.

"Beegie?" Dessa's young face was back. She wasn't somewhere else thinking about her daughter, she was right here, worrying about Beegie.

"What?"

"You stopped walking."

She had? Beegie's feet were firmly planted on both sides of the painted line. Dessa was a good ten feet ahead of her. Something about the way her face was all painted up with concern lit up a new feeling inside her. A better feeling than the one she had been having.

Anger.

Beegie shrugged. "So."

"We have to keep going, Beegie."

"You do. I don't… I don't have to do shit."

Dessa rocked on her feet at that. Like Beegie had pushed her. Beegie liked seeing that—that she had some power, even while she didn't understand why she wanted to hurt Dessa.

The two women stared at each other for a moment. Beegie felt the wind pressing itself on the palms of her hands, pushing its way forward to tug on Dessa's hair, whipping it away from her face. Dessa opened her mouth like she was going to say something…but then closed it. She nodded.

Then she turned and began to walk away.

"Hey," Beegie yelled. "Hey!"

She wanted a fight. She wanted Dessa to beat at her head like Barb or Eric. Push against her. Yell at her. Tell her to fuck off. Tell her she didn't mean anything, so Beegie could yell back at her.

But instead Dessa ignored her. She just walked away. Beegie watched as her body grew smaller as she put distance between them. Another few minutes and Dessa would be out of her sight. Just another person she no longer knew.

Well, fuck her. What the fuck did Dessa mean to her anyway? She was just another someone she'd met after the earthquake. Just like Busman and Not-Charlie, and look what *they'd* done to her.

Beegie shifted her weight from one foot to the other. Her anger retreating with her target. The wind cupped her face, the breath of an interrupted question. And endless "whh"… Never resolving into the "oooo" or the "aaattt."

And then, like it had been waiting for her to be alone, a wave of pain both physical and psychic finally crested over her.

None of this damage was new. But somehow Beegie had not felt the full weight of it until now, watching Dessa walk away. The distance had begun to drain the color from Dessa, so that now her body looked twisted and charred.

Beegie shivered.

Dessa looked like a ghost on the horizon. Her legs twiggy, bent toward themselves, her feet disappearing in the shimmer. Like her feet were no longer touching the ground. Like she was hovering above it.

A clean fear cut its way into Beegie's pain.

Neat as a horror film, Beegie suddenly felt quite sure that if she let Dessa out of her sight, the woman would wink out of existence. The twiggy figure in the distance would pull itself into a small black hole and then…poof, she would be gone.

And everything that Beegie had experienced *with* Dessa would be relegated to the fuzzy world of *maybe* memories… like her mother's eyes in flames or the fuzzy-faced family, things that *might* have happened because she remembered them, but could not have because they seemed improbable, and she had no one to confirm her reality with.

A shock of pain shot up her vagina, lightning strike to her

insides. Her vulva pulsed against the crotch of her jeans. Beegie felt like she could feel every stitch on the seam of her pants, pressing like needles against the bruises on her legs.

She didn't trust her body. She didn't trust her memory. Even this pain. This hurt, this fucked until you bleed feeling, this snapped rubber band loose leg feeling, this *violent* feeling...it would all go away and Beegie would question whether it had even happened at all.

And if Dessa winked out of existence...if she disappeared over the horizon, Beegie would be left never knowing for sure if any of it had really happened. The underpass. Barb. The lion. None of it.

Fuck.

Dessa's body was a small wavering dot in the distance.

Beegie began to run.

Her lower parts screamed between her thighs. They felt wrong, too heavy while she moved. A foreign gravity, working against the motion of her limbs.

As she ran, Beegie imagined that the space between her belly and her knees had been replaced. Body snatched, but just her middle part.

The small dot that was Dessa grew bigger as Beegie moved toward her. Her back still turned, still moving away. Beegie thought about yelling out for her to stop. Asking her to wait up...but something stopped her voice in her throat. She wasn't sure that the woman actually *would* stop. She didn't want to know the limits of Dessa's patience, or if she had run over the edges of them. She didn't want to see Dessa hear her call out and choose not to turn.

So she just ran.

Dessa turned as the sound of her feet slapping the pavement reached her. Beegie slowed to a stop, panting. Her skin felt numb, wind whipped and raw.

"I'm…" Beegie stopped. She had almost said she was sorry. But she wasn't. *Sorry* wasn't why she was here.

But she needed to say something, so she asked the question the wind had been screaming in her ears.

"Why?"

"Why what, Beegie?"

"Why'd you ask me to come with you?"

Something shifted in Dessa's eyes. Like she was doing math in her head, figuring each word and its cost. "It was safer."

Beegie shook her head. "No. After Barb. Why'd you tell me to come with you? Why'd you tell Barb to fuck off? You coulda left me there. I'm nobody to you. You shoulda left me."

Dessa's lips pressed thin. Their color fading into her face. "I said I was sorry, Beegie. You're right. It's my fault. I get it. I get why you don't want to stay with me."

"No. I wanna know why."

She looked away, her gaze slippery. "Why did *you* come with *me*?"

Beegie wanted to say *because you asked me to.* She wanted to say *because I had nowhere else to go.* She wanted to say *because I like the way you talk to me, and about your daughter and I want to make sure she's okay, 'cause once I was a little girl trapped in a room and nobody cared.*

Instead she shrugged. "Didn't have anything better to do."

Dessa's lips turned up at that. A half-sad smile. Just as manufactured as Beegie's peace offering joke.

They began to walk again, but the quality of the silence between them was different than it had been since they left the shack. It was a warmer sound, filling the space between their footsteps. Beegie stayed out of the road, away from the painted lines. She kept her gaze lifted up from her shoes and Dessa in her periphery lest she turn in to a charred and twisted ghost again.

The pain between her legs subsided. Or really what subsided was her awareness of it. Like a tag that should be cut from a shirt, her awareness of the truth of what had happened to her body could be a mild irritation or an excruciating torture. It would always be there, tickling at the back of her brain, but it was possible to pretend that it was not.

Dessa slowed, "Do you see that?"

Beegie followed her gaze to a ten-story building just off the highway. Hundreds of people were gathered at its base.

"The hospital," Beegie whispered. "Jesus."

A chime sounded. Dessa's phone. She pulled it from her bag.

On the screen beneath a long string of numbers with an unfamiliar area code it read:

J says everybody fine.

Another chime. Another message.

@ his house.

Dessa gasped, her body limp with relief. "Oh thank God... Come on, Beegie. We have to go."

29

Joe's house was in Toluca Lake, a small upscale neighborhood tucked into the corner between the 134 and the 101.

But Joe's house was also located in one of Dessa's carefully constructed compartments, kept there so Dessa did not have to think about it too often.

Joe has Olivia. The thought rolled through Dessa's body, a warm tide of relief, as she and Beegie walked as fast as they could toward his neighborhood. *He has her.*

@ his house Amanda's text had read.

@ his house meant the end of this particular compartment. Crushed by the earthquake just as effectively as if it was a real place. The damage would be significant.

You'd be surprised at what you can learn to live with. Her father's voice in her mind. She could live with messy as long as she did not have to live without Olivia.

Beegie kept pace as they exited the freeway, pushing their way past the main strip of businesses and into the enclave of trees and picket fences to the east. Dessa glanced at the girl. Their argument had been another rattling at another door. But one that had held...

When they had seen the hospital, Dessa had been about to let the secret go. To tell the girl to go to the emergency room because she knew that Beegie needed treatment just as badly as any of those people outside that building.

But then the message had chimed, and she had said nothing.

And here Beegie was with her, miles from the hospital, and Dessa responsible again because she didn't know how to say what she needed to say to this girl.

Which was *I am weak. I did nothing. I am sorry.*

That's what was in Beegie's box in Dessa's mind. The thing that had almost come out when Beegie had asked her why she had wanted her to stay: *Because I am trying to fix the unfixable. Because I hate myself for what I did not do.*

Dessa directed them up a street lined on each side with fifty-foot jacarandas. The girl stared up at the canopy they made over the street, the trees' limbs reaching out toward each other in the sky, shuttering the morning sun into a dancing half-light.

"Nice neighborhood," she said, and Dessa nodded, deciding that they would take Beegie to the hospital as soon as she had Olivia again. After she had confirmed the intact reality of her daughter under her fingertips.

The houses grew larger as they made their way deeper into the neighborhood. Typical California real estate moving from the modest million-dollar homes to the slightly less modest two- or three-million-dollar homes.

Dessa spotted a face between two displaced shutters. A bare

impression of a scowl before the space was closed again. Beegie exhaled as the face disappeared. Shaking her head.

Dessa finally spotted Joe's. The white-house black-clapboard shape that lived inside a box in her imagination, every tasteful detail of it clear and undeniable now.

On impulse, she reached into her collar, fingers plunging into her bra and finding the warm circle of metal she had put there the night before. She pulled the ring onto her finger as she broke into a run, ignoring the same itch of insecurity that had driven her to put it on the night before on her way to see Gretchen and the girls. She reached the immaculately laid brick driveway, the perfectly edged beds of all-white roses, and rapped her knuckles on the door painted the ideal shade of red.

Breath held, she bounced on the step. Willing her daughter to run to the door. Listening for the wobbly pattern of Ollie's steps.

Joe answered instead.

Dessa drew a breath as she fell into him. A lover's sound riding the inhale, a gasp of relief at the confirmation of his living breathing self. Her face pressed into the hard valley of his chest, taking in the smell of him, freshly showered and warm. Alive.

He stepped into her. The motion was unexpected, pushing her back with the wall of his body. Dessa stumbled against him, and his hands grabbed her arms, bracing her...no, not bracing her. Prying her off of him, muscling her onto the step as he closed the door behind himself.

"Dessa, what are you doing here?"

Joe's tone was tempered. Lawyer's voice. Controlled calm.

It was all wrong. Ollie should be in his arms. Or on the ground behind him, working her little body between his legs to get at her. She should be calling, "Momma, momma," burying kisses on her face. Joe should be wrapping his arms around them both. Warmth in his voice. Waving her into the house, ready to face the consequences but happy that she was there.

"Olivia," Dessa whispered their daughter's name, hoping that all the pieces of this moment would not click into their inevitable meaning.

"I don't have Olivia."

He said it.

But still a part of her felt it was impossible. No. Ollie was here. She had to be because—

"You were almost there, you said you were on your way when…" Dessa broke off, trying to apply reason to her rising voice. "Amanda said—"

"Is Amanda your friend who called me? Jesus, Dessa. Susan gave me the phone. She was right there."

Dessa felt her head shaking. She was falling through a hole inside her body.

The door opened behind Joe, a dandelion tuft of blond hair peeking past the threshold.

"Joe? What are you doing out there?"

Susan stepped into the sunshine.

Joe's wife was pretty in real life. This surprised Dessa, who had only seen pictures of her online. Social media avatars are usually the most flattering pictures, but Susan was even more attractive than any of the shots Dessa had been able to see in the dark moments when she had googled her.

Well-kept, thin. Hair dyed a shade of blond that didn't immediately supersede intelligence. An easy smile with enough movement in her face to indicate she hadn't given in to the lure of fillers like so many other Los Angeles women of a certain age.

She looked kind. She looked sane.

Not at all the woman Joe had described to Dessa.

Susan's eyes rested on Dessa for a moment, then moved beyond her to the driveway. Dessa turned, remembering only now that Beegie was there. Beegie had witnessed all of this... *Would* witness all of this...

"Sue, I don't know if you've ever met Gretchen from work."

Dessa winced at her best friend's name and looked back at Joe. The lie had slipped so easily out of him. Of course he could not tell his wife who she really was, what he was to her. Susan reached out her hand.

"Joe talks about you all the time."

Dessa took Susan's hand. Shook it. Susan smiled. "Why don't you and your friend come inside. The news said there are riots going on." She waved Beegie in from the driveway, looking up and down their quiet suburban street as if she expected the pitchfork-wielding horde to arrive at any moment.

Dessa noticed a smatter of light on the door as Susan waved her hand. It was small, five tiny rectangles scribing a small arc across the deep red of their front door. The sunlight catching the diamond on Susan's finger.

So like the one on Dessa's own.

Close enough to be identical.

Susan closed the door to her home—*to Joe's home*—behind Dessa just as all the doors to Dessa's carefully constructed boxes burst open.

Dessa followed her, aware that she was still there but also sure that the most important part of herself had lost form...her body was as diffuse and refracted as the scatter of abstract shapes from Susan's ring, losing form the farther they got from their source.

The shapes of her thoughts moved quickly, bending across the topography of Joe's real life. The one she had never really wanted to look at too closely.

Joe had proposed to Dessa a week *after* he moved back in with Susan and the boys. Dessa knew this. All of Joe's world she was walking through was known to her. Then and now.

She had told him to fuck off. Refused his calls for days. She had ripped him up in her mind, made a tiny stack of her love and exploded it into confetti.

But then he had come to her place. Begged to be let in. Begged just to be heard.

"Let me explain," he had said through the closed door.

"I'm sorry," he had said once inside, his hand cupping the ring box.

"Be patient," he had said after she had melted under his logic and his mouth, leaning back while he lifted the hem of her shirt to touch the hot skin of her growing belly.

Joe explained Susan was suicidal. Susan was anorexic. Susan was probably bipolar and likely a drug addict. A danger to herself and the children. He thought she might buy a gun. He thought she might drive drunk with the children. He thought she might overdose, that Cooper or Anders might find her sprawled on the floor of the living room in a pool of pill-speckled vomit.

When Dessa asked him why he didn't just try for custody, he said it would destroy her. Susan lived for the boys. He didn't think she would survive them being taken. Because while his marriage was over, he still cared about his wife as a person. She wasn't bad, just unstable. Joe felt responsible for her insanity... For leaving the way he had the first time. For trying to do it abruptly, instead of weaning her off him the way he should have. The way he planned to do it now.

"You know you're the one I want to be with." He had cried into her body after they made love that night. His tears making a seal between the flesh of her chest and his face.

Dessa had nodded and run her fingers through his hair. A pattern of lights moved in time with her motions on the ceiling and Dessa realized that they were being cast by the diamond he had given her, refracting the dim light of her bedroom lamp. The ring still felt hard and foreign on her hand.

Joe's breathing grew deep and regular. He fell asleep but Dessa could not follow suit because the baby must have been rocked awake by their orgasms. Olivia announced herself with butterfly kicks, bump, bump against the interior of her mother's body. Dessa lay still in her bed, staring at the beauty of the light, bent and tossed against the wall, easing her breath so she wouldn't miss a single kick.

She tapped back with her index finger, pushing on the spot where Olivia's tiny feet were making their presence known. A telegram from the outside world. *GROW BIG, LITTLE ONE.* STOP. *YOUR FAMILY IS HERE.* STOP. *MY LOVE WILL NOT.* STOP.

Dessa remembered that moment because she struggled so hard to let the experience be pure. Feeling her daughter's touch for the first time.

To do this she put away the fact that Joe had simply given her a ring with all its implied promise but had never actually *asked* her. He told her it would get better without saying when or how. He talked about their future without defining its vocabulary.

Those were thoughts Dessa tucked away. They could be dealt with later.

Except that later was now.

30

There was a list of questions about her life that Dessa knew people wondered but did not ask. Speculation and curiosity have a way of staining interaction with their subjects, and Dessa felt the unasked questions lurking under even the most polite exchanges.

She saw curiosity in the face of her neighbor Olga as she passed Joe carrying Ollie on the steps to their apartment.

She felt it in eyes of her coworkers when she explained that she had gotten a call from the daycare, and that she needed to go pick Ollie up, because her daughter was sick and there was no one else who could.

She heard the speculation in Heidi's and Laurel's voices at dinner the night before, felt it when they patted her back and told her how great she looked, their voices thready and high with curiosity.

Dessa knew the questions they did not ask, which were:

Why had she shaped a life in which she could barely afford her rent but wore the expensive jewelry gifted to her by the married father of her child?

Why was she waiting out Joe's bad marriage, allowing him to hide Olivia from his wife and family, when she could just as easily have presented her daughter like an ultimatum?

In fact, the biggest question was why was there a child at all when *not* having a child would have been so much better for Dessa in so many ways.

People wanted to know *why*. They wondered.

But Gretchen was the only one who ever actually *asked*. The only person who ever voiced the *why*.

The first time she asked *why* was on the beach after Dessa's canceled appointment, and she continued for years after, gently, until the final time, just minutes before she had died in the earthquake.

The *why* was as implicit as the love behind Gretchen's prodding. A question so clear it might as well have been written on the yellow slip of paper Gretchen had put into Dessa's purse.

Gretchen's first why, the one that she asked on the beach, came after she had listed the casualties of possibility a child would wreak on Dessa's life. Nothing Dessa did not know. It was a simple question then, much simpler than it would become after Joe moved back in with Susan and Ollie was born.

"Why?" Dessa's best friend had asked.

"Because my parents are dead," Dessa had said, which didn't make sense, even to her. But it was the answer and it was the best Dessa could do.

Grief can unspool itself through strange calculations.

Dessa's mother died on the twenty-third of September.

Her period came that same day. It made its debut while she was on the phone with the hospice center asking what she should do now, reeling from the strangeness of the feeling that she had *not* been alone in the house and now she was, her mother gone without using a door. By the funeral two days later it was at its heaviest, messier and more painful than usual. It leaked after the service, causing Dessa to have run to the bathroom without excusing herself.

In the months that followed, Dessa's period, always regular, became a kind of anniversary marker for her mother's death. It would appear and Dessa would think, *It's been three months.*

Five months.

Seven… before going to the restroom to take care of herself. It was a strange correlation and one that she knew would have horrified her proper narcissistic mother, but the association was strong in Dessa's mind.

This was why she knew there were precisely eleven months between the day of her mother's death and the two purple lines that appeared on her pregnancy test.

When someone reminded her that it was August twenty-third she had thought, *Next month I will have been an orphan for a year*, which was followed by the sudden awareness that she hadn't gotten her period. She bought a pregnancy test on the way home from work.

She was unworried. Casual. Even placing a frozen meal in the microwave before heading to the bathroom to take the test. She was on the pill. Just being cautious.

But as Dessa had watched the urine seep its way into the indicator, she thought of the trip she and Joe had taken that month. Waking late. That night in the pool. Her schedule thrown off. The pills she had remembered to take hours later than she usually did.

The first line appeared quickly, wicking its way up from the bottom of the screen to the top. The box had said it could take up to two minutes for results to appear. Her breath shallow, Dessa began counting. She had one hundred and twenty seconds.

It only took eleven before the damp cotton sent a second line up the screen of the test. The line was dark and hard, finely drawn and undeniably *there*. A demarcation between Dessa's before and after.

Somehow the correlation tied itself up in Dessa's mind. The months during which she was related to no one numbering the same as the seconds to learn that that was no longer the case. One purple line defining the end of her mother's life and the other signifying the start of someone else's.

She cried. Somewhere else in her apartment the microwave dinged, alerting her that her dinner was ready.

She called Gretchen and told her about the result but not about the thought she had had when she had seen it, which was that she was finally not alone. Gretchen did not ask any questions then. There was no why, only how and when, and those questions could be easily answered by a call to the clinic to confirm what slots they had open.

Because of course she was getting rid of *it*.

There was no question. Motherhood, yes, someday. But not now, when her relationship with Joe was so new and she was so young and had so much more to do with her life.

Of course not.

Except from the moment she had seen that second line, Dessa had never thought of the small clump of dividing cells within her as an *it*. The *it* was already a *who* in her mind, a relative she had not yet met...a *someone* who was looking forward to their meeting.

When she explained this to Joe, the night of her canceled appointment, in the front seat of his car, he had nodded. He had two sons already. He understood. He kissed her hands.

Pressed his finger into the notch at the base of her neck. Told her he loved her.

But before he had done those things, he had hidden his face. Palms engulfing his eyes and cheeks. A hitch in his breath. Panic or sadness, Dessa didn't know.

"I will not be a trap," she had said to him. "I love you. I am having this baby. But I will not be a trap." These were the words that unpeeled the hands from his face, that caused him to kiss her and touch her and smell her again.

Because Dessa hated anything that made her feel like her mother.

Odessa the elder was a woman who had prided herself doing everything well, but she had died badly.

Not in the sense that her death was painful (it was) but in the performative sense. Dessa's mother chose to die without grace, angrily spitting venom at her daughter and the world.

It is strange to think of dying as a skill, but the fact of it was delivered daily to Dessa while she watched her mother snipe and snap from the rented hospital bed in the living room.

When one of the hospice workers suggested that her mother's mood might be lifted by looking at old pictures, Dessa had tentatively brought the albums up from the basement. Magenta shifted images of her parents in their childhood, glossier prints of her in her own. Halloweens, Christmases, Thanksgivings. Nothing recent, the digital advent marking the death knell of the physical photograph.

Dessa's mother had thumbed through these quietly. Her face sour but her lips closed. Dessa sat next to her, tentative. In so many of the photographs her childish self looked miserable standing next to her perfectly dressed mother. She remembered being coerced into many of the outfits. Itchy tights and collars, appearance always valued over comfort.

Her mother stopped at a photo. It was of their engagement. Dad holding Mom in a hug, his face buried in her hair. Mother holding the ring out to the camera, her face smug and happy.

"You're in that photo too, you know."

Her mother was smiling when she said this, but there was no kindness in her smile. She tapped the waistband of her younger self's jeans. Her eyes trained on her daughter.

"He was thinking about leaving. I changed his mind." Her mother said this with a shrug, as if it did not matter, but Dessa knew she was boasting. Relishing finally sharing this piece of personal trivia with her daughter, her cleverness in manipulating the man who would become her husband.

But there was something more to it. It was her mother trying to stain the love Dessa still had for him. To muddy her memories of her father, cast each one in a darker light as someone who resented her existence. Whose life would have had a very different shape without it.

Her mother wanted horror. Her mother wanted shock. She wanted questions and statements and drama casting her father as a villain. She wanted tears while Dessa reeled, doing math in her head while she refigured all the stories she had been told about being a honeymoon conception and early birth. Figuring out that she hadn't been the product of love but a tool which had been used to *win*.

So Dessa chose to give her none of it. She made her face blank. She walked away.

Her mother threw the album after her. Its brittle pages breaking as it hit the floor, cellophane ripping, dropping the pictures onto the carpet. Shattered images of the foundations of Dessa's life. Her mother shrieked, "Ungrateful bitch! He begged me to abort you! He cried—"

Dessa didn't hear the rest behind the slamming back door. She sat down on the steps. Autumn was beginning to paint the tips of the elms in the grove where her father had killed himself, cold dipped red on their tops. Dessa let her eyes wander over the ground beneath the trees. Wondering. No one had told her exactly where they had found his body, so she imagined it crumpled beneath each of the trees, different poses. The hunch of her father's back by the fallen tree. The neatly tucked waistband of his jeans peeking up behind a bush.

He had killed himself in June, so the picture she was drawing was all wrong. The leaves should be green, the undergrowth more lush.

But still she persisted in imagining it, while her mother's muffled yelling continued inside.

"It's okay," her father had said that last summer when she told him she didn't think they should go back to the swimming pool. "You'd be surprised at what you can learn to live with when you have to." He had taken her hand after that. Kissed her forehead.

Dessa's awareness of herself split into layers. The overlay that brought her to this moment. The illuminated anatomy of a woman.

The skin: Joe and Susan and their polite offers of ice tea. Their boys, barely looking up from the video game they played to acknowledge that they had been introduced. Dessa's nods. Beegie's strange blank face as she tried to make sense of what was happening. The hot potato way Joe had touched her back when he led her outside, insisted they should sit in the sunshine to chat.

Beneath that the flayed muscles: The slow twitch decisions that had led her to Joe, to this ridiculous farce where she takes the ice tea so that this perfectly sane-looking woman does not suspect that her husband has had a child with the woman in front of her.

And then the organs: Her mother the spleen. Her father the heart. Her best friend the stomach. Her body animated by the invisible functions of dead people and her memories of them.

And then finally, the circulatory and the nervous systems... lacy tracings just hinting at the shape of Dessa. Here was Olivia. Coursing through her. Oxygenating every decision since her conception, feeding the organs, the skin, the muscles.

Beneath it all was Olivia.

31

The boys were playing a video game. Beegie couldn't see them through the window of the back patio, buried as they were in the fluffy couches opposite the television, but she *could* make out the screen they stared at, candy bright and glossy even through the double panes. A yellow car sped through a city awkwardly, stopping and starting, mowing through pedestrians that did not get out of its way.

"I hope apple juice is okay." The blonde woman set a glass in front of her, "It's organic."

Beegie took a sip. Winced at the sour sweetness of the liquid. She nodded thanks, afraid to say anything else before she figured out what the hell was going on.

What were they doing here?

Next to her Dessa was also staring at the game through the

window, but Beegie was sure she wasn't really seeing it. She had that closed-shut look again. Her mind a million miles away.

But the problem was that right next to her sat Joe, the guy from the picture with Olivia, only he was calling Dessa *Gretchen* and this blonde woman was calling him *honey,* and the baby was very obviously not here.

Which was why Beegie couldn't figure out why they still *were.* Shouldn't Dessa have told him to fuck off when she saw he didn't have Ollie, and shouldn't they be moving right now, getting the hell out of this place? Instead they were sitting down in something that looked like one of the catalogs Barb got. Not a back porch but an *outdoor room.* All fancy with cushions on the furniture and curtains even though it was outside and a bougie lighting thing hanging down from the awning, which was something Beegie didn't even know people did.

That must be how you know you're rich, when your house is so big you even got a chandelier in your backyard.

And Joe and the blonde lady, Susan, were acting like they were just pleased as punch to have some *unexpected visitors.* That's what the blonde lady had called them as she introduced them to their sons. "Boys, we have some unexpected visitors! Say hi!" And the boys, who looked about six and eight, had just lifted their hands without looking away from the television. Both muttered lame *hellos* without seeing the people they were supposed to be greeting. Their mother had just shrugged and gestured for them to go outside.

Dessa hadn't said much since the blonde woman had appeared behind Joe. Some yeses, some noes, but all of it sounding like she was pulling her words up from inside a deep well, each one coming a long distance before it made its way out of her mouth.

Susan set a tray with a pitcher of ice tea on the table. "I didn't know if you take sugar or Splenda, so I brought both," she said as she sat next to Joe. Under the glass of the table, Beegie saw Susan take Joe's hand on his thigh.

Dessa blinked hard, but her gaze didn't move from the window, the moving car and running pedestrians.

A moment of quiet settled over the table, like the ash that sometimes rained down after a wildfire. The discomfort of the situation falling on the tops of their heads and shoulders, coating it in a gray snow. Joe and Susan both looking at Dessa and her detached, blank expression, their minds busy searching for the right thing to say.

"How do you know Gretchen?"

Beegie startled, realizing Susan was talking to her. About Dessa.

"We met last night," said Beegie, and their faces fell with an "Oh." She wondered if they'd been hoping for some heartwarming Big Sister/Little Sister backstory. Like one of those shitty "white lady teaches urban kids Shakespeare/math/music" movies Hollywood used to make back when everyone used to pretend that shit like that was okay. Beegie never watched those but she knew what they were about. The story never ended the way it did in real life, which was that in the end little Ms. Shakespeare left the school because she didn't feel *safe* and the kids dropped out or died or had their own babies and never thought about Shakespeare or math or music again.

"Can I use your bathroom?" Beegie stood up, her chair making a scar across the silence.

"I'll show you. The downstairs is being renovated, so you'll have to use the one on the second floor." Susan stood, wringing her hands. Beegie followed her inside.

One of the characters in the boys' video game opened a driver's side door and dragged a caramel-colored woman out by her hair. The sound effects on the game were weird. There was the sound of the car door opening, the man's hollow footsteps…but the woman didn't make a noise when he threw her on the pavement. Not even to curse him.

Beegie thought of the first time she saw Dessa, being dragged behind that broken house. She had not been quiet.

But Beegie knew that violence could be quiet. It could just sound like footsteps and closing doors and squeaking tables.

Susan led her to "the boys' bathroom" apologizing for the mess, dropping the lifted toilet seat and hanging a towel before closing the door behind her.

Beegie didn't really have to go. She just didn't want to be in the middle of three adults all pretending like shit was okay when it was very much not okay. Dessa acting like a bead on a string the minute she saw Mr. Fancy, like she had no choice but to go along with what he wanted.

She pulled her pants down 'cause it felt weird to sit on the toilet with them on. There were plastic boats in the tub. A froggy washcloth puppet laid on the faucet.

Funny to think that the two kids playing *GTA* still used bathtub toys but here was the evidence.

Little assholes, thought Beegie. *Lucky assholes*, she corrected, because they were. To live in this house with a mom who let them play video games, bringing them organic apple juice and cookies.

Why wasn't *this* place crushed in the earthquake? Why the fuck didn't Capricious Nature sit on these lucky motherfuckers instead of all the crushed buildings she had walked past. There wasn't anything more special about them that meant they should get to play video games on a couch in a mansion while she…

A trickle of urine escaped her, burning a messy trail into the bowl.

Beegie inhaled from the pain and patted herself dry… gently…gently.

She pulled her pants back on. Flushed. Washed her hands in soap that smelled like sweet almonds.

She saw Susan the moment she opened the door. The blonde woman stood by the window in the room opposite the bathroom. Instinctively Beegie recoiled, sure the woman had stayed upstairs to make sure Beegie wouldn't steal anything.

But Susan didn't turn to look at her. She kept her back turned from the hall, staring out the window at the backyard.

She glanced at Beegie as she came up behind her, but said nothing, her attention turned back to Dessa and Joe at the table below.

Dessa's lost look was gone. She and Joe were talking to each other, intent, their voices low. The muscles of Joe's jaw tight, like he was chewing each word he said.

Dessa began shaking her head, her eyes large, pleading. One of her hands began to rise from the table, her volume rising with it. Beegie heard shards of her dialogue. Words pointed enough to make their way through the glass. *Family. You. We. Family.*

Joe laid his hand over Dessa's, pushing it back to the table, like a volume knob. Bringing her down. He was speaking again, too quiet for them to hear.

"I know her name isn't Gretchen."

Beegie looked at Susan. The blonde woman's voice had sounded so different without its forced brightness. Ink-dipped shadow, cold as January.

"Then why did you pretend it was?"

"I don't know."

And then below them Dessa was standing. Rocketing up from her chair, her arms held out in front of her. "You shouldn't have cared! You shouldn't have cared about them knowing! Nothing should have stopped you from getting to her!"

Dessa turned, yanking the door to the house open. Joe called after her—her real name—as she ran inside.

Susan moved to the stairs, Beegie running after, almost falling as she made her way down. Both of them pushing to meet Dessa and Joe before they got out of the house.

Their father chasing a woman through their house had finally broken the spell of the video game. The boys were perked up and turned. Tracking the real-life drama behind them.

"You know the worst thing you did?" Dessa was livid, moving, chewing up the space between the kitchen and the door, "You wasted my time. I came here, when every second I spent with you, I could have been getting closer to my daughter."

Her motion slowed, briefly when she finally caught sight of Susan and Beegie on the stairs. Joe stopped short, mouth open as he searched for words to explain this to his wife.

But Dessa kept moving. Her shoes squeaking against Joe and Susan's perfectly clean floor, marring their perfectly clean life. The train was leaving.

Beegie ran after her, the sunlight slamming into her eyes after the tasteful dim of the house. Dessa was halfway to the gate already, as if she planned to run all the way to Van Nuys from here. Burning humiliation and anger as fuel.

"Dessa," Susan called from the steps. The door open behind her.

Dessa stopped. Turned to meet the eyes of Joe's wife. The sound of that particular voice saying her name seemed to have knocked through her rage.

"Is she okay?" Susan said.

Dessa huffed. "I don't know."

"What's her name?"

"Olivia."

"There…there were pictures on his phone. He thought he'd deleted them…"

Beegie stood between the two women, a rock in the river of their pained silence.

"She's beautiful," Susan said.

Dessa's head nodded, a minor motion, but an agreement. Yes, her daughter was beautiful. Even her daughter's father's wife agreed.

A wind set the leaves above them clattering against each other. Beegie shifted, unsure. She had never noticed before how loud that sound was, like applause. A roaring crowd.

"Susan, I need to go." Dessa put her hand on the porch gate.

"Yes. Of course." Susan's tone trying to restore civility, like Dessa simply had an appointment she had to get to. "Let us know how she is…when you find her."

Dessa closed her eyes. Her fingers ironing out the wrinkle between her brows. "Why would you care?"

The older woman's hands flew up to her chest. Little birds flattened against the wall of her heart. "I'm not stupid…but I'm not… I'm not what you think."

Through the door behind Susan, both Beegie and Dessa could see Joe, his body indistinct, shadowy in the murk of the house. He was listening. Afraid to join the women in the full light.

"I don't know what I think anymore," said Dessa and she unlatched the gate, the bottom catching on the sod and pulling a brown divot into the green carpet.

On the steps Susan's face was dark lined, gray. Inside, Joe shrank back into the dim.

"Thank you for the apple juice," said Beegie, and she waved as she moved to join her friend.

32

They got back on the highway. The 101. Straight shot. A needle piercing the heart of The Valley.

The experience in Joe's house had made debris of Dessa's mind. If asked, she would have said she was thinking of nothing, but the truth was stranger. It was as if she was thinking of everything. Her thoughts like objects, detritus bubbling on a current, swinging in and then out of reach. Thoughts interrupting each other.

Olivia's small hunched back, reflected in the mirror of their bathroom. Beegie lifting a chunk of concrete over a man's head. Her father's swim shorts soaked in urine. Gretchen's flowery smoke smell.

Susan's face telling her that she *knew*. About her and Ollie and Joe and his secret life and all the things he had said that had been lies to hold Dessa off, or if not lies, then shifty ways around the truth. Of course she knew. Of course it had all been for nothing.

Fucking lawyers, Gretchen said in her mind. Whiskey perfume by her ear.

Had any of it been true? Susan's instability? Her threats? His worries? Or had it all been just bet hedging on his part? *Do your best not to anger the pregnant mistress, buy time to figure things out.*

At the word *mistress,* an image of a woman in dominatrix gear. Fishnets and leather whip.

She had not been a mistress until Joe made her one.

She had thought he loved her. He had said he did. She had believed him.

And his love for Olivia, she did not doubt… She had seen his face when he looked at the person they had made together. Candle bright smile, catching their daughter in the air and throwing her up again, while Dessa shushed him so that Olivia's laughter wouldn't wake her sleeping neighbors.

This was the child he had chosen not to go to.

It did not figure. Love could only be measured in terms of actions. Joe loved Olivia, but not enough to risk being caught by his wife. Joe loved Dessa too, but Susan also, and neither did he love enough to give up the other one.

And neither of them had asked him to.

Joe loved her, but not enough.

Her mother swam by in the whirling swirling mess of her mind. Her hand decked in the rings her father had given her, tucking in Dessa's bra strap, correcting Dessa's posture. The nasty refrain she had shouted at her daughter in the days before she died. *He asked me to abort you.*

A final volley against the fact that she knew Dessa loved her father more than she loved her mother…she loved her mom, but not enough, as it turned out.

Above them, the hovering green sign. Listing the exits and exchanges. The One Oh One. Never before had Dessa noticed that the numbers of this particular highway looked like a person in distress. Arms raised above the oblong face of the zero. 101. The character emoji of panic, of reaching out for help.

Next to her the girl said nothing. Made soft breathing sounds, exertion as she tried to keep up. Sweat glittered her face. Catching on the edges of her forehead. The sun high and hot now.

Hard to believe she was the same person Dessa had seen laid on the table.

Though in truth, Dessa didn't feel like *she* was now the same person she had been last night. The shivering shifting mass she had been inside the clothing rack seemed ancient. As if the hours intervening had shifted her molecules, reconstructing her DNA until she was now this new thing, and Beegie this new thing. Both of them baptized by the night before.

The Joe she knew last night was not the Joe she knew now. The Girl she had *not* helped was now Beegie, angry and funny and kind, someone more than just a victim on a table.

Dessa thought she should try to explain what Beegie had witnessed in the house. But the words couldn't fix…couldn't stick in her mind long enough for Dessa to form them. She couldn't tell Beegie about Joe unless she told her about her mother, which she couldn't do unless she told her about her father. There didn't seem to be a start to the story she would need to tell her, and if Olivia wasn't alive none of it really mattered anyway…

Dessa choked, her body finding a sound for *that* thought. The dead daughter sound.

"Dessa?"

"OK," she said to Beegie. Not the word, but the letters.

A memorial was collected on the side of the road, propped

up against the barrier. Sunbaked saints' candles, flowers, pink teddy bears. White painted crosses hung with plastic flowers. All the offerings fresh enough to know the loss was new, grief still crisp enough to drive loved ones to park their cars and walk the edge of the highway to leave their gifts.

In her old life, as her old self, Dessa used to pass these memorials and wonder at the foolhardiness of the people leaving them. Why leave flowers and comfort objects for the dead in the places where they died? Weren't there more sensible locations, graves presumably, where those objects would be better laid?

But she understood it now.

The impulse to mark the spot. To broadcast it.

Here our lives ended.

Both for the grievers and the grieved.

"Who cleans this shit up?" Beegie waved a hand at the collection, drawing Dessa back. "I mean, they don't let this stuff stay out here forever. Who decides it's been long enough? Who says when this stuff goes from being special to being trash?"

Dessa shrugged. She was imagining herself and Beegie leaving memorials for their old selves across the map of the city. Carnations and dollar store candles marking their trail like bread crumbs.

"Does Ollie like ducks?" Beegie looked at her.

"I don't know."

"'Cause there's a panda too…"

The girl leaned down to pick up both, sending a pile of grocery store bouquets to tumble from their perches.

She considered the animals. Bean bag corpses flaccid in her hands.

"I like the duck," she said, and tossed the panda back. She whipped the bird against her thigh, clearing the road dust from its body. Its yellow wings threaded through a tiny pink T-shirt with heart-shaped balloons on it.

"Olivia will love it," Dessa said. She would. Would have. Who knew.

They kept walking.

Once, she might have protested picking up an offering to a dead child to give to her own, but now… Beegie's gesture seemed hopeful in a way she knew was an effort for the girl. It had cost her something.

The voice mail on her phone chimed.

They stopped.

"It didn't even ring," Beegie said as Dessa hit Play Message.

A rustling crackled over the speaker. The sound of a receiver in a pocket. An accidental call.

In the muffled background, a little voice. Olivia.

She was singing. "Twinkle, twinkle," her voice a teddy bear lilt.

"Howiwonderwhatchuare…"

Dessa grinned. She always got hung up on that part. Hailey's voice joined, a thin wavery sliver, helping her along, *"Up above the world so high."*

Here came Ollie's favorite part, *"Like a diamond ring in the sky."*

Dessa suddenly felt the presence of the rock on her hand. Thinking of the way Ollie would roll it around her finger while she sang the song. Twisting. Twisting.

"Twinkle, twinkle, little star." Hailey's and Ollie's voices both on this lyric. The singing was smart. Keeping her daughter calm.

Then Hailey yelped and their singing cut off abruptly. A metal crash echoed hollow, a pipe banging. Ollie began to cry, her voice high and tiny over a growing rumble.

There was a moaning sound. Marine almost, dying whale.

Something crashed and Dessa shrieked in time with her daughter and her caretaker, even though she was safe in the daylight on solid ground and they were trapped somewhere dark and moving. Their voices picked up with the other sounds. Wrenching, breaking impacts.

With each crash Dessa's body shuddered, hope fleeing.

Beep. Beep. The message ended.

And then the phone died. A spiraling circle hovering in the darkness before even that disappeared.

Beegie looked up at her. Eyes wide. "She was *alive*."

"She was so afraid." Dessa felt sure her knees were going to give out.

"At the end…" Beegie moved her head under Dessa's so she could meet her face. "Dessa, look at me. At the end, she was crying. She was *alive*."

The message had been left during the aftershock. Old news. If her daughter had died, she had died hours ago…and Dessa had just been pushing forward without knowing. It was an artificial motion, life support forcing oxygen into dead lungs, the motion of her limbs the facsimile of life, because if her daughter was dead then so was she.

She felt the rough tips of Beegie's fingers skim the meat of her palm. Weaving between her own. Beegie's hand was small, like the rest of her, but also like the rest of her, it was strong.

"Come on," the girl said, and used her grip to pull Dessa forward. She staggered into the rhythm of Beegie's steps, expecting her to let go. But she did not. Even when the sweat grew clammy between the mountain range of their fingers, they held fast.

Though she could not see it, by their shadow Dessa could tell that Beegie still held the duck in her hand. It made a strange shape, bouncing against the younger woman's truncated form on the road. Like a butterfly swooping out then in, a lost creature looking for purchase on Beegie's jeans.

Their shadows grew darker and shorter. The sun was condensing them into more concentrated versions of themselves. This distilled simulacra painted the path toward Olivia on the highway, growing shorter with every step.

"Dessa?" Beegie's voice was strained.

She looked up from the foreshortened stumps she had watched grow beneath her.

There was a man.

He paced through the heat-soaked shimmer of the road. Back and forth across all four lanes, his arms swinging wild. Despite the temperature he wore a coat, long and thin. It swung out behind him, exaggerating his movements, punctuating them. It fluttered like an enormous pair of wings.

A splinter of his voice reached them. A raving tone. His face was directed upward as were his invocations. He was mad... in all senses. Insanity and raging anger slithered through his movements.

Dessa imagined his coat suddenly unfurling behind him... spreading out into a pair of dark feathered wings pinioned to his shoulder blades. A sword in his hand, ready to batter against the doors of Heaven.

"What do you want to do?" Beegie was looking back. The exit they had passed miles behind. The one ahead lay behind the raging angel.

Dessa shrugged.

There would be an encounter here. Whether they wanted it or not. She thought of turning back and knew that the angel would follow them, like the man had last night, angered that she had crossed the street to avoid his attention.

In fact, the more she thought about it, she knew there was no avoiding him. Since the earth broke, every time she had sought safety, quiet dark places, she had been forced into the presence of animals, both human and not. She couldn't retreat to the safe corners of her mind, where she calmly discussed mental health public policy with her coworkers over coffee. She could not make her way past this disturbed man with pleasant aphorisms about how she voted for reforms, donated when she could, understood his plight. Right now, he was *her* plight...or at the very least a part of it.

The man stopped abruptly, the wings of his coat folding in on themselves. He had seen them and seeing them had caused him to collect in on himself. To draw his energy in and focus, his hands clasped in front of him.

At the ready.

33

At least this motherfucker did not walk toward them.

That's what Beegie'd thought he'd do when he saw them. Turn and start shouting his shit at them, dragging and waving his hands while he changed his direction so that he could have someone other than God to listen to him.

Instead he waited for them, his mouth tucked up under his nose in that way people smile when they've done something that makes them feel better or smarter than other people. Smug.

That's what he was. Smug ass spider in his web. And she and Dessa were little bugs that didn't have any choice but to pass within his reach.

Fuck him.

"Do you wanna turn back?"

Dessa shook her head. "He'll just follow us... You know he will."

Beegie looked at him. Eyes glittery. He would. He wouldn't want to let them go without at least having a shot at having his say…'cause he had that look.

Beegie nodded and they started walking again. Dessa surprised her by not even trying to steer them away from the man. There was no slipping to the side, like an apology, *excuse us, we didn't mean to interrupt you.* Instead they walked straight toward him. Not like they knew him but like they were just going to pass him in a crowded hallway. Like he was *not* a raving lunatic and this was *not* an empty highway and this was something they did every day.

The man was younger than Beegie had thought. From a distance she had thought crazy, old, homeless…but up close now she was surprised to find that the man was good-looking… he had a face that could have been in a magazine, if not for the wildness of his eyes. Angular jaw, even features. Even his skin, deeply tan and dirty made his eyes bluer, his teeth whiter.

In fact, trapped in a photograph, Beegie thought there would probably have been something magnetic about his wildness. You could admire the lion, when it was behind the glass. But when it was not…when you were within reach of its claws…beauty seemed just like another trap. Another lure.

He said something as they approached. Grinning. Like a greeting, but not. Beegie wondered if he was speaking another language. Another way of saying hello. "Leahanzilpha! Leahanzilpha! Ha, ha!" he clapped his hands as if he had just completed a difficult puzzle, bouncing on his heels.

"I doubted! I doubted, but you came! You came! I was not sure that this was the place but since you have come here, it is! Leahanzilpha, here in the flesh!"

"What is he saying?" Beegie asked, but it was like Dessa couldn't hear her. She just kept walking toward him. Her eyes down.

"The earth cracked like an egg. We are the yolk, spilling

out. Some of us don't know that we have lost our form yet, that the container that holds us has lost its shape, but I do. I know. I've known for a while. I heard the horns when the earth opened. The yawning voice, guttural and strange, and it said to come here and wait and that you would come."

His words made Beegie imagine them all on the porcelain shell of an egg. Burst sac inside, leaking from spider-leg cracks, before the thumb of God pushed its way inside and pulled the whole thing apart.

The man was insane. Tall. Skinny *skinny*. Pants hanging strange on his hips. Coat sloping from his shoulders. He was scrawny but he filled the road with his energy. His madness amplified across the lanes, a web extending out from himself.

Dessa's hand tightened its grip on hers, so hard that her wrist began to shake.

He moved. An almost leap toward them. Grinning bright. Their bodies flinched away, both gasping like he was about to hit them.

Instead he just kept talking. "Leah, raise your eyes to mine." He kept pace about three feet from them. A radius of green stink emanating from him. "You don't need to be afraid. But you need to stop. This is where your sister is coming. And her handmaid. They should be here soon. Leah?"

"Leave us the fuck alone," Beegie said it as calmly as she could.

"Zilpah, that is low language. That kind of language is unacceptable."

"I don't care what kind of language is acceptable to you because right now you're scaring the shit out of us and you need to back…the fuck…off."

The man's eyes seemed to clear for a minute. The deep set smile falling into a look of worry. "Oh dear. I am sorry. I did not mean to frighten you or your mistress. That was the furthest from my intentions."

Beegie exhaled. *This motherfucker.*

Next to her Dessa nodded. Still not meeting his eyes. "Okay...okay. Thank you."

"Leah, do you forgive me? Leah? Leah?"

"Her name isn't Leah." The man looked at Beegie when she said this. Condescending. Like you did when you were indulging little kids.

"Leah?" he said again.

Dessa sighed. "Yeah. Sure. You're forgiven."

He grinned at Beegie. "You should tell your girl not to use foul language."

"Her girl?" There was something happening here. In the way he was speaking. What the fuck was a handmaid? She didn't belong to Dessa. She didn't belong to anyone.

But before she could say this, Dessa was speaking, "I'll do what I can, though I doubt I could do anything about it. If you don't mind, we have somewhere we need to be."

"Yes. Right. Soon. But now you need to be here."

Beegie was getting sick of this. "Jesus, just leave us alone."

"You have to stop, Leah. If you keep going, we won't be here when they get here?"

"We're not stopping."

"I order you to stop." He reached down to grab Dessa's hand. Beegie slapped it away, her skin prickling with rage.

"Don't you fucking touch her! Don't fucking touch her!" The man backed off. His hands up. Beegie's skin was alight. Anger bursting from her pores. Snaking its way out of her. "Don't fucking touch anyone! We are not who you think we are! We are not characters in whatever story you are telling yourself in your fucked-up head! I am a person! I am a person!"

There it was. The phrase that had been swimming under

the surface of her thoughts. *I am a person.* She didn't even know what she meant by saying it. *I am a person.* It was a stupid thing to say. A strange demand. But it felt as necessary as breathing. *I am a person.*

Beegie was stepping toward the man as he backed away. She was so angry. Dessa's fingers tightened around her own. Holding her back.

"I am so tired of this shit. Leave us alone! We are people, not things!"

She threw the duckie at him. It bounced off his chest, an ineffective missile, and fell flat to the ground.

The man held his hands up. Elbows bent. "Okay. Okay."

Beegie glared at him. His face innocent now. Like this had all been a game he had been playing and it was Beegie who decided to change the rules. *Fuck him.*

"Let's go," Dessa whispered in her ear. Beegie felt her hand wrap around her shoulder. Turning her away from the man. Drawing them forward.

"I am a person," she said to the woman. Her anger curling out in smaller waves. The tide receding but still breaking on the shore.

"Yes, Beegie."

They heard a flapping sound before the impact. Like a wing, the hem of his coat beating at the air as he drove his body toward them. Shoulder slamming the small curve of Beegie's upper spine, hip and elbow driving into Dessa's arm and waist. They fell forward all three of them, bodies splayed. Beegie's hand peeled out on the surface of the road, gravel biting into the flesh, just short of driving her head into the pavement.

He was twisting himself between them. Pushing against her with his legs. His hands busy grabbing at Dessa's limbs. All the while he spoke. "I heard the horns. I heard them. You doubt. I heard."

Dessa tried to stand, gaining one foot. He reached for her and she twisted, hitting back at him, trying to free herself. Her fist skidded off his cheek, leaving a bloody gash in the wake of her ring. He cried out, stung.

"I am trying to help you!"

He tackled Dessa to the ground. "It is a kindness I do!" he said pushing down on her. She screamed, trying to bring her hands up from beneath him. Scratching at his eyes.

Beegie moved away from their writhing mass of limbs. Scooting on her ass. He seemed to have forgotten she was even there. Underneath the madman Dessa was barely making a noise. Breath heavy. Her fingers scrabbling at his eyes. Pushing at him.

From where she sat, Beegie watched them. Disconnected. Watched while Dessa wiggled under the man's body. It was like a television show. Distant. Like this was something that had happened before and was only now playing back for her. But the details were wrong somehow.

Beegie watched as Dessa twisted underneath him, crawling away. Her palms grinding under the pressure of his body.

Then she saw it.

At his waistband sat a distinct oval. Wrapped in fraying tape. A gun.

Bang she would shoot the Busman. Bang Not-Charlie. Bang Eric.

The very thing she had been seeking had found them. Only feet away from Beegie's hands was the power to never have anyone touch her ever again.

No. To never touch *them* ever again.

Anger poured into Beegie. *Better to be angry than in pain.* The flashlight had tumbled from Dessa's bag onto the pavement. Beegie picked it up, its metal cold against the skin of her palm.

Dessa had turned toward the man and was on her knees. Something had changed. Dessa was no longer trying to get away, but was instead now trying to get the gun from him. Both she and the man were on their knees. Both of them reaching for the object in his waistband. Plucking at each other's hands. Dessa snatching at the man's waist. The man pulling at her elbows. They were both yelling.

Beegie stood. *Everything would be okay. She could fix it. The gun would fix it so no one ever hurt them again.*

Dessa screamed. The man had wrested the weapon from her grip. Dessa clawed at his wrist, trying to pin it to ground. Her body flattened to the pavement.

They were not even looking at her.

Beegie straddled Dessa's writhing legs. The man's head hovered below her, bobbing with effort as he tried to keep the gun from her companion.

Then, he looked up. His eyes widened.

Beegie drove the flashlight downward. *Once. Twice.*

His hands flailed out, arms swinging upward around Beegie's body, like he was going to pull her into a hug.

Then he fell back. Unconscious. A fresh dent in his forehead.

Beegie reached down, plucking the gun from his open palm. Her heart flared at the touch. *Finally. The thing that guaranteed freedom from harm, cool in her hand. lighter than she imagined.*

Her leg stung.

Her shoulder too.

And then Beegie heard them. Or truly, she *registered having heard them.* An auditory loop playing back an essential piece of information.

There had been two *pops*. Small ones, like the crack of a vending machine bag of chips.

Pop. Pop. The sound played again in Beegie's head. *Pop. Pop.*

Dessa turned to look at her. Blood welled up from the hole in Beegie's jeans.

"I got it," she told Dessa before she dropped the gun and fell to the ground.

34

Dessa had felt the gun before she had seen it. When the man had fallen on her, pressing her down. It pushed against her leg from the waistband of his jeans. A foreign protrusion. She was repulsed at first, thinking it was an erection but then a deeper horror dawned as its true dimensions revealed themselves. A metallic scrape against her thigh. The edges of its handle against her skin.

She had not thought. There was no time for it. She had simply twisted and turned and suddenly she was snatching at his waistband. And he was snatching at her and his gun and she was only thinking, "No." Again and again. *"No. No. No."*

Beegie had been looking for a gun the second time they met and here it was, tucked into a different man's jeans. And here was Dessa again on the ground. And here was Beegie again to the rescue.

It had not turned out so well for them this time.

Dessa tore the Laker's sweatshirt into pieces to make tourniquets. "I'm sorry," she said as she pulled the collar from the sleeves.

"It wasn't my favorite," said the girl where she lay. Her jeans were soaked, a dark red tinge to the black denim. She winced as Dessa wrapped the strips around her thigh.

"I don't know how well this is going to work. It's been a really long time since..." She trailed off. She couldn't rightly say it had been a really long time since she had done this, since it was something she had never done. Only something that she had seen diagrammed out in her father's woodcraft books. Pencil sketched Boy Scouts lying prone on a page of instructions, their faces placid, their bandages clean.

This could not be a more different picture. Dessa's hands caked in dried and drying blood. Beegie shivering with panic and fear, but trying to smile through it.

Dessa threaded a pen through the makeshift bandage and twisted it, tightening it harder than she ever could have by hand. Beegie cried out, but Dessa continued until it felt like she shouldn't.

She could only hope this would help. Or at the very least not hurt.

"Beegie, do you think you can stand up...it will only be for a second."

The girl nodded and weakly pulled herself onto her elbows. Dessa circled her arms around Beegie and helped her to standing. She gasped as Dessa moved herself under her arms, lifting the bandaged wound on her shoulder.

Dessa lifted her. Legs around her waist. Arms over her shoulders. The press of Beegie's small torso against her back.

"Hold on with your legs, sweetie," Dessa said, and remembered that she had said the same thing to her daughter the night before. "Hold on with your legs." While they were playing before she left. Olivia's much smaller body clinging to the same ridiculous dress, lit up now like a disco ball in the unrelenting sun. How strange that she could say the same thing, mean the same thing and yet have the circumstances be so terribly different.

Beegie shivered against her back. Dessa tried not to feel the damp squish of the girl's bandages under the hook of her arms, but it was impossible to ignore the fresh trails of blood it was painting on her skin.

Beegie mumbled something. Her head lifting from the base of Dessa's neck. "We're going the wrong way," she said.

"We'll be there soon," Dessa responded, and with a little pant she hitched the girl up farther.

"Olivia," Beegie said, her breath moving the hair by Dessa's ear.

"I know," said Dessa and she kept moving.

Beegie was light as a child on her back.

Beegie *was* a child on her back.

Dessa bore as much responsibility for this little girl as she did for her own. She had dragged her through this God-forgotten city and it had led her here, carried on the back of a stranger. Holes in her flesh and her soul.

Dessa thought of Gretchen the night they talked about earthquakes. Her best friend's voice whiskey alto in the dark. Cigarette glow underneath. *The real disaster is what happens after.*

This was the disaster.

The disaster was knowing what you are capable of surviving. Knowing what you are capable of doing *to* survive. The voices in the dark you chose to ignore, the ones you do not.

Disaster was the end of wondering *how* you would act and the sudden knowledge of how you did. It was the death of speculation.

She was a woman who did not intervene when she saw another woman raped. She was a woman who was afraid and weak and stupid. She had not pulled the trigger, but she had put Beegie in the circumstances in which she got shot.

Her mind replayed the image of Beegie as she realized what had happened to her. Eyes innocent wide, before the pain brought her down.

The image swept the detritus of Dessa's traumas into their individual boxes. Shutting the doors on her self-pitying swim through her own losses. Even the sound of Olivia's voice, the bang and the scream on the last voice mail. She closed it and pretended that the closure was not her giving up, not her losing faith, but instead it was simply putting it away to deal with at a later more convenient time.

Passing the highway memorial… Passing the exit for Joe's house… Her arms ached but Dessa welcomed the hurt. Better than the shuttering she felt inside herself. Hope was a limp, sun-deprived thing, pale green, flaccid and hungry.

Beegie's legs began to slip as Dessa made her way to the exit. She leaned forward, making a table of her back. The girl hung heavy against her, arms flopping forward. For a brief moment Dessa worried the girl had died, her limbs so loose… but then she felt the compression of Beegie's breath against her back. She was asleep. Her breaths deep and regular. Strong, even…though Dessa felt that to think that word was to invite further tragedy.

The crowd at the hospital had grown since they had passed it that morning.

Or possibly not. It was possible, Dessa supposed, that the crowd was the same size but that it had been pushed back by the arrival of the police. That it now occupied a greater space because the circumference of the hospital was now ringed with police cruisers. Lights on but sirens quiet.

Wooden barriers were also up. Men and women in tactical gear eyed the crowd from behind them, milling together in small groups. Shields up. Helmets.

The police presence made the gathering look like a protest, rabble when in truth it was just people looking for medical care…although the sheer press of them, their confusion from being kept back was setting them to rumble.

"Stay back," a disembodied voice cracked over the mumbling of the crowd. "If you are not in need of immediate services, return to your homes."

Dessa heard voices chattering in response to this as she made her way toward the barriers. "How long do they think I can live without insulin?"

"I make my living with my face! This *is* a fucking emergency."

"Honey, see! They are not going to consider a panic disorder an emergency?" Their necks angled, hands empty, faces wanting.

Dessa made her way past the outside of the crowd without drawing their attention. She thought of using her voice…but it did not seem possible. To say "excuse me" was beyond her capacity. She did not have a voice anymore. If she moved her mouth nothing would come out, just pain on air.

But strangely, after the first few feet of the thickening crowd, people began to clear out of her way. Dessa did not see their faces but she saw their hands and feet as she moved past them. Their arms jerking as Beegie's body brushed up against them, the feet stepping away. If they had been saying something as Dessa moved past them, their voices stopped midsentence, midword, midsyllable.

The quiet forced a path through the crowd. People taking in Beegie and Dessa like some blood-soaked eight-limbed beast. A horrific curiosity.

A few footsteps shuffled toward instead of away. A pair of large blue Converse shuffling into view. "Can I..." A man's voice. "I can carry...if you..."

It took Dessa a moment to realize. It was an offer of help. She shook her head.

"Me," she managed. That was all. Her voice a croak. "Me."

There was a moment of quiet while the owner of the voice took in that she would not be relinquishing the weight of the girl. Then he shouted.

"Everybody clear the way! She needs to get through! Clear the way!"

The Converse shoes stepped in front of her. Shouting. "Let them through."

And they did. Stepping out of their way, silently watching them. There but for the grace of God...

Dessa reached the barriers. Police Line. Do Not Cross. The man with the Converse shoes called to the police. Dessa could see the shadows of his arms flailing, trying to gain their attention. Pointing down at them. Here. Here.

Dessa lifted her eyes as the police officer approached, but just to his tactical belt. Holsters for violence or the prevention thereof. Gun. Club. Mace. Knife. And various other mystery pouches.

"They need to get through." Converse again. Making their case.

Dessa tightened her grip on Beegie's leg and fought against the gravity of her body just enough to look up—

Into her own reflection.

There she was. In the policeman's dark glasses. Twin versions of herself staring back at her. Gray face. Sunken eyes. There was a smear of blood on her forehead. Beegie's blood... the top of whose head Dessa could also see...tucked up against the broken brown wall of Dessa's hair.

The cop didn't say anything, just lifted the barrier and moved it to the side. Dessa dropped her head back down. Thankful to be rid of the sight of herself.

35

Beegie dreamed of black.

This was not an absence of dreams but a dream of darkness. Of floating. Of heat and warmth and safety. Her body covered in light as she drifted to the deepest part of the ocean, where no light reaches even at twelve noon lunchtime, which was the brightest part of the day.

She dreamed the smell of bread. She dreamed the sensation in the palms of her hands when she turned quickly, lifting from their centers, individual pendulums swinging away from her.

Beegie dreamed of a video game car, yellow Lamborghini, hovering and twisting in the living room of some crazy rich people. The rich people laughed and clapped their hands.

Beegie dreamed that the Busman pulled off her pants but there was another pair underneath that and another and another, until finally he pressed into her hips and her bones disappeared under his hands and he fell into her flexing receding body.

She dreamed Barb carried her on the highway, smoking, gin breath. Told her to hold on with her legs. And Beegie wondered where the *other one* was, the woman with skinny arms and brown hair.

In the dream something fell off of Beegie's body…it rattled its way down the leg of her jeans and fell on to the road. A bruised purple plum. It burst as it hit the street, pale orange flesh exploding out from its dark skin.

Beegie told Barb she needed it. That they ought to go back.

"Leave it," Barb said. "It only brings you trouble."

She protested but it was already ruined…and so far away…

Barb swung Beegie down from her back and placed her into a cardboard box by the side of the road. A little girl sat across from her, curly haired and pretty. Thumb stuck in her mouth. There was a cigarette burn on the toddler's forehead. A red bubble blister.

"I'm going to get someone," said the girl's mother. Somewhere else.

"No," Beegie said to the baby.

There was a pink hand holding hers. And her own hand was red.

Beegie shivered. The sky and ground were white and she was lying in snow in front of Jasmine's family's house. Her skin burning hot and cold, flakes melting against her skin. Impossible. Impossible.

"Beegie," Dessa looked down at her.

The ground was hard and cold against her back. The sky now a white-walled hallway. Rectangles of fluorescent lights hashing a line down the ceiling like stripes of paint on a paved road. *Miss Mary Mack, Mack, Mack.*

"Where is the baby?" Beegie asked, tightening her grip on

Dessa's hand. But Dessa was turned away from her. Face angled out down the hall. Toward the milling blue and green people, all of them rushing, all of them averting their eyes. Each wanting her to be someone else's problem...or maybe assuming that she already *was* someone else's problem.

Story of my life, thought Beegie. Always someone else's responsibility, always shuffled off onto someone else's to-do list.

Dessa tried to make eye contact with the people as they rushed past. "Excuse me..." she said. "Can someone..." but she didn't finish.

Can someone—what? thought Beegie. *Can someone find the baby? That's what she wants someone to do. Find the baby. I could do it. She was here a minute ago.*

Dessa looked back at her. "They're ignoring us."

"Am I on the floor?"

The woman nodded. "I'm sorry. A nurse brought us in here. She said she was going to get a stretcher...but she hasn't come back. Please, Beegie. I'll be right back, I just need to get someone."

"I think I was shot."

"You were, honey. I just need to make sure *they* know that."

"Don't leave."

"Beegie."

"Don't leave."

Dessa pursed her lips. Then turned. Her other hand flying out and pointing at a man passing them in a white coat. "You!" she shouted, and the man stopped short. Like Dessa had shouted magic words.

He glanced at Beegie. A strange look passed over him, irritation but also fear. He was afraid of something. Of *them,* Beegie realized. Afraid of her bleeding body and Dessa's pointing finger.

"I'll... I'll send a nurse."

"Are you a doctor?" Dessa asked him.

You could tell that the answer was yes...but that he didn't want to say it for some reason, the way he shifted his weight. Looked down the hall.

Dessa continued, "I need you to look at my friend."

"Look, we have to do things a certain way...we have a lot of patients... I'm sure you have someone assigned. I'll send a nurse." He started to walk away.

Dessa stood suddenly, dropping Beegie's hand. She stepped in front of him.

"I don't want a fucking nurse! I want you to take two minutes and actually *look at her*!"

"Ma'am, with all the trauma from the quake—"

"She was raped." Dessa interrupted him. Clipped. Simple. *Raped*.

"Eleven hours ago. Downtown. After the earthquake. Two men held her down in the back of a shoe store and they raped her. And then she came all this way...she *walked* all this way and another man shot her. I'm going to say it again, because I don't understand which one of those things will get you to treat her like a fucking person. She was *raped* and then she was *shot* and now she is lying on the floor of your fucking hospital and I am wondering why neither of those things qualifies her for two minutes of your time."

The doctor took a step back from Dessa. She looked wild. Eyes wide. Bloodstained arms held out from her body...ready for a fight.

The doctor made a sound like a sigh. He looked back at Beegie on the floor...face painted in shame or one of its cousins. He kneeled down, Dessa's worried face hanging over his shoulder.

"Is this true?" he asked without meeting her eyes...instead

he was scanning her body. Its bandages and bruises. Its other imagined insults.

"Yes," she whispered. It was true. Everything Dessa had said was true, but how had she known it?

Beegie's world was swimming. Lids heavy, skidding against the surface of her eyes. Her fingers tingly and numb. She *had* been dreaming, but she didn't think she was now. But there was just as much that didn't make sense in this reality as there had been in her dreams. How could she be bleeding on the floor of a hospital and have doctors walk right past her, ignoring her...how could Dessa *know* about what had happened before they met, when she hadn't told her.

"What's your name?"

"Beegie."

"Well, Beegie. The first thing we need to do is get you off of the floor."

They did. Get her off the floor, that is. The same people who had been ignoring her minutes before suddenly running to her side. Lifting her onto a rolling bed. Poking her with needles. Slicing off her jeans with scissors.

A woman in a suit apologized for what she referred to as the "unfortunate misunderstanding" and assured them that she would "get to the bottom of it." She stood in the back of the room while almost a dozen people stood around Beegie, cleaning and observing and dressing her wounds.

The shoulder wound was a graze. The leg would require surgery, a doctor who did not bother to introduce himself explained. Beegie overheard another man talking with Dessa about windows of treatment and the possibilities of packing the wound. It drew pictures in her mind of garbage bags filled with her things, Barb tossing them outside her bedroom window so that they burst open on the scrubby bushes below.

Every few minutes a nurse would come in to tell them that a social worker would be there soon… Each time they looked at Beegie like they knew something she did not. Small pout to their lips.

They gave her drugs. Nice ones. She felt good. Floaty again, like the dream, but in the here and now. She still hurt but she minded less.

Finally they were alone. Dessa and her. She had kept expecting the woman to disappear behind the crowd of nurses and doctors. To slip out the door and get to her baby, but she had stuck. Like a piece of glitter on her clothes, too small to be picked up and tossed away.

Beegie narrowed her eyes. "You psychic or something?"

"I was there." Dessa's voice was quiet.

"There?"

"In the store. I saw…"

Suddenly Beegie's heart was pumping so hard. Fists against the inside of her chest. Breaths shallow and fast. She stared at Dessa's eyes. So serious and real and clearly telling the truth. *Two men held her down in the back of a shoe store and they raped her.* That's what she had said. That's what had happened.

"How?" Beegie asked.

"I needed shoes… You were so quiet… I didn't know until… I saw…"

"And you…"

"And I hid."

A sound came out of Beegie's mouth. Almost a hiccup. A gasp. She covered it with her hand. Nodded.

"I'm so sorry, Beegie."

The girl looked away from the woman's horrible face. From her sappy, pretty, tear-filled sorry ass face. Didn't want to see it. Her excuses.

Dessa said, "I called 911, but it was after the earthquake…"

and Beegie's head bobbed. A small repeated motion. Yes, yes, yes. *Of course you did.*

"…and then the music came back on and they ran, and I thought they had killed you…but then I looked and you weren't there—"

She interrupted. "Musta shocked the fuck outta you when you saw me later."

The girl still refused to look at Dessa's face. Her heart thump thumping against her ribs. Ears hot, drugs sliding around her veins. She felt like Dessa had taken something from her, though she didn't know what. Whatever it was, it was a thing she had not known was missing until the woman had offered it back…

"What do you want?" Beegie finally asked. She looked back at Dessa. Her face hard.

Dessa looked confused. "I don't want anything."

"You do. It's why you made me come with you."

"I just… I wanted to make sure you got taken care of…"

"Well, I'm taken care of." Beegie lifted her heavy fingers, eyes scanning the room. "Why are you still here?"

36

Dessa knew that there are some rooms that one can never leave.

She knew that there are some events that fracture souls but leave the body intact. The corpse moves on, lungs still filling, heart still pumping, neurons still firing. The body moves away, but some of the broken bits of the soul stay behind. Shards of spirit caught in the floorboards, beyond reach of the broom. Visible only when the light hits them.

This is the way the living can haunt a place…by leaving behind the bit of themselves that died in that room. That is what trauma is really: A death. The death of possibility. The death of "if only" and "I just could've…"

Would the ghosts of Beegie and Dessa haunt the owners of that shoe store? Every time Dessa flushed at the memory of her instinct to hide rather than shout, would their figures appear? Ghostly apparitions, cold spots, hollow sounds materializing on the garish sales floor. Incongruous among the ranchero music and bedazzled merchandise.

Dessa wanted to be forgiven.

But she was not owed forgiveness.

No one is.

The girl told her to leave.

There was no redemption to be found in Beegie's hard face. Her eyes had gone blank, her cheeks held in a studied slackness…meant to convey anger and contempt and detachment all at once.

And when Dessa tried to explain, she had stopped her. "No…" the girl's voice cracked and she put a hand in front of her face, blocking her eyes for a moment. "You don't know me. I don't know you. You needed to do this thing, you did it. I'm here. But if you think that makes it better…*it doesn't make it better…*"

They were quiet then. The silence of strangers sat between them like a palpable thing, hard and cold under their hands. Beegie had said they did not know each other, and despite the night they had spent with each other Dessa knew she was right.

There was a knock. Soft knuckles rapping against the frame of the open door. Two gentle-eyed women. One in a white coat, the other in a bureaucrat's button-up and sweater vest. The unofficial uniform of social workers.

"See, my new hand-holder is here," Beegie said. "You're off the hook, Odessa Reilly. You can officially get the fuck out of my life."

The girl's words were a slap. A push. A full-bodied confirmation of Dessa's worst estimation of herself.

So she left.

Mumbled a barely audible "excuse me" to the two women at the door as she pushed her way past them. Stumbled into the fluorescent glare of the hallway. Beegie had let her go.

She hadn't forgiven her but she had released her. Olivia could be everything now. Just get home.

So why did she feel so sick? Beyond the exhaustion and hurt there was something else.

"Miss! Miss!"

The social worker. Running behind her. Breasts swinging beneath the soft gauge of her vest. She was out of breath. Dessa stopped for her.

"Please…come…back…" the woman panted.

Dessa swallowed. "She doesn't want me."

"No, um…she's…look, kids like her…they push you away. It's like a test. They push and push to see if you think they're worth fighting for…so I'm just asking you not to give up on her, just yet."

"That's not what's happening."

"That girl disappeared into herself the second you left…she doesn't know what she's doing or why she's doing it but she does know she needs you…that one part of her is telling you to go because another part of her wants you to stay."

Dessa inhaled. The breath skipped on its way inside her body. Hopscotching its way into her lungs. She made a decision.

"I need you to give her something."

It's Saturday, this is what Dessa thought as she made her way past the police barricades and into the crowd. These were people with plans, surely. Los Angeles is a city that loves its weekends. Brunches and trips to the beach. Yoga classes with wait-lists. Runyon canyon turned into a highway of hikers and their rescued dogs on Saturday morning.

"People are a plague," was what Gretchen would say when they reached the top, looking out on the endless sprawl of the city.

"We are people," Dessa would respond, scratching Gretchen's own rescued dog behind the ears.

"My point exactly."

It was so strange to think that it could somehow still *be* Saturday, even though none of the things any person had planned for that day were happening. As if there should be different names for the days that follow disasters until normality was restored…until it was possible to hike and brunch and sleep off a hangover between a set of clean sheets.

Dessa imagined the lunch she should be giving Olivia. The smooshed peanut butter and jelly she would have pulled from her purse at the zoo. The scent of sunscreen on the bottle of water they would share.

That was Saturday. Today was something else. Saturn's day. A day belonging to an older, crueler god. A day when her best friend was dead instead of at the top of Los Angeles's scrubby hills and her daughter wasn't sitting across a picnic table from her but instead was…

Dessa didn't allow herself to finish the thought.

She pushed her way out of the crowd, past the people who would be mowing their backyards and cleaning their bathrooms if the earth had not shaken their plans from their schedules.

She moved past them into the surrounding neighborhood.

And then she heard it.

The sound of a Saturday.

A bike bell.

There were two children playing on one of the side streets. A boy and a girl, their bicycles dipping in and out from a driveway onto a quiet cul-de-sac of a street. They circled one another, shouting and laughing.

They were alone. Dessa imagined their parents were inside—watching the disaster around them unfold on the television if they had power, inventorying their pantry if they did not.

Dessa reached into her bag. Her hand finding the pocket she had retained from the remains of Beegie's extra sweatshirt.

"Excuse me," she said, and both children turned their heads to face her…their eyes wide with wonder, as if she had just appeared in front of them instead of approached from half a block away. In unison their feet dropped from the pedals, skidding against the ground.

In the end, it was a simple exchange.

Dessa had helped the little girl pull the diamonds from the terry cloth they had been pinned to and attach them to her ears. The stones looked incongruously large on the ten-year-old lobes, but the girl beamed as she touched them there.

She passed Dessa the handlebars to her bike when she ran inside to find a mirror. The transaction complete.

Dessa mounted the bike and rode away.

The bike was sufficient. A little too small but manageable. Certainly faster than her feet were on their own.

Dessa got back on the freeway. The tires hummed against the pavement. Plastic streamers lifting and dancing from the handlebars. Someday she would teach Ollie to ride a bike. Maybe this one. Yes. Her daughter would like this bicycle.

She had hung the grocery sack that held her belongings over the wheel. The bag crackled in the wind, buffeted against the tire well. Dessa thought of the earrings Joe had given her, finding a second life in a little girl's jewelry box among the plastic heart studs and kitty cat pendants. She thought of the vanity that had driven her to put them on the night before. She thought of their value…

Yes, the bike had been a good exchange. Any price to get her to Olivia faster.

She recognized a shape on the road up ahead. It had been a

few hours but the man who had attacked them still lay on the road. He had moved. Propped himself up against the barrier between the north and southbound lanes, his body slumped in the small shadow cast by the wall.

Dessa slowed as she approached him.

He was alive but sleeping. His chest rising and falling in a sick wheeze.

Dessa felt a small beat of sympathy before she noticed the spray of Beegie's blood on the pavement. The flashlight lay where it had rolled from the girl's hand. As well as the yellow duck, Beegie's gift for Olivia, where it bounced off the man's chest.

Dessa picked up both items. She stuffed them in the sack and remounted the bicycle, eager to get going.

She stopped after only a few feet. Something occurring to her.

She laid the bike down a second time and went back to the man. The gun lay in his limp hand. He had picked it back up. Dessa knelt next to him, wrapping her hand around its handle and lifting it out of his hand.

She looked up into his open eyes.

He was awake. Wheezing. Watching. He did not struggle to take it back from her, "Leah," he said.

"No," Dessa answered, and then, "I'm sorry."

Because she was.

She turned and left.

As she had leaned over him Dessa had had the impulse to say, "I need this more than you." She had heard the words in her mind.

It was the same thing Jan had said to her as she had picked up the fallen bills around Dessa's body. So strange to be on the other side of it.

Did she? Need it? And if that was the case, did she need it more than him or anyone else?

Dessa didn't know. Couldn't know. Impossible to guess at the hierarchy of others' needs in the face of limited opportunity.

It had been the memory of Beegie after their first meeting that had driven her back to take the weapon. She had been looking for a gun. Dessa thought about the absurdity of giving it to Beegie. The gun that had fired the bullets that pierced her body.

What a strange present.

The tires droned on the pavement beneath her as she turned onto the 405. A zipping hum, both high and low. Almost like those throat singing monks. A meditation beneath her.

Dessa felt foreign to herself. Distant. It was a strange sensation. Not like her mind was clear or empty…but rather that she had had all the thoughts there were to have and that her brain was now done with thinking. It could only perform the basic operations of respirations, circulation, neuron impulse—but that it was going to absent itself from any other observation.

The throat singing tires began to drone a single word.

Home. Home. Home.

She noted details. These were the same ones she always noticed on her way home. The single dead acacia tree poking up from behind the highway wall, among its live companions. An orphaned couch cushion, orange with black stripes. A single boy's shoe, blue and red with spiderwebs. A graffiti tag, the word *seldom* in spray paint—if it was a name or description Dessa did not know.

And then she was at her exit.

Her neighborhood.

Her block.

Her street.

Her building.

There were people milling around outside it. Their faces grim. Mouths open. Dessa drew to a stop, the bike falling between her legs. She pulled through the crowd, finally seeing what they had been staring at.

The whole front of her building had sheared off. Behind the fallen facade, the part of the structure that was still standing looked...wrong.

It was too short.

The bottom floor the building was gone. The remaining levels had swallowed it, and they hung angled impossibly over the alley.

Somehow Dessa did not scream...instead she kept walking toward her home...her daughter...

On the driveway someone had painted a large red circle. An "x" struck though it.

"What does this mean?" she asked no one in particular. Her voice didn't seem to be her own.

She heard a whisper. A fragment among the crowd. A distinct, "He lives here." She turned and saw suddenly that everyone in the crowd was staring at her. Their faces even grayer than before.

"What does this mean?" she asked again. This time her voice strident. These people knew.

"The firemen came, they pulled out the survivors and then they put this on the ground." It was a man. She recognized him from the neighborhood. Dessa had seen him walking his little dog.

"God," Ollie had said when they saw him with his small companion, the consonants switching in her mouth. *"Godggy."*

"Was there a little girl? Did they get a little girl?"

The man's face went white. He shook his head, "I don't

know." Dessa searched the crowd. Shouting, "Was there a girl?"

Her eyes caught familiar ones. Pilar. Their neighbor. *"Ai, mi niña. Porque tan triste?"* she had said to Olivia.

But it was Pilar who was *triste* now. It was Pilar who was *llorando.*

"No," she said. The same word in both languages.

Dessa howled. Feral pain echoing out of her. The sound was bigger than her body. It knocked her over and she drowned in it. Tumbling end over end in a tsunami of grief. Her eyes ceased to work, the gray scream swallowing even her sight for a moment.

Her knees broke, touching the pavement. Her vision came back to her here, on the ground. A view of her hands. Between them the newly sprayed X framed between her outstretched thumbs. She gulped air. The X beneath her making a strange totem on the backs of her eyes. When she blinked it was still there…in reverse. White floating in a field of black.

She was not home yet.

But she would be.

37

Dessa stood.

Her feet seemed so distant from her on the pavement…a miracle that she had the capacity to make them run and pedal and swim her way to this very moment. It seemed like they should have stopped by now. Divorced themselves from their connection to her mind.

But they had not.

She moved, heading toward the alley that threaded its way between the buildings.

"You can't go in there."

This she heard distantly. Like someone was shouting at her underwater. A hand snaked itself around her arm, holding her back.

"You can't go in there." The neighbor's grip tight on her bicep. He of the little "god."

Dessa rounded on him. Her eyes wild. "My daughter is in there… She *is in there.*"

She pulled against him and his fingers slipped against her arm. Dessa felt the traces of his touch against her skin and she ran toward the building.

If he said anything else, she did not hear it.

The corpses of her neighbors' cars stuck out from under the building. Like the Wicked Witch's sister, their fenders reaching out from under the collapsed overhang like a pair of ruby slippers. The tail ends of sensible Corollas, Saturns, the five-hundred-dollar beaters with the screeching timing belts that woke Dessa at 2:00 a.m. when their barback and waiter owners came home for the night.

Some of the stucco had crumbled in the fall. A litter of debris across the alley and the remains of the cars.

The door to the stairwell had disappeared as cleanly as if it was something that had only existed in Dessa's imagination. So completely swallowed by the building that the stucco was barely cracked where it was supposed to be.

Dessa stood in the blank gap where her car would have been had she stayed home. She could almost hear the sound of the Korean soap playing out of the apartments above…the melodramatic swell of music before cutting abruptly to a deep-voiced commercial pitch.

The only way in was up.

She picked up a chunk of concrete that had rolled into the setback. Her hands pricked on the stucco mesh, some of the trowel marks still clinging to its sides.

She threw it at her neighbor's window…more of a push than a throw. The image of Beegie performing a similar action flew into her mind.

The rock sailed through the glass. A bright ringing shatter.

The window burst onto the remains of a maroon Honda with a sticker on its fender. *Aloha* it read, a bird of paradise etched out next to it in white.

She climbed. Her feet slipping for a moment off the edge of the trunk.

Aloha means hello and goodbye. Her mind gifted her with this thought as she caught herself against the wall. *Hello and goodbye*, she thought again as her knee scraped against the rough surface of the building.

From this vantage Dessa could almost see into the apartment... The glass had broken cleanly, in large shards, from a single blow. *Cheap...so Goddamned cheap...* Dessa thought. The glass should not have broken this way. It was dangerous.

Of course this cheap glass had survived the crumbling of the building...only to be shattered with a single rock.

Dessa hefted herself up, straining against the ledge, fingers biting into the metal brackets that had held the window. She hooked her ankle and swung herself up...

Into someone else's obliterated world.

A television cabinet lay across the width of the apartment. Solid oak. Cables hung limp from the wall, stripped and dusty, like they had tried to cling onto the aging technology as it had toppled to the floor.

Dessa's soap opera loving neighbor lay beneath the cabinet. Dead.

Dessa gasped and recoiled, her hand flailing out and hitting against the wall behind her. She rocketed up, the force of her horror almost causing her to tumble back out the window.

She had not known this woman...but she had been her neighbor.

Just. Get. Home.

Dessa was one flight of stairs and a hallway from her daughter...or if not her daughter then...whatever answers waited for her up there.

She picked out a path toward the door, wincing when the cabinet shifted under her weight, pressing down on...

Do not think about it... Gretchen's voice in her mind...or was it Beegie's?

The chain lock was still attached to the door. Peace of mind. Dessa unlatched it and the dead bolt both. The door stuck for a moment in the frame before thrumming open. It swung toward her, the knob vibrating in her hand.

The hallway beyond was pitch-black.

Dessa stepped into the pool of light cast through the broken window. She would not make it far without a flashlight...and her own, the one that had been with her all night, through so much, was now lying on the street left behind in the plastic bag.

She turned back into the apartment, into the small standard kitchen, its appliances identical to the ones that sat in her own kitchen. The cabinets had opened spilling food and plates, cans and packages of dried noodles on the floor. Dessa ducked by the sink, "Please, please..." she whispered, her fingers quick, sifting through the wreckage on the floor.

She found it. Under a package of unopened sponges and cockroach traps. Thin, plastic, small and red. Its light was weak but present.

It would have to do.

Dessa shone its watery beam into the darkness of the corridor, illuminating the path to the stairwell.

The ceiling had fallen in chunks onto the floor, exposing the straining wood beams and metal ducts above. Insulation fluff reached out from the gaps, showers of plaster dust cascading from their edges.

Dessa's eyes caught on the wallpaper. Its stripes had been...

derailed. Thrown off course by the shifting and cracking drywall affixed to its back.

She stepped into the hall.

A loud wooden creaking resounded. The ducts above her popping and vibrating under the strain.

Dessa held her breath.

Just get home.

The sound stopped, petering out until there was only the soft shushing sound of the plaster dust hitting the floor.

She took a step. And then another.

A piece of insulation brushed the top of her head as she moved under it. Like the building was reaching out to caress her...*there, there, my dear.*

Dessa reached the dark void at the end of the hall. The open stairwell connecting the floors with each other. It took her a moment to make out exactly what it was she was seeing in the flashlight's feeble glow. It looked like the stairs had grown away from the floor, shifting upward, leaving a pile of debris below. The second story landing had been pushed up to waist height by the remnants of the first flight of stairs... *No*, she thought. *It was the floor that came down.*

Dessa shone the flashlight up into the remaining hollow of the stairwell. The second flight of stairs still hung from the wall. She hoisted herself upon it, ducking herself into the narrow space between the doorjamb and the top of the landing. Without pause she stepped onto the first tread.

Beneath her foot the staircase *bounced*.

Dessa lifted her knee, shining the light onto the steps...a half inch of rebar lay exposed between the wall and the poured concrete form of the stairs. The bulk of the stairwell canted out from the bending threads... These thin black pieces of metal were all that were keeping the enormous weight of the stairs from crashing into the pile of rubble below.

Dessa inhaled, flattening her body against the wall, toes kissing the void between the risers and wall.

This was a bad idea.

But there were no other options.

She slid herself against the wall. Willing herself lighter with each step. Afraid to breathe for fear the small weight of oxygen in her body would be the difference between balance and disaster.

Step.

Step.

Step.

She reached the landing, the sound of her relieved pants echoing around the dark. Dessa laid her cheek against the cool of the wall, heart thumping. *Just get home.*

Something brushed against her leg.

Dessa yelped and twisted. Two glowing eyes looked up at her from the darkness. She shone the light downward.

A cat.

The same one Ollie had tried to lure out from under a car yesterday afternoon. The creature looked up at her mournfully. It meowed and again rubbed itself against her ankles. Dessa's heart was thundering against the walls of her chest... she felt like it was rocking her whole body.

As she opened the door onto the third story hallway, the moment overlaid with hundreds of other homecomings; Work bag slung on her shoulder, Ollie on her hip or in her car seat. Drooling up at her in the cheap blue light of the corridor.

The building growled again...but Dessa did not stop.

She reached their door. Hand on the knob. Turning.

It stopped in her hand.

Locked.

Instinctively, Dessa reached for her purse...but of course it wasn't there.

She screamed. *The key. The fucking key.* Her fists connected with the door, like she was knocking. Bang, bang, bang! "Please! Please!"

The halls groaned in reply, protesting the insult of her fists. She could not have come all this way only to be stopped here, in this broken building, by a cheap lock in a cheap door.

And cheap walls...

Dessa ran her hands across the wall beside her front door. Feeling for the fracture, the give, the cracks beneath the surface. She sensed something beneath the palms of her hands, a long thin bump threading its way under the wall paper... she pushed on it...

...and it gave. The Sheetrock folding into the cavity beyond, like origami. She wrapped her fingers around the torn edges, ripping at the paper and the drywall. The material bit at her hands, but it broke, dry and hard, revealing the framing and the backside of the walls of her home.

Dessa lifted her heel and kicked, driving all her strength into the wall. Again. And again. The surface beneath her foot becoming friable and dusty until it suddenly wasn't there anymore and her shoe flew out into the air above the space where her daughter had learned to crawl. Dessa had held Ollie's little fists up in triumph and sung a song when she had first cleared those few feet of carpet. Ollie's drooly grin looking up at her.

The song wove itself into her consciousness as she reached down to rip a space for herself to pass through. *And we'll keep on fighting 'til the end...* Almost there.

One foot. Two feet. Three feet cleared.

She turned sideways and put her leg through. It touched the floor and she ducked her shoulder into the space beyond. A kind of breech birth, sideways from the dark womb of the hallway into whatever new world lay waiting for her on the other side of the door. She brought her head through, shutting her eyes for the brief pass through the wall—

The sunlight hit her face, for a moment painting her vision orange. She opened her eyes and gasped. "Oh my God."

The living room from the apartment above had *fallen* into her own. The ceiling was gone, or rather the ceiling was on her floor. Broken two-by-fours and MDF subfloor blanketing the shabby remnants of her life. Her neighbor's furniture lay broken and tumbled on top of the rubble.

Above, improbably, her neighbor's carpet *still* clung to the wall… It hung down like a curtain. Draped over half of the disaster, like some slow-moving reveal.

"OLIVIA!"

Dessa stepped into the debris. "Olivia!" Was her daughter buried under all of this? She waded through it… Afraid of what she might step on…

Her eyes snagged on something in the kitchen. The remains of dinner. A half-eaten grilled cheese sandwich. A sippy cup. The ceiling had not fallen on that end of the apartment.

"Olivia!"

Dessa moved toward it. Desperate for any sign of movement. Flailing for hope. The door to the bathroom lay open, the seat up. Dessa imagined Hailey bringing Ollie to it after she had vomited…brushing her hair back.

In their bedroom a section of the ceiling had fallen…but the floor above it had held. A piece of drywall obscured Ollie's bed from view. Dessa hauled it off…

Revealing only the dusty bodies of Olivia's stuffed animals. "Olivia!"

A small noise followed. Mouselike. Dessa looked around. Her eyes skittering, looking for any small movement.

"Mommy?"

Her daughter's voice, but far away.

Dessa thought for a moment she had imagined it. That despair had sent her autonomic system reeling, and in order to keep her from dropping into insanity it had sent her an auditory hallucination…a minor madness to prevent the larger one that threatened if she did *not* find her daughter.

"Olivia?" she asked.

The closet. *They were in the closet.*

Dessa turned. Fallen bits of drywall leaned up against the door…her bed stand had toppled. She moved toward it…still not sure she hadn't pitched into a fantasy…

Her hand touched the handle of the door. "Ollie?"

"Mrs. Reilly?"

It was Hailey's voice. Shaky. Joined by—

"Mommy?"

Dessa cried. Her hands shaking. Her breath fast. "Oh my God…" *Thank you…thank you…*

She pulled on the handle, but it slipped between her fingers. The door was wedged somehow, jammed between the frame and the floor. Frantic, she began clearing the ground. Hefting the broken wedges of Sheetrock, toppled nightstand drawers, everything out of the way. Ollie called to her from behind the door. *Mommy. Mommy. Mommy.*

She tried again. It didn't budge. The knob again slipping through her fingers, scraping past them. Ollie began crying.

"Hold on, honey… Hold on…" Dessa ran her hand beneath the lip of the molding. The wall was connected fast with the door.

"Hailey, can you kick the door for me?"

"I think so." The girl's voice was thready. Unsure.

"All right, aim for the hinge, down low… I'm going to pull." Dessa braced her foot against the wall, tightening her hold on the handle, "I need you to kick with everything you have. Ready. One. Two. Three."

The door pulsed as Hailey rammed her legs against it. Dessa pulled, her arms straining, fingers slipping, sweaty against the metal of the knob.

Dessa flew backward as the hinge finally gave, stumbling onto her bed.

A small hand appeared in the dark crack where the door had been dislodged from the floor. Chubby wrists. Followed by a head of dust-strewed curls.

"I'm hungry," Ollie said when she saw her.

Dessa laughed, reaching for her baby's beautiful body. Pulling her up from the floor. Skin on skin. Confirmation of living flesh.

38

Moments after Olivia was born, the doctors had placed her pink screaming body on Dessa's own. Dessa had looked down and seen her daughter for the first time, the vantage skewed so that Ollie looked like little more than a wet screaming face. For a brief moment, she feared she had given birth to a human ball, that the ultrasounds had lied when they had shown two long sets of limbs and that her daughter was actually malformed, damaged somehow before the world even had its chance at her.

She bristled.

It was not disgust that Dessa had felt but the momentary call of the war drums. A mother's impulse. Her badly made daughter was threatened by a cruel world, and if she so needed, Dessa would defend her to the death. Her bristling impulse was only anticipating how hard she would need to fight.

Naturally, it did not last. The moment Dessa's hands swept down, she felt them. Ollie's legs. Ollie's arms. She confirmed it all as she pulled her daughter's perfectly formed body up to her breasts. Dessa's eyes were not enough to banish that first initial horror...she needed to touch every tiny knuckle on Olivia's hands. Feel the joints of her elbows beneath her skin. Run the tips of her fingers along the seam of Ollie's back. Her daughter was fine. She was here. They were together.

Sweeping Ollie up from the floor of her broken apartment, Dessa felt their first moments twinned. Ollie's sweat-damp toddler's body, tiny quick fingers, perfect small chest. Seeing wasn't enough. Dessa needed to run her hands across every inch of Olivia's flesh.

But there was not time.

The door caught on Hailey's back as she made her way out of the closet. Hooking her for a brief moment while the girl struggled to free herself, like she was being held back. A victim from one of those bad horror movies Hailey had no doubt auditioned for.

Dessa let go of Ollie—*too soon*—to help her through, wrapping her arms around Hailey's shoulders. Finally the door gave, whatever had held the girl breaking and releasing her. Ollie's babysitter sobbing great relieved sobs, gasps of freed air.

But accompanying her freedom was an unsettling crunch within the wall above the door. A splinter-rending sound muffled behind the walls of the closet.

We need to get out of here...right now.

"Can you walk?"

Hailey nodded, climbing to her feet. Dessa swung Ollie up into her hip.

She led Hailey back through the hall, to the kitchen, to the living room, or what remained of it. Her feet careful on the boards, seeking the floor. Avoiding edges.

Something slid beneath her foot and it caught her eye. A photograph. Her mother's carefully crafted smile looked up at her from the debris. Somehow the box containing all her parents' photographs had broken and spread itself like a net under the crumbled ceiling. Somewhere under all of this were pictures of her entire past. Her childhood. Graduations. Photos of birthday parties.

And every photo of her father.

"My Dessa. Hello. Strong girl. My strong girl."

He had thought she was strong.

Dessa kept moving. Olivia was the only thing that mattered. Everything else was just paper.

When they reached the stairwell, Dessa shone the light on the gap between the stairs and the wall. "You need to keep your weight close to the edge," she whispered to Hailey, handing her the flashlight.

The girl hugged the wall, her face almost pressed against it as she made her way down. Slight panicky breaths reverberating around the darkness.

"Just stay calm, Hailey...move slowly..." Olivia shifted on Dessa's hip. Whimpering into her mother's ear.

Hailey reached the bottom with a little cry, shining the light back up toward them.

Dessa took the first step.

The staircase shifted with a groan. Sliding farther out of the rebar.

Dessa shrieked and stepped back onto the landing. With Olivia she weighed too much.

She knelt down. Prying Ollie's clinging arms away from her body...there was only one way this could work.

"Honey, did you just see what Hailey did?"

Oliva whined around the thumb in her mouth. Her arms reaching back for her mother. Begging to be held again. "Mommy needs you to go do the stairs just like Hailey did. Really, really slowly."

"Uh-uh," her daughter shook her head.

Dessa tried to regulate the panic out of her voice. They were almost there. "Please, honey? Mommy really needs for you to be a big girl and do this... I'll come down right after you."

"With sugar on top?"

"Yes, the prettiest please with twenty tablespoons of sugar on the top of it."

Ollie nodded. As if that was precisely the correct amount of sugar.

"Okay. Show Momma."

Olivia put both hands on the wall...

She stepped down.

Dessa waited for the sound, the swift crumpling action and drop.

But nothing happened. Dessa's whole body was screaming with alarm, but she kept smiling at her little girl. Certain everything would crumble at any moment...

But Ollie kept going. Smiling back at her from each stair. Small bare feet shuffling back together, back together. A game.

"See, Mommy?" Voice bright and sweet and unconcerned about the danger.

"I see, sweetie...keep going."

She reached the bottom, hopping from the final step into the shaking beam from Hailey's hand. "Now Momma's turn!" She pointed up at her.

Somewhere something cracked...distant. A shot fired in one of her neighbor's apartments. They were running out of time.

"Hailey, there's an open apartment down the hall. Take her. Wait for me. I will be right there."

"But..."

"I need you to go!"

Ollie suddenly aware of what was happening began to cry. She threw herself back onto the first step, desperate to get back to Dessa. The stairs made a grinding protest in response to Olivia's small weight. Dessa shrieked, "Hailey!"

The babysitter suddenly snapped to, grabbing Ollie and running into the hallway. Dessa could hear her daughter crying for her. Angry. Betrayed. *Momma. Momma. Mommy.*

Dessa listened to her daughter's voice fade as Hailey carried her to safety.

Olivia *was* her home.

The sound of Dessa's breath echoed through the darkness. She was blind without the flashlight, but her daughter was waiting for her at the end of the hallway.

She placed her hands against the wall. Her forehead brushing the uneven concrete. She took a step.

And another.

And another.

The staircase slipped a little. A small bounce. Dessa cried out. Her panicked breath reflecting back onto her face.

"I can do this..." she whispered.

My Dessa. Hello. Strong girl.

She took a breath...and another step.

Another.

She was sure there were only a few more left... The gray rectangle of the doorway was close.

There was a screeching sound. Unnatural and *everywhere.* Echoing up the spine of the building. Rolling over her.

The stairs were letting go of their restraints and they would take her with them.

Dessa leaped into the dark.

She hit the landing, fingers crunching into the edge of the wall, just as the stairwell dropped. Dessa rolled, falling through the doorway, her body striking the floor of the hallway.

The entire building rocked with the impact behind her. Dessa found her feet and ran, toward the distant well of light from her neighbor's open doorway, surrounded by the building's death rattle. *She would hand Olivia to Hailey...then climb out herself. They could make it.*

She reached her neighbor's apartment.

They weren't there.

She had told them to go here, but there weren't there!

"Olivia!" Dessa voice was lost in the cacophony of the building breaking. She whipped around. Where had they gone? Hailey couldn't have climbed out, not by herself, not with Olivia in her arms.

"OLIVIA!"

The sound of breaking lumber picked up. Screeching. Bending. Tearing holes in the air. Dessa turned back...had they missed the apartment? Fallen in the hallway? Had she run past them in her rush to get here?

There was a fireman in the doorway.

He was shouting something, but Dessa could not hear him over the roar.

Dessa tried to move past him, but suddenly he was lifting her...like her weight was nothing, he was lifting her and throwing her over his shoulder and running toward the window.

Dessa screamed at him. Beat at him. Reached past him. She screamed her daughter's name but now she could not hear it. Not even the faintest sound could be heard so that her daughter's name had been reduced to a series of movements with her tongue and her mouth, *O-li-vee-ahh*. Her daughter was nothing but movement and desire.

More hands wrapped themselves around her limbs. Pulling her out of the building. Setting her down on the ground. Pulling her away from the bumper of the car as she tried to climb back up, desperate. Screaming.

The fireman who had been inside swung himself out. The men surrounding her yanked her up, away from the ground as they ran.

Dessa reached... Behind her outstretched fingers she could see the building collapse upon itself.

It was over quickly. Only seconds really, before the structure swallowed itself. Loud. So terribly loud.

And then silent.

So *terribly* silent.

They dropped her. The firemen. Tried to set her on her feet but somehow her legs were no longer there. They disappeared beneath her like the building. She folded herself into her hands and sobbed.

Olivia had been there. And then she wasn't.

Momma had failed.

Just get home.

Home was gone with Olivia.

Dessa heard Beegie's voice in her mind. Reflecting back from the night before. *Even if she's dead she needs you. Even the dead need someone to care.*

Something small pressed itself to her back.

"What's wrong, Momma?"

Dessa looked up into her daughter's concerned face. Small furrow between her brows.

Behind her Hailey hugged a fireman. She was crying, clinging at the man.

Dessa swept her daughter into her arms. Folded her into

her body. Olivia's rump in the well between her legs. Olivia's head in the space between her breasts. Her shoulder beneath them. Her daughter slid into her body like she was molded from it, her natural home.

"Oh God…oh God…" Dessa whispered.

A prayer. An exclamation. A giving of thanks. Dessa did not know. But it was the only word in Dessa's mind. The only word for this moment.

AFTER

The social worker brought back Dessa's ring.

The woman held it in her open palm in front of her, the diamond still tinged pink with Beegie's blood. Beegie had looked at it for a long while before the woman said anything. Not understanding.

"Your friend asked me to give this to you... She said that a ring is a promise."

Beegie didn't understand.

The woman said, "She said she would come back...for you."

And even though there was a part of her that wanted to believe what the woman said, Beegie didn't take it. She looked away, turning her eyes out the window.

She felt the woman take her hand. Soft fingertips against her own.

And then she felt the ring slide onto her finger.

It was too big. Loose around the pole of her index. But Beegie cupped her hand around it anyway.

"Let yourself have this, Baby Girl," whispered the social worker. "You need to let yourself hope."

Beegie's face was wet now. Her cheeks damp and hot. *Hope* was for other people. For people with different histories. Hope didn't belong to her.

And still somehow it had been placed in her hand.

She did come back. Or rather *they did*. Dessa and her Ollie. The little girl was dirty, her hair covered in dust and holding the yellow ducky Beegie had picked for her from the highway memorial.

She had been through a lot but she seemed fine. Running around Beegie's room. "What's that, Momma? What's that?"

When she climbed into Beegie's bed, Dessa had reached over to pluck her off...but Beegie had stopped her. "It's okay," she said. The little girl fell asleep there, curled up at the foot. Small and sweet.

"She's probably cold... Can you?" Beegie asked Dessa, gesturing at her blanket with her good arm.

And Dessa pulled the blanket so it covered the little girl's body.

"Thank you," Dessa said.

"I'm sorry," Dessa said.

And Beegie nodded. "I know."

When she thought of the incident in the back of the store, a strange thing began to happen. She was still angry that Dessa had not done *something*...though when she played the scenario of Dessa doing *anything* out in her mind it always turned out worse than it actually had. One or both of them dead, killed by the Busman and Not-Charlie. Ollie never rescued, left to die in her mother's apartment building.

This way of thinking made Beegie feel cold inside. Sterile and cool like a metal countertop. To think that what had happened was the best possible outcome of the many that could have resulted from Dessa doing something, *anything,* it made Beegie feel like she was supposed to feel *lucky.*

And she did not want to feel *lucky.*

But in a small way the whole thing changed in her mind just knowing that Dessa had been there. It made the memory of the assault less *lonely* and somehow that made it feel like something Beegie could bear.

Dessa and Olivia went to live in her dead friend's house. Beegie came a few days after, with so many bottles of pills it took the doctors almost an hour to tell Dessa how to give them to her.

Dessa had warned her about her friend's dog, Kitty. That he had been strange since they had gone to Gretchen's home. That something had fallen on him during the earthquake and he was limping. And that he was sad and scared, waiting for his owner who was never going to come back.

But if Kitty was sad, he didn't seem like it to Beegie. He accepted her fine, sitting on the couch with her when she let him. Sitting on the ground next to her when she didn't.

She thought it was funny. That she was meeting another dog named for a different animal. Rooster. Kitty. Maybe somewhere there was a chicken and a cat named dog.

There were a few times that Ollie asked if they could go to the zoo. Beegie and Dessa were always silent for a moment after that…before Dessa would tell her daughter, "Someday, honey."

Someday when the power came back. When the rules applied. *When the animals were back in their cages.*

It was quiet for a very long time. The electricity didn't come back on for weeks. So they went to bed with the light. Played games by the window. Ollie drew pictures with Gretchen's ballpoint pens on sheets of yellow paper.

They wore Gretchen's things because they didn't have any of their own. The dead woman's pants and shirts were too big for both of them, slipping off of their shoulders and hips. Making Dessa and Beegie look like children in their parents' clothes.

Beegie searched through the stacks of Gretchen's books for something to read. But everything she tried seemed too slippery. Her mind wandered away from the book until she realized she had been running her eyes over the words without taking in a single one of them. She missed the company of books.

She hoped someday they would come back.

They avoided answers. Resolutions. Plans.

There was no talk about Olivia's father. No talk about Beegie returning to Barb. It was as if the earthquake had shaken the world like a snow globe and assigned them this new reality. These new people. Thinking about the steps that would follow belonged to another time.

Instead they lived the way they had managed to survive. By putting one foot in front of the other.

★ ★ ★ ★ ★

ACKNOWLEDGMENTS

I would like to thank: Brandi Bowles at UTA for her tenacity; Margot Mallinson and the team at MIRA for their trust; Kat Hjelte for her caregiving; Laurie Frankel for her counsel; Stephanie Kallos, Deb Calleti, Erica Bauermeister, Kevin O'Brien, Lynn Brunnelle, Chris Van Etten, Brandy Rivers, Martha Brokenbrough, Ted Kosmatka, Tim Lebbon and Josh Malerman for their encouragement; Shannon Malabuyo for her camaraderie; Baba and Papa for their support; Harper and Haven for their patience; and Stephen…for everything.

Bridget Foley, August 2020

JUST
GET
HOME

BRIDGET FOLEY

Reader's Guide

1. Have you ever experienced a natural disaster? If yes, what was the experience like? How did it make you feel? If no, how do you think you would react? Are you prepared for one?

2. There are a lot of intense events in the story. Which scene stuck with you the most? Was there anything that stood out for you?

3. What about each character did you most relate to? Dessa's maternal instincts? Beegie's longing to belong?

4. Did your opinion on the characters change throughout the book? What about their choices influenced your view of Dessa and Beegie?

5. Have you ever been in a scenario when your fight/flight/freeze response kicked in? Were you surprised at how you reacted? If you've never experienced this, do you think you have an idea about how you might react to danger?

6. Dessa felt she owed Beegie a strong debt for not acting when she might have. Do you think that's right? Did Dessa

owe Beegie anything more than the obligation we all have to help a fellow person in distress?

7. Do you think it was important for the story to depict the assaults? Do you think it would have had the same impact for the reader without experiencing these things alongside Beegie?

8. Beegie's resilience, and her support of Dessa, allows both of them to get through the night. Do you think Dessa would have made it home without Beegie's help? Do you think Beegie would have made it home without Dessa?

9. In the aftermath of the earthquake, the novel saw the absolute worst of humanity come to the forefront. Do you think that's accurate? Or do you believe that there would have been more helpful people?

10. Both Beegie and Dessa are quite stubborn in their own ways. Do you think this helped them or hindered them in their challenge to survive the night? What about during their everyday lives?

11. What do you think will happen with Beegie and Dessa in their futures?

RESOURCES

Together We Rise
A nonprofit organization dedicated to transforming the experience of foster care for kids in America.
www.togetherwerise.org

National Sexual Assault Hotline
1-800-656-4673 (HOPE)
www.rainn.org

National Center for Victims of Crime
1-202-467-8700
www.victimsofcrime.org